THE VEIL BETWEEN WORLDS

The Ladies of the Labyrinth
Book 1

Hope Carolle

ARE YOU SIGNED UP FOR DRAGONBLADE'S BLOG?

You'll get the latest news and information on exclusive giveaways, exclusive excerpts, coming releases, sales, free books, cover reveals and more.

Check out our complete list of authors, too!

No spam, no junk. That's a promise!

Sign Up Here

www.dragonbladepublishing.com

Dearest Reader;

Thank you for your support of a small press. At Dragonblade Publishing, we strive to bring you the highest quality Historical Romance from some of the best authors in the business. Without your support, there is no 'us', so we sincerely hope you adore these stories and find some new favorite authors along the way.

Happy Reading!

CEO, Dragonblade Publishing

PART I

CHAPTER ONE

How should I be merry or glad
For fair promises men to me make,
But when I have most need, they me forsake?
Everyman [Anonymous], 1485.

"H E'S GOING TO kill me," I said, frozen, too scared to move. The sour expression on his loose lips and creepy devil eyes indicated that I was not at all a welcome presence on his field. I didn't know sheep could have horns, but this one sure as hell did. Extra-long, potentially lethal. Drops of rain dripped off its bedraggled wool, its hollowed-out ears pointed sideways.

He growled at me in a deep "baa," grass clinging to his chin. Multi-tasking.

Sheep always looked so small from the side of the road. In nursery rhyme books. On mobiles, fluttering over cribs, playing a melody. Harmless. Fluffy creatures.

This one was huge. Over two-hundred pounds. It could take me down. Or toss me up in the air and spike me on top of the nearby fence post.

"He's not going to kill you, Ellie," Jane said. My best friend was laughing at me. Friends do that—at least mine do. *That's normal, right?* "He's just a sheep. They have brains the size of peas."

"So did the dinosaurs," I argued. "You don't have to be smart to kill somebody. History's shown that time and again."

"Walk around him," Jane ordered.

I shook my head, staying firmly planted in the frosty grass. "If I move, he's going to charge. This whole 'gentle sheep' thing is a myth. They're plotting an insurrection. I'll be their first victory in a sheep takeover. We're outnumbered."

Jane sighed as she walked over to me, took my elbow, and escorted me past the sheep, commenting, "You, my dear, are a true wimp. I guess you never got out to the countryside much when we were at King's."

My kids were so busy jumping in the puddles they had no idea of the brush with death their mommy nearly had. "Why would anyone leave the theater, museums, and libraries of London for muddy fields?" Culture always won out over nature in my book.

Jane had corralled us into going on this "scenic walk," on the way to her local pub for lunch that morning. But we'd been walking for what seemed like miles in a cold, wet wind, and I didn't think that wet, murderous sheep ranked that high on a scenic scale from 1-10. My feet were cold, my boots and the bottom of my jeans were covered in mud, my cheeks were raw, and my children had run out of snacks to keep them going. No doubt when she tired of trying to impress Leila, the nanny for Jane's girls, I'd have to carry Sophie when her energy ran out. At five years old and forty pounds, her weight would grow heavier with every step.

Come to England for January break, Jane said. *It'll be fun*, she said. *Don't go to that wretched, tacky Florida. You see your parents all the time! I need girl-time with you. Guy will be away, and it would be just us girls. Being on sabbatical is so utterly boring!* Through the hooded lens of my windbreaker, the giant hill we had to climb loomed, and I thought, *yes, why would I want to relax on a warm, sunny beach when I could get soaking wet in rural England?*

Jane had enticed me with visions of fresh, country air for the kids, a great big house for us to rattle around in, a trip to Winston Churchill's country house, a behind-the-scenes tour of the new British Library (new to me, anyway), copious amounts of wine, and the use of her long-time, as-good-as-Mary-Poppins nanny Leila when we wanted a lay-in. It had sounded nice from the confines of our 1,000 sq. foot bungalow rental.

Since I couldn't have a pina colada beachside, I needed that stick-to-your ribs pub lunch. "Please tell me civilization is near. Where's *The King's Arms*, or *The Queen's Head*, or *The Stag Inn*, or whatever this pub is called?"

"Don't make fun of our ancient publick houses—there are more than just those three names. The food is excellent and makes every list of Top 10 you can imagine. And it's just over that hill," she said.

"So, what's this one called?" I challenged.

Jane murmured something.

"What's that?" I asked again. "Couldn't quite hear you."

"The Queen's Head," she admitted.

"Aha!" I shouted. "I knew it!" The sheep looked at me again. So over me. "Are we going to make it before it closes?" Pubs stopped serving food at 2:00. As an American used to getting food whenever I wanted, this was a hardship.

Jane pulled out her Burberry encased iPhone and checked the time. "Yes, if we keep up a good pace." She looked over at my two girls. Abby, aged eight, was three years older than Sophie and infinitely wiser, with gorgeous chestnut-brown hair. Sophie's blond curls, normally just wavy, were coiling up in the wet. They walked arm-in-arm with Jane's two girls, Cordelia and Alice, one year younger than each of my girls, having the time of their lives. "Girls, the pub is just over that hill. Race you to it!" Jane yelled. They took off, squealing, rubber boots flying and bright yellow and pink raincoats getting splattered with mud. So far, their energy was holding up, but the bathwater was going to be filthy tonight.

AFTER I HAD polished off my shepherd's pie and taken a bite (or three) of Jane's bangers and mash, I sat back in my chair to allow room for the enormous stodge of food we had just consumed. I'd missed English food. Even though I'd forgotten how cold and rainy England could be, it was so good to be back.

There's nothing like an English pub. This one oozed history with its wide plank floors, timber-beams framing the ceiling, cracked stucco walls, and high-backed chairs. It was over five hundred years old; the plaque on the outside dated it back to 1505. I could just picture a man from times past coming in, sword belted to his waist, ordering up some ale at that very bar in front of us.

When the kids started getting antsy, we cleaned them of any visible food on their faces and sent them off to play on the playground accompanied by Jane's nanny, Leila.

Jane and I then enjoyed a bracing cup of English tea and enjoyed the calm that had befallen the place now that our noisy, impish troops ran amok outside.

"I wonder if I could get your opinion on something?" Jane asked.

"Fire away," I said, preparing myself for a tale of professional malfeasance. Jane and I were professors in Middle English; she at King's College in London, me at Wellesley in Massachusetts. We'd met at King's as PhD students. She had been kind enough to be friends with the likes of me, an American, even though many of our classmates found Americans loud, imperious, and ignorant, and automatically didn't want anything to do with me as a result of their preconceived notions. I spent many a night in my room alone reading and watching horrible excuses for game shows on English telly (what? No cash prizes?!) until I met Jane.

"It's about John…"

His face immediately popped front and center into my

memory. "John, your brother?" I coughed, surprised... choking a little on my tea.

Jane hit me precisely between the shoulder blades with one hand.

John had once been my everything: my reason to get up in the morning, the one who made my pulse race, my safe place when I curled up against his chest, sharing secrets.

"Look, I know that he was a complete idiot to you, and I'll never understand why. I do love him because he's my brother, but..." Jane paused. I knew she'd felt terrible when he broke my heart, which had sent me running into the arms of the next man. Unfortunately, he did much of the same, only worse.

"Seriously, Jane," I said, trying to suppress the tremor in my voice, "the past is the past. I'm over it. What is it about John? Problems sharing the house?"

"It's not that—he's rarely there, and he's respectful enough of our privacy to keep to his side of the house. He always knocks when he comes over to ours." It had been hard for me to visualize how two adult siblings, one with a family, the other a single man who had an endless supply of new girlfriends, could share a house. But then I saw the "house" and realized it was not a bad problem to have. Jane's side of the house was enormous and modern but made to look like a Norman castle. John's side of the house was actually a ruin of a real Norman castle, part of which was livable. They'd inherited the place from their parents last year.

Jane and John had been raised there—John had never stopped living there. But when their mother died, Jane and her husband decided they were tired of not having enough space for their children to run around in their small house in London. And my God, they had plenty of space now. Ten bedrooms. A pool. A great medieval hall. A library....

"I think John is in trouble," Jane continued, her eyes appearing more enormous than ever. "Sales dropped off years ago from his book, and yet he still seems to be rolling in cash. He's making these insane purchases; he bought an Aston Martin last week, and he's got a *riad* in Marrakesh—"

"*Riad?*"

"It's like a villa, with a courtyard—very grand. I just don't know where he's getting the money. He's got that art gallery in Tunbridge Wells that his friend runs for him, but I can't imagine that makes much of anything. I never see anybody in there." Jane picked up the red paper napkin under her teacup and started folding it into triangles. "Yet he's fixing up his side of Wodesley with plumbing, electricity, masonry-workers there all the time. I'm worried he's making money in ways that aren't legal."

"What about his inheritance?"

"Oh, long since gone. Took a gamble on a tech business and it failed."

"Have you asked him about it?" I hated to think of the man I had once known so well, back when he was seemingly innocent, now mixed up in something bad. *Is he dealing drugs?*

"Ellie, you know I'm not shy, but even *I* can't get a thing out of him."

I knew that was true: Jane could make the hardiest of her entitled male colleagues shake in their wing-tipped shoes when she came striding down the hall with an agenda in-hand. And yet to me, she was the one friend with whom I felt the most comfortable. Even in the two days since we'd been at her house, I was beginning to remember the fun-loving twenty-somethings we used to be, before work and kids. And oh yeah, a horrible divorce (on my part) that had occasionally made my head threaten to explode.

Jane continued, the red napkin now torn into tiny pieces, "When I ask him where he's getting the money, he just says 'Investments,' smiles, and walks away. I thought maybe *you* might be able to talk to him? I know he's still got a soft spot in his heart for you. I learned more about John when you dated him than in our whole lives growing up together."

Talk to John? The food in my belly seemed to start audibly groaning and puffing outward, straining the waist of my skinny jeans. I reached for my Tums at the bottom of my handbag.

I had a strict "no-contact" rule when it came to ex-boyfriends. It brought nothing but heartache. And heartburn.

Jane reached for my hand. "I invited him over to dinner tomorrow night, along with a couple of friends. I hope that's okay with you?" she asked, her huge eyes pleading. Who could resist? No wonder Guy had fallen so quickly for her once she set her sights on him.

But she knew what a big deal this would be to me. She knew I had *specifically* asked her if I could avoid seeing him when I'd made plans to come over.

Why in the world would I want to have dinner with a man I despised? Who'd made me look like a fool?

"Sure, um, of course. I'll talk to him."

I'd bitten my tongue. I'd been used to biting it so long with my ex, sometimes I worried that I'd been tamed, like a dog. I used to be a wolf, and now I was a lap dog. Or maybe a sheep.

Being tossed up in the air by a sheep and maybe impaled on a fence post might be preferable to questioning my ex-boyfriend about his nefarious ways. What a fun trip this was turning out to be.

"Great." Jane patted my knee, letting out a big sigh of relief, putting the shredded napkin into the empty teacup. She had passed the baton. Old reliable Ellie was on the case.

I freaking hated old, reliable Ellie sometimes.

LATER THAT NIGHT, Jane and I were sitting in the Great Hall of the modern wing of Wodesley Castle, the kids safely asleep in bed. The room was a replica of a medieval hall, with wood-paneled walls, stone floors, and a timber-lined ceiling twenty feet above. Giant logs crackled and burned red hot in the large stone fireplace, rising fifteen feet high. We had pulled two leather wing chairs close to the heat. It seemed to me the builders of this mansion could've done a better job to insulate and heat the place, given modern technology and all that. Or maybe Jane might have rolled in some space heaters. I was never, ever, warm when I was in England, not even in this gorgeous house.

"It may look beautiful," Jane agreed, "but it's a hell of a thing to keep it running. Thank God people will never quit using toilet rolls."

Jane's grandparents had made a fortune in the toilet paper business. Went to America once, realized the toilet paper there was infinitely softer, and started importing it. Soon everyone abandoned the flimsy sheets of sandpaper-like rolls they had been using, and the rest is bum history. Jane had wisely invested her trust fund, while John had blown his.

Jane brought out a second bottle of merlot when we finished the first, as well as a pair of cozy fleece blankets, probably because she caught me shivering.

"Do you remember the time when Burley Newton gave his never-ending paper on the use of horses and donkeys as representative of class in *The Canterbury Tales*? I thought I was going to die. And the look on Roberts' face as she realized we had twenty more pages to get through."

"Thank God for all the ass puns we got to make later," I said, burrowing further under the blanket, finally beginning to relax in her presence again. The yellow glow from the flames flickered around the room, casting odd shadows in the corners and making things that had appeared normal during the daylight hours into phantasmic, shadowy objects. Jane, however, stayed much as the Jane I'd always known, except for a few crow's feet around her eyes and possibly blonder hair…

"People never believe me about Chaucer and his fart jokes!"

I thought of an appropriate quote. "*This Nicholas anon leet fle a fart, As greet as it had been a thunder-dent…*"

Jane laughed in response. "One raised eyebrow from you in tutorial was enough to set me off. I was trying not to laugh so hard tears slid down my face."

A noise stopped our laughter. It was a cross between a knock and a scraping noise, coming from the front door.

I jumped out of my seat. "Jesus! What is that?" I asked.

Jane's eyes widened. She took a deep breath and started walking to the front door. "What's that noise?"

I grabbed a fireplace shovel and got out my phone, ready to dial 999.

A voice came through the door, "Jane, let me in! I need help!"

My heart did a cartwheel in my chest. I knew that voice. *Oh no, not him. Not yet.*

"John?" Jane ran over to the door, slid back the bolt. In the door came John, looking like he'd been beaten up. He sank to his knees. As I drew closer, the sweetly rank odor of the truly soused reached my nostrils. I stepped back.

"Thank God you're home," he said, thickly. "I need your help to get me out of…" he twisted his body around to show her.

"Manacles? What the hell? Why are you shackled up like somebody who stole bread in *Les Miserables*?" Jane said, crossing her arms and standing over him.

"Try 1344—" He put up his arms; a solid iron hinge gripped his hands about ten inches apart, locked on one side. His right hand had bled, and the stain of old, rusty blood ran underneath the metal.

Jane squatted down next to him, examining the manacles up close. "Did some girl leave you like this? Is this some kind of bondage thing gone wrong? Honestly, John, I'd prefer you not bringing this into my house. The children could see you and ask all sorts of questions."

John winced as his sister touched his hand, and when he opened his eyes, he was staring directly at me. He blinked a few times. "Ellie? Oh yes, Jane told me you were coming." His polite act wasn't winning me over, as though he didn't recognize how ridiculous and scary he looked. "How have you not aged at all? How long has it been?"

"About 17 years," I said. "But to be honest, you're looking a little rough tonight, John."

Yeah, it wasn't nice to say that to him, but it was true. His once-short hair was now long and scraggly, like he hadn't washed it in weeks. His face was dirty, his beard not long enough to be shaped, and not short enough to be rugged. And his clothes: loose, red, drawstring pants, with roughed-up suede boots, and a long, once-white linen shirt open at the neck, revealing his dark-blond chest hair.

Jane put her hands up between the two of us. "Okay, let's just stop with the reunion for one second. Who's got the key for this?"

"We can't get it," John said. "No one has one anywhere near here. You need to call Harry."

"Who's Harry?" I asked, taking a closer look at the manacles encompassing his wrists. *How are we going to get this off him? I wondered. The fire department? The police? A locksmith? A blacksmith?*

"Harry's our friend from when we were growing up," Jane explained. "Lives on a farm not too far from here. Yes, maybe he would have some blacksmithing equipment? Some tools?" She whipped her phone from her jeans muttering, "This is going to be an awkward... Hi Harry?" Her voice was pitched high, and she walked away.

John slumped onto his side on the floor, his arms still forced behind him. "Things look very swirly to me now. Too much traveling—back and forth—not good for the head..." With that, his eyes rolled into the back of his head.

Well, crap. "Jane!" I yelled. "He passed out!"

CHAPTER TWO

Right as an aspen lefe, she gan to quake
Troilus and Cressida, Geoffrey Chaucer

JANE INSISTED WE not call an ambulance. "He's just drunk, not injured," she insisted. I suspected she wanted to keep the fact that her brother was trapped in manacles out of any report that might be made, in an effort to keep her family business private from the prying eyes and ears of the local village.

John's snoring supported her supposition; he appeared to be sleeping and would occasionally mumble and fuss when we jiggled him, and then fall back asleep again. We placed a pillow under his head and used one of our fuzzy blankets to put over him while we waited for help.

I shook my head at this bizarre scene. So vastly different from my quiet nights at home—me, alone in my vast king-sized bed, and the girls wrapped around each other in Abby's double bed. We lived a small, quiet life, which was about all I could stand after the emotional upheavals that Alex had put us through. He loved us—no, he hated us—no, he wanted to stay at home. And finally, no, he needed to be by himself. Living with Alex was like being strapped to a rollercoaster, with all the highs and lows, some thrills, and a lot of upset stomachs.

I walked back to our chairs to down another glass of wine,

while Jane paced back and forth.

Minutes later, we heard crashing pebbles in the driveway as a car furled through them.

A light tap at the door, and a man came through the unlocked door.

He didn't look like any farmer I'd seen before. Dressed in dark jeans, oxford shoes, a button-down shirt, a Barbour waxed jacket, and carrying a bag full of tools, he appeared very posh. His cheeks were ruddy, his eyes blue but with dark circles under them, his chin strong, and his lips full. I looked away, trying to find something else to stare at, feeling instantly like a dumbstruck teenager too nervous to take in the good-looking boy in her midst.

"Thank you for coming, Harry." Jane walked up to give the man a kiss on each cheek. She was tall at 5'10," but he was a good five inches taller than she and she needed to stand on tiptoe to touch her lips to his face. But his focus was on John, as he moved to the floor beside the unconscious man.

"Let's see what we've got here," Harry said.

John remained on his side, his two hands behind him, quite clearly alive as he snored loudly. Harry put a hand to his head to check for a fever. Then he leaned over him to examine the manacles.

"Good God, these look ancient," he said. "Not machine made—hand-hammered. Where would the key go? Ah, here." He pointed to a hole at the opposite end of the hinge, and then looked over at me. "Oh hello," he said, noticing me, standing nearby. "I'm Harry."

He reached out a hand, and I shook it. It enveloped mine in a warm, solid grip.

"Hi, I'm Ellie. An old friend of Jane's from university."

"Oh, sorry guys," Jane piped in, as though she'd been some-place else. "Where are my manners? I should've introduced you."

"Pleased to meet you," Harry said, as if I had just walked into his place of business. "Would either of you have a hair pin?"

"I do," I said. Abby had earlier taken two sections of my hair to braid and then pinned them at the back. She loves playing with my hair like she's a teenage girl, says it relaxes her; so long as she doesn't pull it, I love it too.

I removed the bobby pins from my hair, handed them to him, and started untwisting my hair. I caught him looking at me a second longer as my long, red hair swung down to my shoulders.

I cast a quick look at his left hand. No ring. It was a new, reflexive habit.

Harry bent the bobby pin into a hook and started inserting it into the keyhole. He took it out, bent the pin a different way, and tried again. Finally, on about the tenth try, the hinge popped open. Harry eased the manacles from John's wrists. He then checked for broken bones and rolled John onto his back. "John, mate, wake—up. It's Harry." He eased open one of John's eyelids, and grabbing his phone, turned the flashlight on, and flashed it into his pupils. They dilated.

John screwed up his face and reached up a freed hand to cover up his eyes. "What's happening?"

"John, you're home with Jane, and me, Harry. Everything's okay. Would you like some water? Tea?" Harry asked, his voice deep and lush, the kind that could read poems and make women swoon.

He grabbed an arm to help John to his feet, and I came up to the other side, holding onto his elbow.

Maybe I should have joined farmerdates.com instead of Match.

John cleared his throat. "What I need," John said, "is meat. I need iron."

"Iron, hmmm. That's specific. Okay," Jane said, "I've got some leftover steak pot pie. Does that sound good?"

"Perfect," said John. Then he squeezed my shoulder that his hand was draped over as we walked him to the fire. "Ellie, there's something I've been meaning to tell you. I tried to tell you this many years ago…"

If the sight of my ex-boyfriend in manacles wasn't enough, the promise of an explanation more than caught my attention.

◈

CHAPTER THREE

I am right sorry for your heavinesse.
Troilus and Cressida, Geoffrey Chaucer

JOHN STAFFORD AND I had had a brief but combustible romance when I was twenty-four and he was twenty-nine. We'd met through Jane, of course. I was a PhD candidate at King's, and he was writing a book and working at an art gallery. We had amazing chemistry—couldn't keep our hands off each other. I loved his tall, angular body and his wavy English hair that seemed to defy gravity. We shared a similar love for Middle English history and literature and went to all the plays and concerts we could, thanks to my student discount. Every day I woke up with a smile on my face, knowing that I would see or hear from him, and he'd make me laugh.

But it ended just as quickly as it began. One day John just didn't show up for a date we'd had planned to visit the Bodleian Library, home to some of the most precious manuscripts and books in the world. I waited at Paddington Station for the 11:06 train to Oxford, at Platform #6, calling his phone on my cell. He never picked up. I decided to just get on the train, figuring he must have been stuck in the tube somewhere; the trains were always breaking down. I'd go on ahead, he'd call, and we'd meet up there. But despite numerous calls and texts, I still didn't hear from him. I wandered around the Bodleian in a daze. *Had he gotten into an accident?*

Upon my return to London with still no word from him, I contacted Jane. She didn't know where he was either, nor did their parents.

I wanted to contact the police and file a missing person's report, but when I told Jane what I was about to do, she confessed that this sort of thing had happened with her brother before. "I'm so sorry Ellie, I wanted to warn you, but I was really hoping that with you, maybe he wouldn't do it." She told me he'd periodically gone missing for weeks at a time since he was seventeen years old. The first time it happened, their parents had freaked out. They contacted the authorities and got his picture in the newspaper. But then he showed up, apologizing, saying he needed to get away from all the stress of exams and gone camping. This happened again and again over the years, and he always showed back up with an excuse, apologized for upsetting everyone, and the episodes were swept under the rug. "I've been on pins and needles the whole time," Jane said, "worried he might pull something like this on you."

I stopped eating. I barely showed up for classes, which was very unlike me. One of my professors handed me a card with the name of an eating disorder specialist, "In case you need it," she said.

Six weeks later, when John reappeared at the doors of my one-room student apartment, soaking wet, begging for forgiveness, I could not. He looked ten pounds heavier, and his cheeks were rosy, but his eyes wouldn't look into mine. "Let me explain, Ellie, please." I folded my arms and asked him to leave.

I would not forgive him when he met me outside the college library three days later, nor when he met me at Jane's flat that she shared with her fiancé Guy the next week. "But please, Ellie, you've got to listen to me. The place I go, it's hard to believe, but…"

I refused to listen to him and sent him packing. He sent me

emails, but I deleted them. Jane never stopped apologizing. "I shouldn't have let you two get involved in the first place. You're too good for him," she'd said, holding me around the shoulders, "I shouldn't be saying that because he's my brother, but it's true."

His actions were unforgiveable. *You don't do that to a person you love.* Him disappearing showed that he didn't truly care about me. How could he not even pick up the phone, send a text, an email? How selfish he was to keep me worried about him, questioning our relationship, questioning his character; what he could possibly be doing? All the songs that I used to love suddenly I had to turn off. I could listen only to the news about wars around the world, putting my own heartbreak neatly into a mental box I labeled, "It could be a lot worse."

The truth was simple: he'd made a conscious decision, day after day, to not contact me. That was no slip-up, that was six weeks of *choosing* not to care about what I'd thought and how I was.

John gave up contacting me after that. And I'd been able to keep a safe distance from him ever since, until now.

NOW THE MAN I'd hated for so long sat before me in one of the wing chairs where Jane and I had been reminiscing not an hour before. He'd gobbled up Jane's steak and kidney pot pie, his cheeks were pink again, his dark-brown eyes had that familiar twinkle of the exceedingly brilliant, but his long, dark hair was lank, and his skin still filthy. He needed a shower, but he would not yet leave until he spoke to me, alone.

Harry and Jane excused themselves to sit in the kitchen. I could hear Harry singing something that was cracking Jane up. Was that a Bee Gees song? *Who sang Bee Gees songs? How did his voice get so high?*

I wanted to be anywhere but here but remained in that wing-backed chair.

"Please do relax, Ellie," John said. "You look like you're about to spring away like a gazelle who spots a lion."

I sighed, and curled up onto the chair, tucking my feet under me, trying to stay warm. "Well?"

"Jane told me you're divorced."

"Yes, three years ago," I said. "Sophie was two, and Abby five." Alex had left parenting all in my lap and ran away. That seemed to be an unfortunate pattern the men in my life shared.

Maybe I'm the one who's toxic? That thought kept me up many nights.

"I've always regretted what happened to us," he said, reaching for my hand. I looked down at his hand and kept seeing it still bound in the manacles. I shoved both hands under my arms. "I know you think I'm a stupid playboy now, but for me, you'll always be the one who got away."

Too little, way too late. "You don't get to say that. You made a conscious decision to not be in touch with me."

"That's exactly why I want to explain myself to you. I'm not heartless. I'm…" he stopped. He cleared his throat again. Something he did quite a lot. "When I disappeared on you, and my sister, and before they died, my parents, I go to a place where it's physically impossible for me to have contact with the outside world. You have seen evidence of that, tonight."

"The manacles? What—do people lock you up? Are you… some sort of spy?"

"It's not *where* I go that gets me into trouble, but *when* I go…" He gestured to his drawstring homespun pants, his linen shirt, his odd boots.

"What do you mean, *when*?" I asked.

Before he could get any more words out, he went pale, his eyes crossed and then rolled back in his head. In slow motion, his chin hit his chest, his jaw dropped open, and he slumped over the arm of the chair.

"Jane!" I yelled.

Jane and Harry came running out. Jane took a look at him, and he let out a snore. "Let's get him to the couch in the library," she said. "Maybe he just needs to sleep it off."

"Yeah, I think he's okay," I said, looking down at him. "Maybe just exhausted? It's so weird, one minute he was talking to me, and the next he just…"

With fainttyng & feblenes he fell to þe ground, in a dede swone.

He was feeble all right, thinking that by telling me I was "the one who got away" would make me change my mind about him. And what did John mean about "when" he was going? A time zone difference? I just didn't understand. And what was with the homespun clothes he was wearing? He was dressed for a Renaissance fair. Did he peddle turkey legs? Was he one of those guys who danced in town squares? I searched back in my memory for the name—a Morris dancer?

Harry ended up pitching John over his shoulder like I've seen soldiers do in the war to evacuate their wounded brothers. I marveled at his strength. Farming, I guess, could make you that strong.

Jane directed Harry to put him in her library, where there was a nice cozy couch. We covered him up with a blanket and turned on a low light so he would not be startled if he woke in the middle of the night. Then we crept quietly out of the room.

"Whoosh, that was intense," I said, sitting down on a nearby chair.

"What did he say to you?" Jane asked. Harry stood next to her chair.

"I'm not sure—he didn't get to say too much before he passed out. Something about 'I was the one who got away,' and that it's not 'where he goes, but *when* he goes when he disappears.' Had he disappeared on you this time?" I asked.

"Yes, but he knew I was throwing a party for you tomorrow, so he was showing back up for that. But the manacles? That's new."

"I'm sorry that you still have to go through this with him. It must worry you an awful lot. I only had to deal with it for a short while." I was relieved that I'd been wise enough to step away from it, years ago.

But Jane couldn't; you can't abandon your brother.

"Ellie." Harry reached out his hand and placed it on my arm. "You look a little shaken up. Are you okay?"

I looked up at him. He had such piercing, beautiful, blue eyes. "Oh, you're sweet to ask, but yes, of course I'm okay!" I forced myself to look away quickly. Away from those eyes.

We may have taken the manacles off John, but that iron cage around my heart was still firmly in place.

❖

CHAPTER FOUR

For many marvels they had known, but such a one never;
So the folk there judged it phantasm or magic.
Sir Gawain and the Green Knight, Anonymous

JANE IS A fantastic hostess (her guest beds were incredibly comfortable, the towels thick, and there were hot water bottles at night), a dear friend, endlessly interesting and fun to talk to. Add to that list: fantastic cook. We'd had a full English breakfast the next morning—fried eggs, fried toast, baked beans, bacon, fried mushrooms, fried tomatoes—basically a heart attack on a plate. But it was perfectly suited to sustain my crew to do a tour of nearby Hever Castle, the former home of Anne Boleyn. The girls and I were going off on our own—I'd borrowed Jane's "safe-as-houses" Volvo, guaranteed to shield us in the event of a crash (if I forgot which side of the road I was driving on). Jane stayed at home to cook up an authentic medieval feast for her guests and us that night.

The food was the only thing I was looking forward to when I thought about the party. I had no desire to see John again or hear whatever crazy excuse he was trying to shill off on me about the manacles. I planned to put on my best Connecticut bullshit shield and keep it raised, no matter what he might say to me.

Jane had also invited Harry (she gave me a wink when she

said that, and when I asked what she was on about, she just shrugged with a cheeky grin), along with the local rector of the village church and his wife, and another neighbor, a former "football" star, and his partner. It was ostensibly a party to celebrate me being in the UK, but I think it was just an excuse for Jane to go all out and cook up a storm. Jane liked to be busy. She needed papers to grade, undergrads to intimidate, faculty meetings to rule, lectures to give, and new shoes to buy for the purpose of doing it all while looking fierce as hell.

When we returned from Hever Castle (I highly recommend it—moat, ghost stories, furniture, portraits, and archery practice and painting little crowns for the girls—pasted-on "jewels" extra.), Jane had platters in warmers, sternos lit under chafing dishes, a bar set out, and ballads from the 14th century playing on her multi-room Bose system. While Jane was placing ice in her chic, copper ice bucket, I unleashed a tirade against the crazy drivers that were out on the roads. "Somebody didn't have their lights on when it was raining, and I flashed them a half dozen times and still they would not change!"

"You just can't stand it when people don't follow the rules, can you? Let it go! Let them drive the way they want to drive," Jane advised.

"It's just common decency. That's all I'm after—common decency." Then I had a comeback, "And *you* should talk. I thought on your sabbatical you were going to finally read Tolstoy and learn how to meditate. Instead, you're throwing dinner parties and painting rooms. And trying to save your brother's soul. Geez, that's relaxing!"

Jane held a piece of ice in her hand and studied me. "So, the conclusion here is—you need to lighten up and give people a break, and I need to chill out."

"I'll accept that," I said, closing Jane's fingers over the ice cube. "Chill out. Starting now, with this cute, little cube. And the next person who breaks the law, I'll simply look the other way."

"Americans say 'cute' too much," Jane complained.

"Chill!"

The girls and I went up to change. They were having a special dinner with their BFFs Alice and Cordelia and the nanny up in the playroom, followed by a movie after. Professor Jane did not allow for much TV in her house, so this was a special treat for all.

I had to gear up for a night with my ex and Farmer Harry. How did one dress for such an evening? Well, I didn't have much choice as I'd only brought over two dresses for the week in case we went out to a West End show or something. So, it was between a red, off-the-shoulder dress that was midi-length, and a fitted black dress, that showed a little cleavage and a lot of class. I decided on dress #2 and spent a bit of time on my hair and make-up, something I hadn't even thought about doing the night before.

And then I reached for my pair of sexy slingback heels—not too high, because I can't walk in heels that well. I teeter.

They were not there. I could see them now, clearly, still tumbled saucily on my bathroom floor, waiting for me to pack them. One of the girls I'm sure interrupted me, and my mom brain declared I was done packing. My only two choices were my tall leather riding boots, or my hiking shoes. There was only one answer. I'd look like a sophisticated woman on top, and a horsey woman on the bottom.

"Mommy, you look pretty tonight," said Sophie. "I wish I had your blue eyes."

"Mommy always looks pretty," chided Abby, pushing her sister a little too hard.

"Hey, hey, don't push Sophie please," I said. My two loved each other, but Abby was very bossy to her little sister, and Sophie was a big-time attention seeker. Sometimes the combination could be combustible, and distraction was the name of the game to keep the situation from escalating.

"I have time to read you a little bit before we each go to our parties," I said. Abby sat to the left of me on my bed, and Sophie sat on my lap. We didn't have to bring many books with us since we knew the Percy girls would have millions of great books. We settled into a chapter of *The Lion, The Witch, and the Wardrobe.* We came to the scene where Lucy and Edmund meet up in Narnia.

"Oh, Edmund, I am glad you got in too. The others will have to believe in Narnia now that both of us have been there. What fun it will be."

"Mommy, what would you do if I went to Narnia?" asked Abby.

"Oh my gosh," I said, "I would be so worried if I didn't know where you were. But I would come find you, wherever you are."

Sophie put her baby-soft hands on my cheeks and kissed me on the forehead. "Mommy don't be sad, I kissed it better. We would never leave you."

I squeezed her into a hug and smiled. "Thanks honey, my brain did need a kiss. I think sometimes I get too caught up in books." The girls nodded; my nose was always in a book when they were playing independently, because I was always trying to attain more knowledge. Life was quickly ticking by, and I felt like I needed to cram as much information in as I possibly could. There was so much out there I didn't know, some secret to our existence that I needed to find out—and maybe by reading just the right thing, I could find it.

"Now it's time for you to go off to your party." I set Sophie down, and then gave Abby a hug. "Are you excited?"

"Yes!" they both shouted. They'd heard the other girls talking about all the fancy things they were going to have at their party. Cucumber sandwiches, scones, pink tea, and pigs in a blanket.

"You have fun too at your party, Mom," said Abby. "I like it when you dress up."

I curtsied. "Well, it makes a change from normal, right? And thank you for doing my hair again! What would I do without you?"

We parted at the top of the stairs, laughing and throwing kisses at each other.

"WHY DO TWO smokin' hot birds like you two get involved in anything as boring as bloody Chaucer?" Roger Field asked. The famous soccer player (soccer to an American, "football" to the rest of the world) was rich as Thebes and used that as a license to say whatever he wanted. His wife Jilly, young, blond, perfect make-up, perfect boobs, sat beside him, and gave him a sharp look.

"It's not exactly a practical vocation now, is it?" murmured Mabel Goddard, wife of the local Rector, hand on her chin. Mabel personified practicality in her wool cardigan, print dress, and sensible shoes. Her husband, on the other hand, tall with black and white hair, found everything fascinating. He said upon meeting me, "An American? Fascinating!" and shook my hand vigorously.

Jane and I looked at each other to decide how best to answer the soccer player's question, and I stole a quick glance at the real hottie in the room—Harry. While Jane and I were not usually given the "smokin' hot" qualifier, we did often get asked: *Why study and teach Middle English?* What in the world drew us to devote our lives to the study of a dead language and a bunch of snooze-worthy tales of knights and quests?

Jane turned her head, her dark-brown hair styled into a sassy and fashionable bob, and winked at me. It was my turn to give our standard response. I got up.

"Oh no, here it comes," said John, who knew the routine from days of old.

I walked over to the kitchen island and boosted myself onto the top of it then started reciting, in my most dramatic voice, with as accurate an accent as I could muster and with the assistance of two gin and tonics. "From the Prologue of *Canterbury Tales*:

> *"Do come," he said, "my mistrals*
> *And gestours for to telln tales,*
> *Anoon in myn arming*
> *Of romances that been royales—*

Of popes and of cardinals
And eek of love—likinge."

Then Jane clambered up next to me, as lithe and glamorous as she'd been before she'd married Guy and had two kids:

Who so shall telle a tale after a man,
He moste reherse, as neighe as ever he can,
Everich word, if it be in his charge,
All speke he never so rudely and so large;
Or elles he moste tellen his tale untrewe,
Or feinen thinges, or finden wordes newe.

Jane and I bowed to polite applause and a couple of "huzzahs" from John, hopped down from our perches, and rejoined the group at the long table.

I overheard Roger say, "What just happened?" to Jilly. She shushed him.

"To me," I said, "it's all about the romance of the time. Courtly love, chivalry, pilgrimages. I love that during what was supposedly a primitive time, great literature—and some very raunchy poems—were written, in the midst of death, plague, and famine...."

"Yes, and cheers to the written word for giving us comfort in the face of all the bad news out there," Jane raised her glass. My glass met hers in solidarity.

"Amen to that," Reverend Goddard said. Mabel crossed herself.

John raised another toast. "To my dear sister, Jane, and the lovely Ellie. Smart, beautiful, and loving women. And to the glorious, medieval world that inspires them." I shifted in my seat, uncomfortable with him implying any sort of ownership over me.

Harry and the others raised their glasses of wine to join the toast, except for the Reverend's wife, who was six months pregnant.

"Mommy?" I heard Sophie's baby-like voice call me from the other side of the room.

"Sophie? Come here, sweet pea." She walked over to me, looking at the other people in the room slowly and deliberately. "What's up?" I asked. "You're supposed to be with the other girls." I pulled her warm body into my lap.

"I just wanted to say hi to your fwends," she said—she still had a problem with pronouncing those r's.

Sophie never met a stranger and loved to be appreciated as the adorable little girl she was, as well as make people laugh. After I briefly introduced her to everybody, I said, "Now, time to get upstairs, and no more interrupting, okay, sweets?"

"Okay, Mommy," she got down off my lap, paused, and then said, "and you all, have a fantastical night! I'm off to Narnia!" She made one twirl, leaped into mid-air, and then skipped out of the kitchen.

I blushed. She was a ham, but you couldn't help but think that was endearing. Or at least, I couldn't.

I hadn't gotten much of a chance to talk to Harry, but he did seem happy to see me when I came into the room. Or at least, happy to see my somewhat-revealing dress. And now I could see his eyes twinkling at my youngest's antics.

"Your olde English—that was marvelous. Better than what's on the telly," Jilly said, nudging her husband in the gut. "Don't let ol' Roger here give you any guff. Unless it's got cars and sports in it, he ain't interested."

I needed to remember to ask Jane why she had asked the soccer star here again.

Then Jane said, "How are your girls enjoying Mrs. Hart's class? Alice loves it." Ah now, I remembered: Jill's twins were in the same class as Alice, and Jill and Jane chaired some sort of parent fundraising group for the school.

Reverend Goddard, on my left, turned to me as I passed him the cheese board. "So, Ellie, have you had any 'spooky' experiences since you've been up here at Wodesley?" He held his fingers as imaginary quotation marks over "spooky."

I raised my eyes in surprise. "Spooky? Why no, this place is like living in a hotel," I said, thinking of my cozy guest bedroom waiting for me upstairs, far nicer and neater than my messy bedroom at home, where books and papers covered every surface.

"Well, local gossip has it…" Reverend Goddard leaned in, in a conspiratorial manner, "that strange things have occurred in and around Wodesley Castle for generations."

"Such as?" I pressed, suddenly more awake. This was more fun than talking about the declining church-going populace, a subject we'd already touched on a bit too long for my interest.

"I've heard that when the Staffords' parents built this modern addition to the castle, the construction workers said the smell of smoke used to waft through the house, when there was no fire anywhere near here. They heard thundering hooves, even though there were no horses anywhere near here. And then there was the clanking…"

"Clanking?" I asked.

"Yes, like the clanking of swords. Said it sounded like an old Errol Flynn movie, er, what was it called…?"

"*Robin Hood*?"

"That's the one!"

Jane's parents had inherited the toilet paper business, and its earnings, when John and Jane were small. Romantic in nature, they'd decided to buy the broken-down Wodesley castle and fix it up. The whole country had been mired in recession, so they were able to negotiate the property that held the ruins of the castle for a very reasonable price. They built the new house next to it, incorporating the stone exterior of the old castle into the new "manor" house.

"Reverend Goddard, this house was built over thirty years ago," I argued. "Why are people still talking about it?"

"Doesn't matter how old the tales are—it makes for a good story, doesn't it? You hear a lot, believe me, down at the public house."

Harry nodded. He had been listening quietly across the table.

He didn't have much to say for a large portion of the dinner, but maybe he was shy. Or—the horror—boring? A statue-worthy face and an outstanding body will only get you so far, in my book. But still, when he did cast the occasional glance my way, my heart did a cartwheel.

We were interrupted by Jane bringing out Course #4: smoked trout. I took a polite but small portion and nibbled at it. We'd already had a cheese course, a soup, roast pheasants, scalloped potatoes, sorbets to clear our palates, and now fish. Jane had made sure we each had finger bowls between us to cleanse our fingertips and delighted in having us use just knives and spoons—no forks—to eat with. Forks weren't used in England until the 16th century, which was the end of the time period we studied.

The Reverend's wife was gnawing thoughtfully on a celery stick, turning down the buttery rolls being passed on a tray with a sad look in her eyes.

"Mabel," I said, hoping to engage her, "what do you make of your husband's assertions about ghosts at Wodesley?"

"Ghosts? We say Father, Son, and the Holy Ghost—he is always at the table with us, is he not? As for the other spirits who might be tagging along, well, they aren't that important, are they?"

"Well," I said, "that might be true Biblically-speaking, but a real-life ghost in the house? That could be pretty cool."

"Not really," said Harry, sadly. "Not if it's somebody you used to know."

What a strange comment. I almost wished he'd made an innocuous comment about the weather.

The vicar tapped me on the shoulder, and whispered in my ear, "Harry's seen some awfully bad stuff in Afghanistan. Just retired from the army. He's been spending a lot of time at the farm, I think. Trying to reset his compass, you know."

Oh, God. I was being so obtuse, trying to be witty about my Middle English skills and ghosts, and here poor Harry was suffering from PTSD. Jane hadn't told me. She'd only said they'd kissed one day under a tree at school when they were twelve, and they both agreed it was weird—like kissing your sibling.

Finally, Jane served the sinful dessert of sticky toffee pudding. Who needed anything more in life than sugar and butter? I lapped it up with gusto, emitting soft groans of delight, intermingled with whimpers as my expanding stomach pushed against the tight waistline of my dress.

The two couples with children got up to leave soon after, and the mood lightened considerably thereafter. Harry, John, and Jane had an easy rapport from having had years of adventures together and funny stories to recall. Jane and I had been best friends since university. And John and I… well, I tried to be a grown-up around him. Let bygones be bygones.

We started a silly game where we made hats out of cloth napkins (*Sailor! Turban! Pirate! Crown!*) and acted out charades.

When we took a break from laughing, talk returned to the pleasant Reverend Goddard and his sour wife. "Oh yeah," I remembered, turning to Jane, "he mentioned some funny rumors about Wodesley Castle, but then we got sidetracked. Clanking swords or something?" I tread carefully, not wanting to upset Harry, who seemed much happier now that the others were gone. Maybe he was an introvert who did better in small groups.

"Those idiots down in the village with their stupid rumors," Jane scoffed. "Surely there are more interesting things to talk about. How about Brexit? The crazy cost of housing in this country? Honestly, it's shocking that you can still leave school at the age of fifteen. We need more education, not less—"

"So let me be clear," I said. Once Jane starts on a political rant, it's hard to reel her back in. "You've never heard or seen a ghost or anything out of the ordinary since you've been living here?"

"Don't be daft, Ellie." She swatted me on the hand. Jane was a swatter, especially when loaded up with gin. "Poor Mum and Dad were forever having to debunk some silly story by some village drunk, but I never—"

John interrupted, looking up from his phone. "You never did, Jane," he sighed. "Always too busy, with your nose stuck in a book, naturally." The smile fell from his face.

Jane went pale.

I tried to intervene—keep the mood light. "So, there's something to these rumors?"

"Oh, more than just something." John turned to me, deadly serious. "It turns out that when you're a curious lad like I was when we first moved here, and your parents are busy building a house, and your sister is too busy buried in her studies to play, well, you explore on your own. I tried to tell them about all the odd things going on around the house, but they just laughed. No one took me seriously." He stopped, taking a look at our expressions now. "I've seen you all giving me strange looks today after you saw me last night, handcuffed. It wasn't the time or the place to do this before, because you had guests, and your little daughters were about. But now I want to show you all the magic that *paying attention* to your surroundings can bring. Follow me," he ordered as he pushed his chair back and stood.

Harry stood up, looking distinctly uncomfortable. "I think it's about time for me to head home," he nodded at me and Jane, and backed away from his chair. "I'm sure this is just for family."

"Harry, I want you to see this too. You helped me last night. We've been friends for years. You need to see what I'm talking about."

I don't think John gave him any choice, so Harry shrugged and stayed put.

John stood up, weaved tipsily, and then steadied himself. I leapt up and grabbed his elbow, but he shook me off, and lurched down the hall.

"Follow me!"

CHAPTER FIVE

For thogh we slepe, or wake, or rome, or ryde,
Ay fleeth the tyme; it nyl no man abyde.
Wife of Bath, Geoffrey Chaucer

W E FOLLOWED JOHN down to the old castle. Jane had offered to take us for a tour when he was gone, but I didn't want to see his bachelor pad. Part of the *no-contact* rule was the *no-see* rule.

Taking a key from his pocket, John opened the giant oak door that led from Jane's modern house to his semi-renovated castle.

Jane whispered in my ear, "I have a key too. I'm not sure why he locks it, but I respect his privacy. Privacy is paramount to John."

The rush of cold air hit me—it must have been a good fifteen degrees colder in the old castle, and there was a smell of damp in the air, as though the old stones could never fully dry out. John turned around to look at us, wrapping our arms around ourselves. "A bit cold, isn't it? It's still a work in progress. My own apartment here, though, is quite snug."

We followed him up a tall, winding, stone staircase. It had no railing—nothing to stop you to tumble to your death two floors below. I started to hyperventilate a little, picturing a fall that would be impossible to stop. As I clung to the inside column, I got slower and slower, the higher up we went. Thank goodness I'd forgotten my slingback heels.

"You all right, Ellie?" Harry was behind me, probably fed up with my slow progress.

"You can pass me if you want. I'm just a little…"

"Cautious?"

"Um, I would probably categorize it as 'scared,' to tell you the truth. Not a fan of heights. It's stupid, right?" I turned around, very carefully, to look at him, to apologize. "You can pass me if you want," I repeated.

"I wouldn't dream of passing you," Harry said. "I'll stay right behind you to make sure you don't fall. You do have to watch your step, though, there are a few cracks here and there." He placed a reassuringly warm hand on my back. With his farmer's muscles and strong physique, I knew he could stop me from falling. Or at least make a valiant effort.

Jane and John were already looking down at us from what might have been the tower.

"Get a move on, woman!" called Jane. "What's wrong with you—we're not *that* old."

"It's not because I'm out of shape, Jane," I said. "Do you not remember that heights and I don't mix?"

"Almost there, Ellie," Harry said softly. There was no sarcasm in his voice, no exasperation.

At last, we reached the last four steps, and a reasonably safe balcony with a railing. Safety. "There now, Ellie, you did it. I know a fear of heights can be crippling," Harry said.

"It's the sole reason I decided against a career in roofing," I said.

Harry laughed out loud. "That's a damned shame—you would have made an excellent roofer. Might be more practical than teaching a bunch of acne-ridden eighteen-year-olds Chaucer though, right?"

Oomph, that hurt. I was just beginning to like him, and then he joined the soccer star in dissing my career. Yes, not all eighteen-year-olds fell in love with Chaucer… but when those few did, I know I'd helped uncover an essential part of them. This mysterious force that resonated with a medieval poet's words. Truly, when it happened, that was magic.

"Well, yeah, I guess if you put it that way, it doesn't sound—"

Harry tried to take it back. "I didn't mean to—"

"I guess I'm no hero soldier," I said, "saving lives and things like that. Like you do. Or did."

"That part of my life is over now," Harry said. "It was the worst part, but quite possibly the best as well."

"Holy shit, John!" Jane shouted from down the hall.

We turned the corner and came into a room that John had just opened with another key.

The place was a treasure trove: gold and silver chalices, plates, urns, swords, shields, gowns, robes, coins, flags, furs.

And books. "Jesus Christ!" I said.

"Ellie, come see!" Jane held open an illuminated manuscript—a beautifully, hand-painted illustrated book. "Mid 1300's, don't you think?" she asked.

"It's a good starting point," I said, pointing out the curve of the "s," that was long and shaped like a modern day "f."

Jane turned her head to stare at her brother. "Where did you get all this, John?"

"Is it all real?" I asked.

"Have you been stealing?" Jane asked. "Good God, if you've been stealing, I don't know what we're going to do with you. What would Mum and Dad think?"

John shook his head. "I think they'd be proud of me. Because this is what I was telling you about, Jane. I was *paying attention*. All those noises were trying to tell us something when we moved here. Because I listened, and did research, and investigated what you, Mum, and Dad, ignored and it led me to this." He gestured around the room, smiling.

"This stuff belongs in a museum," I said, "and a library, and the Victoria and Albert, the National War Museum…" So many curators would love to have their hands on these precious items. They should be on display in public, not locked up in a ruined castle. *How dumb is that?* Unless he intended on selling them.

Jane and I went through more of the books; they certainly looked authentic. The script was true to the period, the ink, the vellum used for paper, the spine of the book carefully sewn together. Harry was running his fingers down the armor. John stood back like a proud father, surveying us all.

Beyond the books, there was a beautiful silk green dress on a hanger, laced up the front, with long bell sleeves. I looked at the seams. Hand sewn. The silk was rough, not manufactured, the way modern silk was. Gold thread was woven through the neckline.

I heard John's voice behind my ear. "Please, try that on for me. There's a bathroom just over there, and a big mirror."

"Oh, that's crazy," I said.

"If you put it on, I'll tell you where I got all this stuff from." John's breath was boozy. It was impossible not to drink too much at Jane's. I indulged, but you can't ever have too much if you're a parent—you never know if there's going to be an emergency. But John was still cohesive enough to make a bargain.

Ethically, it's wrong to put on a fragile, antique dress. Plus, how could I, an American woman born in the 20th century who ate fast food once (twice) a week, possibly fit into something made to fit a tiny medieval woman? I held the dress up—the dress was laced. *Of course!* It was designed to fit women of all sizes, with panels at the side to be laced too. Fabric was so precious, it had to be able to fit many different women as it passed down from mother to daughter, sister to sister, or employer to servant. Also, with women being pregnant nearly all the time thanks to no birth control, the waist had to expand to fit a baby bump.

"Okay," I said, "but only because it's going to go to a museum after this, and I'll never have another chance. Jane, you put on one too. It'll be fun."

"You've gone and lost your head, woman," said Jane. "What

on Earth would make you think that I'd ever be an accessory to this madness? It's bad enough this thievery is taking place in my house—"

"This-is-not-your-house," John said slowly and deliberately.

"*Next* to my house, then," Jane huffed, and dipped her head back into a book she held with her long sleeves so as not to get her fingerprints on the delicate paper.

Far be it for me to get between a sibling fight, but I did want to see how Jane would look in a golden circlet with a chiffon-esque covering. I was hoping she'd look like Maid Marion from Robin Hood. "Come on, Jane, not even this?" I said, waving my hand QVC style around the hat, trying to make it look enticing.

I will refrain from telling you what Jane called me at that moment but suffice it to say it was not at all polite.

"Harry, come try this armor on. It'll be like that summer I made you participate in that Medieval Festival as swordsmen," John said, playfully punching him in the shoulder.

"I can't believe I signed up for that. I felt like such a fool per-forming in front of everybody."

"Well, you certainly got into the spirit. Everyone who took you on ended up on their backsides. Good thing we weren't fighting with real swords."

That armor couldn't possibly be big enough to fit Harry, with the average man being about 5'6 back then. Although a lot of armor was custom-made for the wearer, this armor—a chest plate and shoulder plates—looked like they too could be laced up as well.

Jane and I exchanged glances of wonder, concern, and dismay all at once. I sheepishly looked at the dress I was holding in my arms and said, "Well, it can't hurt to try it on, right? I've always wanted to see what I'd look like as a medieval lady. Research?"

She gave me a weak smile. Her mind must have been whir-ring a million miles a minute, agog at the books in front of us, and aghast at the thievery that her brother must have been up to.

The bathroom was rustic, but had modern lights and plumbing, and a large mirror. I stripped out of my dress, and slipped the long dress on, lacing the leather ties closed. It was not too short—whomever had worn this must have been as tall as most of the men of her time. The green was definitely the right shade for this redhead, and the design flattered my curves. The floor was too cold to be without shoes, so I put my brown leather riding boots back on over my socks.

I heard John say, "I'm not saying anything until Ellie comes out, Jane. Just wait!" His voice was insistent, dark. He was running this dog and pony show. I'm sure Jane hated that.

I came out of the bathroom. Harry was still trying to adjust the armor over his shoulders. But John saw me, and he put his hand over his chest as if to contain his heart. "Ellie, it looks like that dress was made for you."

Jane squeaked, "Ellie, you look more beautiful than I've ever seen you—even than at your wedding to Evil Alex!" She came over to me and gave me a squeeze.

Harry didn't say a thing. I was hoping maybe his mouth was hanging open just a little, or maybe that's just the way his mouth always was? Maybe he was a mouth breather, and I hadn't noticed.

"John, okay, time's up," Jane said. "We've admired your things and it's fun playing dress up, but tell us, where are you getting these antiques from?"

John briefly pulled his phone out of his pocket and checked it, then put it away. "I've been there," John said.

"Been where?"

"Come and see. I can only go back briefly, because I got in trouble the last time, and I'm not in the best of shape, but I want you to come and see it for yourself…"

"See what? Go back where? It's really late," I said, torn between wanting to know and a desperate tiredness that came with a mixture of jet lag, wine, and young children.

"The answer is just in the garden. Come with me right now, or else I'll…"

"Or else what?" I asked.

"For the love of all that is good and holy, just follow me!" he pleaded, clasping his hands together. "Then I'll let you all go to bed."

We had followed him once already and been rewarded by the sight of all this treasure, so why not take one quick trip to the garden?

"Let me change out of this first, John, I don't want to get it wet," I said.

"No, leave it on, I want you to have it. Take your clothes, though, so you don't have to come back up these stairs," said John. "I forgot you hated heights." I wasn't sure if he was scoffing at me, or being sentimental. My radar was definitely off having two men in the room, one whom I didn't know at all well, and one whom I knew all too well. "You too Harry, I want you to have that armor. Keep it on. I'll help you take it off in a tic."

I grabbed my modern clothes. Jane said, "I'm taking this!" she said of the book she was holding in her hands. John turned off the lights and locked up the room, tucking the key into his pocket.

CHAPTER SIX

And gladly wolde he lerne, and gladly teche
The Canterbury Tales, Geoffrey Chaucer

I TOOK THE steps one at a time, with Harry descending in front of me, holding my hand and creating a human buffer between me and falling. His hand was calloused, the kind that came from hard labor, and as they laced through mine I saw a soft covering of blond down coated his fingers. He was thoughtful. Sweet. Quiet, though. So quiet. And he made fun of the fact that I was a professor, which irked me.

But what did it matter anyway? He was about to go home to his farm and process the war, somehow, and I had just six days left in England.

And John with his treasure room! He really seemed so different than fifteen years before. Stealing things, probably selling them on the black market to who knows what kind of unethical people, when these amazing works of art needed to be seen by all who loved the period.

When we walked back into Jane's part of the house, a child's wailing came from the upstairs rooms. I broke into a half-run and started to climb part of the way up the stairs. *Were my girls okay? Did something happen while we were in the castle, and they got scared?*

"Mummy! Mummy!" It was one of Jane's daughters. I blew

out a breath of relief, and turned to Jane, who was right behind me. "I need you, Mummy! There's a strange sound in our room."

"I'm coming, darling!" Jane charged up the stairs before turning around and saying to me, "Don't worry—I'll make sure the girls are fine. Probably that branch squeaking again."

"Ellie, come on," John urged me. I looked up the stairs, wondering what I should do. "You can tell Jane about what you see in a few minutes."

"Okay, quickly though. I don't want Jane to have to handle whatever drama's going on up there all by herself." Sometimes my girls got up in the middle of the night and came into my room. *Would they remember where they were?* I set my little bundle of clothes on the stairs to take up with me when I got back.

"Yes, yes," he mumbled, walking out the front door.

It was cold outside, with a light mist falling. There was not much outdoor lighting at Wodesley.

"How's that armor feel?" I asked Harry, walking next to me, with John leading the way. He had shoulder plates on that ran down past his elbows, and a chest plate that hung from around his neck and tied at the back.

"It's ridiculously heavy." He started tugging at the laces.

"Yeah, I'd like to get this dress off too. I keep feeling like I'm going to trip in it." The dress didn't quite make it to the ground, but still I managed to keep stepping on it with my boots.

"Come along, Ellie, Harry!" John interrupted. "You've got to see this."

"Jesus, John! It's freezing out here. Can't this wait until tomorrow? I'm totally knackered." Teeth starting to chatter, I thought about the word *knackered*. It's a British phrase for exhausted, but its actual derivations come from sending horses to the glue factory. Very sad, really, when you think about it. People bandying about the word when it—

"Woman, stop with your complaints," John said.

"All right." I stopped in my tracks, the heat rising to my face, placing my hands on my hips. "Now I *really* don't want to come if you're going to speak to me like that. I mean seriously, after the way you treated me when we dated, and now this? No, I'd really rather not be here," I sputtered. All the anger I'd tried to keep in the past came roiling up again. My hand clenched up, balling into a fist.

I would not stoop to violence. I turned on my heel to go back to the house, shouting over my shoulder, "Harry can tell me and Jane about your 'big secret.'" I felt a tug stop me. John had grabbed my hand and fell at my feet on his knees. John's hand was smaller than Harry's, softer.

"Please Ellie, I apologize," he said, his face filled with re-morse. "I've had too much to drink. We're just going over there—to that wall." He pointed to a wall not thirty feet away. "Nearly there. Please? It's really important. I didn't mean to be rude."

There and then, that was my mistake. I should have turned around. Why the hell would I have given this drunken man at my feet any of my time? I was cold, it was late; my girls would get me up early the next day. Was I pathetically still harboring a thing for him? Or was it Harry being there, and knowing that I only had a few minutes more with him and I'd probably never see him again, and it was just nice to spend a little bit of time with this sweet, quiet guy who cared whether or not I was scared of heights? Or was it the excitement of what John was offering to reveal? Maybe it was all of the above. The Gods of Fate had given me the perfect excuse to back out of that situation and go back to my safe and mundane existence, but at that moment, I chose not to.

"Fine, but I'm just walking there and then I'm done. I want the executive summary, and then I'm in my bed with one of Jane's hot water bottles."

"Promise." He let go of my hand and stood up, hurrying us now to the wall. "It's here," he said, pointing.

"Wait, this is a labyrinth," I said, looking in front of me at the expanse of the grassy path and the pebbles that outlined the way, in a kind of Celtic circular knot. It was large—maybe thirty feet in diameter.

"John, we used to play here as kids," said Harry. "But what does it have to do with your stolen loot? Was it buried underneath?"

"What you two buffoons don't see, is that there is a key in here—a secret passage back in time." John started walking the outline of the path, carefully, going around to the right, and then back to the left.

"Oh my God. Are you high?" I sighed. "A labyrinth in your parents' garden is a time travel portal? Are there magic mushrooms that we're supposed to take to go with this whole experience?" I rubbed my eyes, tired and itchy. I didn't know if I had the energy to deal with John's issues, no matter how crazy they were.

"It's a Thin Place, Ellie. *Not* a hallucination. Were those jewels, that dress, those books... a hallucination? Do you remember us talking about Thin Places, back when we were dating? But I was too scared to tell you back then the truth. I was afraid you'd think I was crazy. That was my biggest mistake."

Harry turned to me, looking for an explanation.

"Um..." I said, "I do... but I can't remember the details so well. Celtic mythology, is that right?" A realization washed over me. Maybe all of those weeks he'd left me alone, he'd been through this Thin Place? He wasn't staying away from me on purpose, and maybe he couldn't get back? What was the mythology again? My mind was shifting through decades' worth of knowledge, trying to find the storage box in my brain in which it had been filed.

"Yes!" John's eyes brightened. "The ancient Celts believed that a Thin Place is a special place in the world—there are rumored to only be a few—where the place between Heaven and Earth, or in this case, the present and the past—are only a few feet apart. You can almost touch it the space in between is so thin. I'd been playing out here for years as a boy, and then I did research when I got older, until I finally unlocked how you can bridge those few feet."

"How?" Harry asked, direct and to the point. I was hyper-aware of him being close to me and suddenly didn't know how to stand properly anymore if his eyes came back to me. I shifted my weight to the back of my feet, then to my toes. Put my hands under my arms to keep them warm, but then worried that made me not stand-up straight.

"You have to walk the labyrinth the number of times that there are curves in the path," John said, now walking around the path carefully, as Harry and I stood just outside, standing side by side. "Labyrinths exist all over the world—even aboriginal cultures with no knowledge of the outside world have built them—so there seems to be an innate power known to man about them. You just have to figure out the trick. When I was 17, I made my first trip back in time. And I've been going there ever since. That's why I disappeared on you back when we were dating, Ellie." He looked at me, straight in the eyes. "I had an appointment back in time, but then I couldn't get back to you. I never know how fast the trip back home is going to be."

Ordinarily I wouldn't have believed an inebriated man walking on a path in the dark, but where *did* those treasures come from? I had once loved and respected John—thought he was brilliant, funny. So, I was now either a witness to his complete and utter downfall before we sent him to an in-patient clinic for treatment, or the most amazing thing was about to happen, and his brilliant discovery would be revealed. I didn't know what to feel. What if he had really done it and was not crazy, and had loved me all those years ago, but actually had been stuck back in the past?

"One more time," John said. "I'm going back once more, and you'll see what I'm saying is true. Don't be worried, I'll be back soon."

"John," I said, my heart suddenly catching in my throat at what was happening, "if I went along with what you're saying, and you really are about to disappear, then what about the fact that you appeared at Jane's doorstep in manacles? Would you be in danger?"

"I need to take this risk," he said, now nearly in the center of the maze. I felt Harry come closer to my side. Was he just as anxious as I? No, he was rock solid, and not freaking out, and that helped me to stay calm. John continued, "I can't go any further in my life without telling anyone. The burden, the lies—the covering up… It's hurt those I love for too long. I need you two to believe me, and Jane. Now, there's one more important thing to tell you before I go, make sure…"

John grabbed at his chest and fell over. *What happened?* With a gasp, I raced over to help, and Harry was one step behind me.

And that's when we discovered that John wasn't crazy. He'd had too much wine, but he was not crazy.

Because I was falling through the depths of an inky, black universe. The Thin Place had opened up, and took us through those few magical feet, separating past and present.

PART II

CHAPTER SEVEN

For time y—lost, may not recovered be.
Troilus and Cressida, Geoffrey Chaucer

THE THIN PLACE in concept sounds like you can just reach out and get through to the other side, effortlessly. The reality was a lot scarier. I could not see what was above or beneath me, but I shut my eyes tightly and braced for impact. I grabbed at the air, grasping for something to stop me from falling. But there was nothing.

A horrible screeching penetrated my brain, as though a subway had just rolled into the station and applied its brakes. I was praying for a quick death to end this torture. "I'm sorry! I'm sorry!" I shouted in vain to my girls, knowing that I was dying and leaving them without a mommy.

Just when I thought I couldn't scream anymore, I landed. But it was not in the bone-and-organ-crushing way I was dreading, but one that placed me down softly, pooled in that long dress, as though angels had lowered me.

While I hadn't smashed into a million pieces, my gut was not sure the emergency was over. My cheek pressed against the ground, and I felt the sweet pleasure of its solidity. My arms and legs felt as heavy as logs. My ears continued to ring. Would I ever be able to hear again? Move?

But then I heard, "Ellie!"

Harry's voice. His knees pressed up against my body, then I felt his hand on the side of my forehead, and his other on my wrist to check my pulse. "Are you all right?"

I held up a hand to indicate I was alive. But I wasn't ready, or maybe even able, to talk.

"What happened?" I heard Harry ask, the ringing slowly fading to the background in my ears. "I feel terrible. I might... puke."

I heard retching. I *smelled* retching.

I rolled over onto my back. I had to see where we were—where that awful black rollercoaster ride had taken us.

Wodesley Castle loomed over us. Wodesley *Castle*.

The castle. Completely intact, smoke rising from its chimneys.

I shut my eyes again, tightly. I couldn't breathe.

We were actually back in time.

This is not real. This must be a dream. I must be hallucinating.

My stomach lurched.

If I'm back in time, how can I get back to the girls? What did that idiot John do?

I took another look. Fifty-foot-tall towers, guards on rooftops, icicles lengthening in the freezing rain. My head was too heavy to lift, but with one cheek on the frosty grass, I realized an amazing thing about the brain and the heart—two totally opposing thoughts and emotions can exist simultaneously.

One thought: *I want to go inside and see my dreams come true— be amongst the knights and ladies of medieval times, hear how they speak, see them interact, live actual history. All my years of studying about the time's literature, the language, the history, the people, right before my eyes.*

The other thought: *This is a nightmare. I am far, far away from my children, who depend on me and who I love more than life itself.*

I started to shiver. I told myself to take some deep, yoga breaths like I had been taught in a mini retreat for over-worked professors at Wellesley. Breathe in for five, hold for five, breathe out for seven. Place your hand on your belly to make sure you're breathing deeply enough. I could hear the instructor's voice, see her lean muscles that I ached to have, if only I didn't like food so much.

It wasn't working—this was not the clean country air I was used to at Wodesley Manor. It was fetid, reeking of open sewers and farm animals' waste. I clamped my hand over my mouth. Could I crawl to a place where we could escape the awful smell?

Adrenaline filled me. "Harry—we need to go back. Right now. I can't be here!" I tried to stand up, but dizziness got the better of me, and I fell back down to my knees, sweat pouring over me. I rolled back onto the cool grass again for comfort, to stop the world from spinning violently. This feeling was way worse than any hangover.

This might be what dying felt like.

"Ellie, you're in bad shape," Harry whispered in my ear. "If you give me a minute, I can help you get into that castle. You're going to freeze if we stay out here much longer. We need shelter."

The cold actually felt good, but then again, I couldn't feel my hands or feet. I tried to clear my head and think properly. "We can't go into that castle—it's too dangerous. We're strangers. We need to find John. He can get us back." My mouth chattered as I spoke.

"No sign of him," Harry said flatly.

How could he be so unemotional? Not freaking out? But then I remembered—*a soldier. Trained to be calm in a crisis. Will probably freak out later. In his man cave, or out farming.*

Did John come back in time with us? Was he back at Jane's, cozy with a water bottle? Was it just Harry and me? We didn't even know how to work the labyrinth. That seemed like such a ridiculous phrase: "work a labyrinth." *How had he walked around it again?* He'd said that there was a special trick to it. I couldn't remember. *Crap, I couldn't remember!*

My brain seemed only to be running at half-speed, which

wasn't good, because if we were to run into anyone, I would need my full faculties. "Just give me a minute, and then let me try to get up again. Maybe we can run into the woods and hide until we figure this thing out—and track John down. If he's even here."

Harry was still on the ground next to me, his brows knit together. "He must be here if you and I came through that Thin Place. But I can't understand why he would have left us."

"Because he's an irresponsible bastard," I said.

He shook his head, rubbing his eyes. "No, Ellie. I've known him since we were boys; he's always been a good friend. A good person. He may have a few problems, but—"

Another voice came across the grass. "Be you friends of Chronicler John? Are ye come to save her story?"

Those were the last words I remember hearing before the screeching in my ears overpowered me again. Just as the world around me started to turn black, though, I could make out a pair of eyes, shining in the darkness.

CHAPTER EIGHT

"Do come," he said, "my mistrals
And geestours for to telln tales,
Anoon in myn arming
Of romances that been royales—
Of popes and of cardinals
And eek of love—likinge."
Geoffrey Chaucer

THE BED WAS lumpy. Fur tickled my chin. I inhaled an odd mixture of must, cloves, lavender, and animal skin. People were speaking nearby. True Middle English speakers.

A dead language, now alive.

Keeping my face immobile so that I would still appear unconscious, I tried to shake myself awake on the inside. *Listen to it carefully: Middle English spoken by the natives.*

Academics had pieced together what Middle English should sound like, and that knowledge had been passed down through the generations and debated *ad nauseum.* We knew that different regions had different dialects, depending on the invading forces—French, most recently, Vikings before that.

Through my closed eyes, I listened for patterns, inflections, usage. It was total immersion Middle English that was now more than just a drinking game Jane and I used to show off with, or something I used to try to instill a love of the language and its literature to my students.

A man and a woman were talking about Harry and me. About how brave Harry had fought off a gang of kidnappers and thieves, and how I must have been separated from my household of knights and servants. I had been struck on the head and had not come out of a "swoon" ever since.

Ha! Swoon. Divorced moms with sole custody don't have time to swoon.

I don't know how Harry had gotten us to wherever we now were, and how much time had passed. I prayed for the strength to face this new/old world and thought of my daughters' sweet faces for inspiration. I needed to come off as though I belonged wherever I was, whenever I was.

I opened my eyes. There was a woman dressed in a roughly made woolen dress and clogs, her brown hair tied up in a scarf. The man next to her was sporting a tunic that looked like it was made from a stiff silk, a fur cap on his head, and with large gold rings on his fingers. Harry sat by the fire, nodding off, looking slightly green. Daylight flooded into the room through the slats on the stone walls.

I needed to let them know that I was awake. "Sir?"

(Let me note here that I am translating what was said from both sides from Middle English, so you don't have to spend years learning a semi-dead language in order to understand what happens next. While I try to persuade my students that it's time well-spent, what this book is about is really all about how we spend our time, and I realize you may have other priorities.)

"Dear lady! Are you well?!" The man came to my side and kissed my hand in a way that I thought only French men could pull off. "My name is Dagworth, Lord of Wodesley Castle." His hands were large and fleshy, but warm. He held my fingers so lightly, as though worried he might break them. Then he placed my hand back down on the coverlet and went running out of the room. "Lady Elizabeth! Lady Elizabeth! The lady is well!"

I heard cheers erupt from a distance away. I stole a glance at Harry, now awake, looking for a sign from him. He gave me a subtle thumbs up.

"What has happened to me? Where am I?" I asked, when Dagworth returned.

"You were struck on the head by a most wretched and cruel band of robbers. They who had no sense of what is right and wrong left you to die out on the road, in the cold depths of winter." The man shook his head at the calamity that had befallen me. Then he turned to Harry, who had gotten up and walked over to the bed and clapped him on the back: "Yet this good man here witnessed the entire wicked scene and came to your aid with the greatest of kindness, chivalry, and courtesy. He did fight off the villains, and brought you here, into our castle."

"Good sir," I said to Dagworth, "would you be so kind as to introduce me to him?" I asked.

All the courteous use of titles were commonplace at this time, although they may seem tedious now. But back then, titles were earned the old-fashioned way, with lots of blood, sweat, and tears.

"This strong man is a knight by the name of Harry DuMont," Dagworth explained. "He tells me he has recently been traveling the world on a quest, although I have yet to find out what that quest is in search of. He speaks mostly French, *vous connaissez?*"

I nodded. *"Je connaissez bien."* I'd taken French throughout high school and college, never knowing until my first courses in Middle English how the two languages had clashed and merged, at least in England. Whereas the French language mostly stayed the same, English has changed enormously.

The French (Norman) invasion of England in 1066 led to most of the nobility of the Middle Ages speaking French. It was considered posh. This change in rule brought about Middle English, which is an amalgamation of Old English and French.

"My lord, sir knight." I held out my hand to Harry, and he walked over to me, still wearing his fisherman's sweater and jeans, having taken off his armor. I'm sure the people here thought he looked pretty strange. I said, "I most humbly offer a thousand thanks for rescuing me and keeping me safe." I piled on the flowery language, and I hoped that Harry would pick up on my lead.

Harry responded in French, "Madame, it is my honor. I pledge to you to do everything I can to make sure you are returned home safely again, if you should have no knights or family to take care of you." French must have been easier for him than trying a stab at Middle English. It was a good, safe choice. He'd probably already figured that out while I was passed out.

"What a good man has found you, lady!" Dagworth said. "Beautiful sentiment, Sir Harry," he said, placing a hand on his back and smiling wide. "Please be assured that you may rest here as long as you require, Lady, and we shall do our utmost to take care of you in a manner that befits your gentility."

This man, with his chivalrous manners and speech, his dress, even his look (clean nails and hair, red face), was a gold mine to my eager professor's brain. Lord Dagworth had to be in his late fifties, and seemed strong and vigorous, despite living well past the life expectancy in the Middle Ages, which was forty-seven. Of course, the instances of dying in childhood without any vaccines or antibiotics drove down that number quite a bit, so if you lived past ten, it was likely you would live a good while.

It was my turn to think up something plausible on the spot, when my head was still operating under protest. "I am Lady Eleanor of Hartford." Sure, I could pass for a noble woman, right? In that green dress John had given me? I knew by looking at the rough clothes the woman was wearing that that kind of dress was a rarity.

"How is your head, Lady Eleanor?" asked Harry.

I attempted to sit up, but when I did it felt like my brain had been pulled out of my head and shoved back in, sideways. That Thin Place might be "thin," but it's earth-shattering for the body. I quickly laid back down. "I fear my head ails me yet. And you, sir?" I asked Harry. How could he be up? Why wasn't he lying, listless on a bed like me? "Were you hurt last night?"

Harry acknowledged that he had a mild headache, a *mal de tete*.

"Mary, bring forth mead for the lady," Dagworth said. "I will not have this woman waste away." The maid brought over the mead for me to drink, and as she held the cup to my lips, I took a few sips. It was warm and soothing, and helped me to regain a little equilibrium. I would have liked about seven glasses of water, but anytime up until the 20th century water was dangerous stuff. The bacteria in the water could cause dysentery. Alcohol and boiled drinks were the only things safe to drink unless you had a nice clean well.

Oh God, why was I even having to worry about this crap? Who spoke what, and when? What could I drink that was safe? What was my plausible backstory? *Why couldn't I just wake up and this would all go away like some weird dream?*

A richly adorned lady entered the room, sounding like she was talking the whole way to an army of people. "Isobel, you get the dresses ready, and Claire, please see to our provisions. We need to be well stocked for our trip—I don't want to be hungry. Plenty of cheese and bread, and some of those oranges too! And bring my guitar!"

The woman focused her honey-brown eyes on me. I took in her unbelievably beautiful dress: crimson red in a weighty silk. It must have cost a fortune, because not only was she tall, but she was wide. Her silver hair was elaborately braided and pinned in circles all around her head, and she had two enormous keys on a chain around her neck. "Now, now, now, does there be a woman in our house who is awaken? The woman who gave us all a fright in our night?"

Lady Dagworth sat in the chair next to my bedside. She put a warm hand over my forehead, the same way my mother used to. Her eyes blazed with both energy and kindness. "Ah, here you are, awake and alive! I am Lady Elizabeth Dagworth, mistress of

Castle Wodesley. How do you fare this morning?"

This woman seemed sharp as a tack. She might be able to see right through my medieval act. "Dear lady," I said, hoping to employ my best manners, "I am sorry to inconvenience you and your great house. You and your husband have been very kind to lend me such gracious quarters until I was well. I should not dare to intrude upon your hospitality any longer, as my ears have heard you are to be embarking on a journey." I got up onto my elbows, and it felt like all the blood rushed out of my face. Lady Dagworth swiftly lowered my head back down to the pillow.

"Dear…" she said, looking to her husband to supply her a name, which he stage-whispered into her ear, "Lady Eleanor. Your accent is very odd indeed. From where do you hail? You cannot have me send you back onto those dangerous roads until I know that your head is healed. Tell me, where are your family, and the rest of your traveling party? Your servants?"

Before I could try to relay my tale, another man entered the room.

I clamped my hand over my mouth to wipe recognition off my face and restrain me from yipping with glee.

"Lady Dagworth, I have come at your bidding," John said, as he took his eyes off me and bowed to our hostess.

John is here—thank God! He can take us home! All I had to do was figure out a cure to this vertigo, get out of bed, and we could go.

Lady Dagworth introduced him to me. "Lady Eleanor, may I present to you my chronicler, John Stafford. Stafford is here to write the stories of our family, and to collect important works for our library. I thought he need hasten to hear your story, and that of your rescuer knight. We will bring it to the king when we visit Windsor."

I tried to attempt a look I would classify as nonchalance in meeting this "stranger," but apparently, I was not carrying it off, because Lady Dagworth began to give me an even more quizzical look. However, she had responsibilities and did not have the time to satisfy her every curiosity. "I wish that I could stay to look after you myself, Lady Eleanor, and hear the story of how you arrived in our home. I am most curious. But there is simply too much to arrange! I will be back as soon as I can. Mary will help you soon, but first, please come with me, Mary, and Lord Dagworth, you also. I have need of you." Lady Dagworth arose from my bedside, turned on her heel and rushed from the room. The others followed demurely, clearly used to following her directions.

John, Harry, and I were alone.

"John! Where the hell have you been? Why did you bring us here?" I hissed. I pulled my legs out from under the covers and tried to get out of bed, and instead of standing, my vision went black again, and I heard howling in my ears.

"Give yourself some time, Ellie," John said through the howl, and I was back lying down again. "Horrible way to travel, isn't it? What you need is what finally gets me out of my daze—red meat. I usually carry some in my pocket, but I've already eaten my share. Wasn't thinking you two would be carried along with me. My apologies," he murmured, looking down.

"Apologies? I might have believed you, you know, without you bringing us here for proof. And now you've put my and Harry's life in danger. It's amazing we even survived, you complete asshole," I spat, my voice as low as it could possibly go.

"Messing about in time travel has something to do with iron, but I'm not sure what," John said, ignoring what I said. "I'll arrange for the cooks to send some meat to you so you're up and running again."

He continued, "I gather from the buzz around the castle last night, Eleanor, that you took everybody's breath away in your gown 'with your *longen* red hair, tumbling down the lady's pale bosom.'" John looked me up and down in bed, as though I was still his lover.

I literally couldn't stomach that kind of look from somebody who had intentionally or unintentionally ripped me away from my family. And then what he said hit me.

"People saw my boobs?" The dress I was wearing, wait, I checked. I was now in a white shift. The dress that I *had* been wearing? Please God, tell me Mary had gotten me in that and not Harry. I turned to him, "I'm so sorry Harry. Did you have to carry me? I must have weighed like…" when was the last time I had been carried? In college, before I had kids? "I must have weighed like a thousand pounds of dead weight."

Harry shook his head while I flushed. "Nah, you don't weigh any more than one of our 100-pound travel packs in the army. Well, not much more." That plus, 40 pounds, I knew, and he knew it too. No wonder he looked so wrecked. It was a miracle he hadn't herniated a disc in his back. He continued, eager to clarify, "And no fears, Ellie, nobody saw anything they shouldn't have, er, I think. But in my defense, I only have two hands, so if your dress got pulled down so that it was quite low, then I'm sure you might have had a very appreciative audience…" He cleared his throat. "And I did have some help."

"Help, oh that's good. Do you know who it was?" Not that it mattered; besides John, we really didn't know anyone here. But I did want to know who helped save me from freezing to death outside.

"I don't know—some short, weird guy down at the labyrinth. Lacking some fingers, I think."

Well, that messed up that romantic vision of Harry carrying me in. It was Harry *and* a short man with not many fingers?

What did it matter anyway? I'd never see these people again, and I'd run naked through the castle to get back to my girls, if I had to.

I looked back at John. "How could you leave us like that?!" If I could have been anywhere near mobile, I would have moved to have slapped him. Or strangled him. Or kneed him in the balls.

"It was an accident. I'll explain it all later, after you're up and around and feeling better. I'm sure you're too woozy now, and Harry here is not looking much better. Let me go make sure they bring you some food. Like I said, that will bring you around, I promise."

"But wait—we need to get back to our time. *Now*. My kids are going to be looking for me—it's been…" I looked around for my phone. *Not here. I must have left it on the stairs at Jane's house with my clothes I'd changed out of…* "How many hours since we got here?"

Harry looked at his watch. "I can't tell you—my watch stopped."

John said, "Oh, it's probably been about ten hours."

"Oh my God, no!! Jane's going to be worried sick. My kids will be freaking out!" I wanted to hold in my emotions, but tears have a mind of their own sometimes. I blinked back as many as I could.

"Time doesn't pass the same here as it does at home," John said, seeking to reassure me, sitting on the chair next to me. "It changes every time I come. Sometimes it's the same, sometimes it passes more quickly here than at home, so it ends up being—I dunno, about a 5/1 ratio. So, when it's like that, for every five hours that passes here, one hour will have passed in our time. Therefore, if we left at eleven last night, and it's now about nine in the morning here, that's just about one hour at home. If the Thin Place is working like that, hopefully Jane wouldn't have even noticed we're gone and will have just gone to bed."

"My girls are going to wake up very soon and find I'm not there. They're going to freak out." I could barely speak, torn between anger and fear and homesickness…

"You're afraid of leaving them alone for *an hour*?" John seemed incredulous, and now his temper flared. "With Jane and the nanny in the house? Jesus, Ellie. Can't spend even one hour away from your girls to—I don't know—experience the wonders of time travel?" He held out his hands to show off the timber-walled room, the fireplace, the four-poster bed, the Norman chair. "My God, I'm so glad I didn't tell you back when we were dating. That was an excellent call on my part. You have zero sense of adventure."

There could be no happy medium for me. Sure—John was right—this was an off-the-charts exploration that a person like me would have died to experience. But now I had kids to take care of. Sure, I'd like to bungee jump and go on safari, but I had to stay home with them and raise and protect them.

And I was stuck on this bed, unable to move. In the wrong century.

John continued, "Look, if we had it your way and walked out right now onto that labyrinth, in full daylight, people will see what we're doing, and maybe even imitate us later when we disappear. God only knows what kind of troops we'd have arriving on Jane's and my doorstep."

"How many people look out over the labyrinth? Surely not that many?" Harry asked.

"This is a fortified castle with people manning the towers. Once we get you back on your feet, I'll show you and we'll come up with a plan then. But first, Ellie can't do anything anyway until she can sit up without passing out. So let's get her and you some iron."

Harry nodded.

"But—" I started to argue.

"I'm pretty sure Harry's back doesn't want to carry you out."

I glanced at Harry. He looked down.

Nobody would volunteer to carry an adult human around if they could wait a little while and see whether they could walk on their own. Hell, I even get tired of carrying around a five-year-old.

John turned and left the room.

"Well, I guess you can see now why the two of us never worked out...." And then I could feel the tears starting again. "Harry, I'm sorry. I'm just going to have to lose it here for a minute." I pulled the sheet up over my head and started to bawl. "It's not about John..." I said, wanting him to know.

Finally, after a little while, I told myself to pull it together. Again, following that lean yoga teacher's example of slowing my breaths, I calmed down.

I dried my tears with the sheet and pulled the covers back down again.

"I'm back. Sorry," I said.

Harry didn't look much better. Sitting on a hard-backed chair that looked very uncomfortable, dark circles had formed under his eyes.

"How are you feeling?" I said. "You look tired."

"I'll be all right," Harry said. "Just trying to think out our next move."

I sighed. "I guess we don't have one until I can move without passing out. I'm really sorry." I hesitated. "If it weren't for me, you'd be going home already."

"No, please don't think that way." He patted my shoulder through the blanket. "I can't do anything without John showing me how, and as he said, not during daylight hours. We just have to hold tight until we get our food. Besides, this isn't a bad place to recuperate, right?" The room was cozy, with a fire roaring away in the fireplace, a tapestry on the wall of a lady and a unicorn, and my double bed, covered in fur robes. "Compared to the army, this is—"

"You've taken your armor off," I said, seeing the shiny metal pieces stacked up in a corner. Thank God he'd been wearing them so he could fit in, but he didn't look very medieval without them now. The watch on his wrist would certainly elicit many eager stares. And his razor-short haircut could never have been achieved with a pair of dull shears. "I think you'd better put that watch in your pocket," I said.

"Oh, you're right," he said, slipping it off.

"Did you see how people were dressed when you came in? What were they wearing? Am I going to stick out like a sore thumb?"

"Well," Harry said, stretching into a yawn, "you and I both have a lot more teeth than the average person here. But this place is remarkably kitted out for the 14th century. John's got a lot of restoration work to do on his castle if he's going to get close to what the original looks like."

I laughed, then felt guilty for Harry sitting in that wooden chair. "Hey, you're tired—do you want to lie down and get some sleep? I can make room?" I asked, and then I felt stupid for asking. Was he going to think I was trying to seduce him? No, right?

"Thanks for the offer," Harry said quickly, "but it wouldn't look very wholesome if you were caught in bed with a man you didn't know."

"I didn't mean—"

"I know. Neither did I." He winked. Harry pulled a fur off my bed and wrapped himself in it, curling up on the floor. "I've been awake for two days straight and we'll all be better off if I can get a quick kip until the food gets here." He closed his eyes and fell asleep in seconds.

He had the experience of a soldier who knew when it was safe to sleep. The fact that I had an ally here in my room who seemed dependable, could think on his feet, and best of all did not abandon me made me pretty lucky.

Unlike John, who must have gone running off the second we came back in time. Who would do that to his friends, and why? I was disgusted.

Harry had the wherewithal to get us the four-star treatment here at Wodesley Castle, despite him not knowing Middle English, and everybody thought he was a true courtly knight. Not bad work for having to slog me around like a sack (or three) of potatoes.

I tried to get a good look at Harry now that he was asleep. His light brown eyebrows furrowed as if he were concentrating really hard on something in his dreams. There was a scar just under his hairline on the side of his neck. Was that something he got in childhood, or was it a war injury? His lips parted and he started blowing out soft breaths, his chest moving up and down, with his enormous hands crossed over his chest.

I had a huge pang in my chest feeling helpless and unable to move, and the second one sank deep down from seeing Harry on the floor like that. I was too tired and sick to figure out why, it just made me sad.

$$\bullet\!\diamond\!\bullet$$

CHAPTER NINE

"Would you heed well my words, it were worth your while—
You are rushing into risks that you reck not of
Sir Gawain and the Green Knight

I T COULDN'T HAVE been much later when somebody knocked.
It was Mary, who slipped back into the room before I could
think of the right words to say in the language. She had a platter
of cold meat, cheese, bread, and an orange. *Where did they get an
orange?*

There were no forks, but there was one knife, and a finger
bowl for washing. Jane would have been pleased at the accuracy
of her medieval dinner party reenactment.

Mary curtsied, and said, "I shall return after you are done, and
help you to get dressed, madame." She left the room.

Harry was awake now, and said, "Oh, damn. I thought *I* was
going to help you get dressed," he said with a raised eyebrow.

He was flirting with me. Under normal circumstances, that
would drive all my senses into over-drive, but I was too busy
thinking about the next few hours until we got away to put more
than thirty percent of my brain power on it. So I threw a large
pillow at him. "By the sound of it, you got more than an eyeful
last night."

Harry picked up the platter and brought it closer to me. He

cut up the meat in small pieces, as I did for my girls who were too young to cut up their own meat. I closed my eyes as I started to chew—I tasted what I did not expect to find in food coming out of a medieval kitchen—garlic. The meat was spiced, and juicy, with a bit of pink in it. It was actually good. I wasn't expecting medieval food to be good. Even English food from twenty years ago was terrible—who knew that it was better 700 years earlier? Harry kept those little pieces of meat coming; I was famished.

"You do enjoy your food, don't you?" Harry asked, barely able to suppress a smile.

"Don't fat shame me, man. Keep it coming. I think I'm feeling better…"

My ears and head cleared, the dizziness evaporated, and I began to feel stronger. I sat up, and with one hand on Harry's arm, and a fur blanket wrapped around me, I began to walk around. Two steps later I let go of Harry and jumped in the air.

Harry let out a whoop and we exchanged a spectacularly awful high five—my hand met his forearm, and he ended up hitting me on my temple.

But that was okay—*Yes! I'm back*! I had no desire to be a swooning lady stuck on a bed. That was way too boring. I'd take a swift look around the castle and absorb as much as I could before we got the hell home.

I needed to get dressed—I saw "my" green silk dress in the corner. What would have happened to us if I came through in my little black dress instead? I'd have been deemed a harlot instead of a lady and turned out on the streets. Instead, I was here in the lap of luxury. Clothes really did make a woman back in this time. And an accent, which I had to work on. I sounded weird and could tell by their reactions to me that I did.

Harry excused himself to sit in the hallway outside my door, and Mary was there waiting. I wondered if she heard us laughing and worried as I had no chaperone. Was I being too familiar with this savior knight? I'd been getting dressed by myself since the age of four. But if I were truly a lady in that day and age, I would have a servant who dressed me. Did she hand me clothes and then watch me put them on? Or did I act like my little girls and raise my arms up to receive the dress?

Mary was all business as she laid out a small sheet of linen, that she called a "foote sheete." She gestured me over to the fire. Luckily there was no getting naked, as the clothes simply went over my linen shift. My bra and underwear had been left on—I'd hate to be without them. But what might Mary have thought of my padded Calvin Klein bra and printed happy face emoji underpants if she'd seen them?

"This is a handsome room," I commented, deciding to raise my arms to let the dress slip over me, trying to look like I was used to this.

"It is one of *eleven* guest chambers," Mary said proudly. She swept the green dress over my head and through my arms, and the dress dropped down to the floor. Mary started tightening and tying off the laces on the sides of the dress.

"Eleven? That is very grand." Most castles of the period were likely to have a private bedroom just for the lord and lady, and that was about it. Everybody else had to rough it out in the hall, sleeping together on the floor. Eventually, more bedrooms were introduced when knights could focus more on luxury and less on protection. The Dagworths must have been very wealthy.

Mary looped the belt around my waist and adjusted it so that it hung at a jaunty angle around my hips. She brought in a sleeveless surcoat to go on top of the dress, and I was finally beginning to get warm. My boots were brought over. "I have never seen these before." She pointed to the rubber booted soles, and the zipper. She played with the zippers and pulled it up and down. "Magick?"

"Oh no, they have fine shoemakers where I come from," I said.

Fishing a hairbrush out of her apron, which was wooden and probably made from boar bristles like my modern Mason & Pearson brush, Mary stood in front of a chair and indicated that I was to sit. I'm sure she was used to doing this for all other ladies, but it was certainly the first time I had been given such lavish attention, except at the hairdresser's.

Mary's sure and competent hands started brushing and winding, twirling and manipulating the sides of my hair, while the rest hung loosely down my back. I put my fingers up to feel the ridges and braids and coils and waves that had been produced with a few deft touches of an expert. "Oh Mary, you are very good."

"Thank you, Madame."

Then Mary stood before me, admiring her handiwork. "Such beautiful hair, but you do not pluck your forehead," she clucked, pulling out a rough looking pair of tweezers from her apron pocket. "Would you like me to?"

"Ack! No!" I put up my hands to protect my hair. I'd seen enough pictures of Queen Elizabeth Ist and her freakishly high plucked forehead to scare me off of that. Mary backed off, surprised, but she complied and put the tweezers away.

"Do you have a *husband*, a family?" I asked.

"I had a *husband*," she said, "but he did die in an accident some time ago. I have four boys who liveth still, and three that are with the angels. But the ones who grew, they have all gone from Wodesley now, young men."

Mary didn't look older than 35. She had four adult boys. She must have married very young. "And you, my lady? Your family?"

"I have two little girls," I said, "and I miss them terribly."

"Where are they, Madame?"

"They are safe and well with…" I paused.

Where were they now? Still sleeping? *Please, girls, still be sleeping, and don't wake up to find out that I'm not there.*

My hands were constantly reaching for my cell phone. I was terrible about constantly checking it—obsessive even. But had I not left it at Jane's, it would do no good to me now—I doubted there was service that got through the Thin Place.

"They're with my sister," I finally answered. Jane was as close to a sister as I would ever have, and aside from my parents, no one I'd trust more with my kids.

I teared up, again, and then got mad. *I need to woman up and stop crying! This is my reality: I need to get out of this chair and get home.*

"I am a widow as you are," I said, using Mary as the first to test out a cover story I was inventing on the go, "and I have lived abroad with my *husband's* family in Provence for many years." That would help explain my weird accent, and why nobody in England, maybe, would have heard of Lady Hartford. "When my husband died of the ague—" the ague is a kind of fever, usually associated with malaria—"my youngest daughter too fell ill." I paused, thinking up the rest of the story, and Chaucer's *The Canterbury Tales* came to mind. "I have come to England on a pilgrimage to pray for a return of her good health. I met up with a group of pilgrims in Canterbury, accompanied by my maid and my men. One of my men told me about the springs near a high ridge near Pembury. I thought if I could capture some of that pure water for my daughter on my way home, it might help."

"But Lady Hartford, you were not dressed as a pilgrim when you came to us," Mary said, shaking her head in dismay. My story didn't match up with my clothes. "Did you not stand out from the rest? What happened to your badge?"

"Yes…" I said, thinking up another lie. Pilgrims wore simple clothes—far from the silk that I was wearing—and wore badges, or trinkets, to denote the fact that they had been on pilgrimage to Canterbury. "I went to the cathedral plainly robed, but my husband's family insisted that I respect their family name with the appropriate clothes elsewhere. I promised them that, but as I rode with the other travelers, one odious man kept talking to my maid and my men. He must have paid them off to leave my side when I was attacked. I did not see who did it, but I was carrying gold with me for my passage home, and wore the rubies that my husband had given me. I never take them off. I'm afraid I don't remember much else. But all I have appears to be gone, except for this necklace and…" I reached up to my throat. I'd felt it there the whole time—it was like a piece of me. A piece of gold with my initials and Abby and Sophie's, intricately scripted together, with two rubies and one emerald embedded within, our birthstones. The stones were small, but it symbolized our life as *The Three Musketeers*—what we'd become after Alex had left.

Mary put her hand over her heart. "My lady! I knew that you had suffered hardship with being attacked by bandits, but now, what will become of you? How will you get back home with nothing but the clothes you wear now and that *smallen* necklace?" I guess, compared to what Lord and Lady Dagworth had, the necklace wasn't much.

It did sound pretty dire for Lady Hartford. She could get a message out to her family in Provence to send money to bring her home, however months and months long that would take. Ellie Hartford, on the other hand, had to rely on the unknown laws of a labyrinth in the middle of a garden in Kent to get back to her family, seven hundred years in the future.

Maybe to lighten the mood, Mary turned the discussion onto another matter. "What do you make of Sir Harry, then? Coming to your rescue, right out of a tale of romance from King Arthur? Do you not think he is very handsome and strong? All the ladies downstairs can talk of nothing else. You should have seen the way he carried you into the Great Hall last night, as if you weighed nothing and were no burden at all."

I blushed, relieved to hear he was not struggling and cursing, near to dropping me on the floor. I had pictured him dragging me along the ground, heaving me as he stopped every ten yards to catch his breath. "And he was so gentle with you, as if you were the most precious gift in the world. If it pleases your lady, you might see whether you can hold on to his knightly service to you as long as it is required." Mary smiled. "Traveling back to Provence with that one at your side would make for a very sweet journey. It is clear that he cares for you very deeply, even having only just come upon you. What do the minstrels sing about 'love at first sight?'"

The two of us jumped when we were interrupted by three knocks on the door, and then Harry's deep voice called in French, "Lady Hartford, are you ready? May I escort you downstairs?"

Mary and I exchanged glances like a couple of schoolgirls; had he heard us talking about him? We couldn't help but open our eyes wide. Jane would have said, "OMG!"

I whispered, "Do I look all right?"

She winked at me and whispered some phrase into my ear that I had never heard before in my studies. But I believe the modern-day interpretation would mean: "Work it."

CHAPTER TEN

Some say wommen loven best richesse;
Some saide honour, some said jokinesse
Some riche array, some saiden lust abedde,
An doften time tob e widwe and wedde.
Some said that our herte is most esed
When that we been yflatered and yplesed—
He gooth ful neigh the sooth, I wol nat lie:
A man shall winne us best with flaterye,
And with attendance and with bisinesse
Been we ylined, bothe more and less
The Wife of Bath, Canterbury Tales, Geoffrey Chaucer

WHEN I WAS in the sixth grade, I had a pretty big role in our school musical. For two months, we sang and rehearsed. I was confident that my starring role was going to make me the most popular girl in school, and I fantasized every night before falling asleep about the triumph my performance would be.

A 103-degree fever intervened. My mother tried to persuade me not to go to school, but I declared in a croaky voice, "The show must go on!"

After twenty minutes of standing in the chorus singing, it was time for me to make my triumphant entrance on stage. I said one line, swayed like a very slight birch tree in a strong wind, and proceeded to fall in a heap right off the stage.

So instead of being celebrated as the "most popular girl in school," I became "the girl who fainted at the Christmas play."

Now in a completely different century—the 14th—I had become "the lady who swooned" yet again, and (might have flashed her boobs), thanks to my entrance last night. When I stepped out into the vast hall with Harry behind me, the noise and activity came to a complete stop, and everyone stared. I didn't know if people were looking at me with pity, curiosity, or amusement. I had wanted to slip through this castle unnoticed and get the hell out of there, but now that plan had gone up in smoke. I was *news*. Thank goodness nobody had cell phones, or I'd already have become a meme on social media.

Lady Dagworth spotted me. "My dear Lady Hartford! How well you look!" The people who had been staring at me seemed to realize that the boss lady was on the case, and it was time to look busy again. Our hostess came over to us. "You must forgive our household, my dear. I'm afraid you and your knight have given everyone here much to discuss. And that is most unfortunate," she declared, looking sternly about her, as she raised her voice, "as there is SO MUCH TO DO."

Lady Dagworth noted the effect that her presence and words had on the activity levels around her with a nod of her head, and said to me, "Madame, my most sincere apologies. We are all turned upside down because of the arrival this very evening of the Earl and Countess of Salisbury, the King's own favorite friend. They are coming here to spend the night before we all head to Windsor tomorrow for the great tournaments that the king has arranged. Although why," she said in a conspiratorially low voice, "our king insists on having a tournament in this foul, freezing, and frosty weather, is much beyond my simple female brain."

As Lady Dagworth talked, she took my hand, looped it through her arm and started walking. She had one eye on me to make sure I was feeling healthy, and the other eye on what seemed like fifty people in the hall, busy at work.

There were some large, beefy men setting about different tasks: heaving wood next to the enormous fireplace that must have been twenty feet wide, moving great tables, and erecting a dais. There was a smaller group of men dressed in tunics with some chain mail on, heading out the door. Female servants swept and scrubbed the floors in dull colored-dresses, and women who had on far prettier gowns were carrying in greenery, folding cloths, or directing others on what went where.

We walked past all this activity and back beyond the great fireplace to the kitchen, a large room with an enormous fire, and massive black pots hanging inside it. A large pig on a spit was turned by a small boy who sat on a stool. Beneath the pig stood a pan to catch the savory drippings. Two large, rough, wooden tables were surrounded by women chopping vegetables, arranging platters full of cheeses and fruits, plucking birds, peeling potatoes, and rolling dough. In a corner, away from the fire, a girl of about twelve churned butter, her skinny arms moving up and down, over and over again. I wondered if my Abby would have the strength to do that. She definitely wouldn't have the patience to keep at it for long. But maybe if she had a boss like Lady Dagworth, instead of a mom like me? I probably spoiled my two, feeling sorry for them that their father had left…

Harry had followed us back into the kitchen, two paces behind me. He and I had agreed before we left our room that we would stick together. But Lady Dagworth would have none of it. She turned around to say, "Sir Harry, the men are out in the yard practicing their swordsmanship, while others have gone hunting. I am sure you would like to join them, and not follow behind the skirts of two women, charming as the Lady Hartford may be."

I did not want to be separated from Harry. I didn't know where John was, and I needed at least somebody I knew in this other world with me. I stopped and looked at him, about to open my mouth and say something. But Lady Dagworth interrupted. "No need to worry, lady. I know you are coming off a terrible misadventure with the ruffians outside these gates, but I assure you that you are in safe hands here in my castle. This knight needs to be around other men, not acting like your lady's maid."

There was no way around this unless I wanted to look really weird having a man follow me around all day; it was not normal for these times. I nodded to him that it was okay, although I didn't know what he was going to do out there. Practice sword-fighting? Go hunting? I knew so little about him—how was he going to get along? He turned on his heel so fast I expected sparks to see skid marks on the floor from his boots—I guess he did want to see what the men of the 14th century were up to. I was nervous for him, though, even with his enthusiasm and newly elevated status as the medieval equivalent of a comic book hero.

"Oh, and speaking of ladies' maids, how did you get along with Mary? I see she did a beautiful job with your hair. You really do have the most radiant shade of red I think I have ever seen."

"Your compliments make me blush, my lady." And indeed, the familiar heat on my face had come up to match my hair. The curse of a redhead was that every feeling we had was telegraphed when the blood rushes to our pale faces. "It was very kind of you to lend me your maid, after mine abandoned me."

"Good; you shall continue to have Mary for the rest of your stay. She was recently looking after my daughter, but there seems to be some friction between the two of them. Perhaps they need some time apart, and another girl shall go to Yvonne." Lady Dagworth stopped and surveyed the kitchen, scrutinizing the staff and possibly talents of the women and girls before her.

"I thank you very much for your hospitality and care, but I can't stay here, Lady Dagworth," I said, firmly. "You have been very gracious to a stranger, but I need to make plans to leave very shortly so I do not inconvenience you and infringe upon your household much longer."

Lady Dagworth was just about to respond when a pack of giant, barking dogs ran by us, thwacking me with their furry tails.

"Tiresome, muddy beasts!" shouted Lady Dagworth, swatting one gray wolfhound-type creature on the rump. "Please excuse them, Lady Hartford. They follow my husband everywhere. Sometimes I do swear he loves those dogs more than his own children. And the mess of them—dirt and fur all over the floors, on our new rugs! The whole castle reeks of wet dog."

Women have been apologizing for the state of their houses probably as long as we've had a home to call our own, no matter whether it was a cottage or a castle, spotless or truly dirty. As a good guest, it was my job to reassure her. "Indeed not, Lady Dagworth! I smell nothing but sweet herbs and good cooking smells, and see only a beautiful, well-run castle."

Lady Dagworth stopped for just a split second, acknowledged my compliment, and then a look of pure exhaustion came over her face as her stern smile suddenly sank. She finally took a deep breath for the first time since I'd been around her. Women of this time period got up well before sunrise. I'm sure she was longing for some time alone, in her room, with her eyes shut, but did she ever get it? Was there such a thing as leisure time for any woman in the Middle Ages, even with all her wealth?

"Is there anything I can do to assist you, Lady Dagworth?" I asked.

"Oh my dear, you are very kind to offer, but I fear we would just trample you underfoot as you do not know what to do and where to go." She squeezed my hand and said, "What I would like very much is that after all this whirlwind is for you and I to sit together and have a goodly chat. You seem like a dear, sweet thing, and I would like to get to know you better, and hear about your family, and where you come from. And we need to figure out what we are going to do with you! But first, I'm afraid, I must deal with the Earl's visit, and our packing...."

She seemed to will herself back into action, and I was her first order of business. "Lady Hartford, I must now send you up to John Stafford, whom I believe you already have met. I have instructed him to take good care of you. We must get your story down while it is fresh in your head, and before we all leave for

Windsor. Evelyn—" she said to a nearby kitchen worker—"would you escort Lady Hartford to John Stafford? No doubt he is in the scriptorium."

John. That was exactly who I needed. Perfect. I took a quick look around the kitchen to let it sink all in for my memories, was patted on the back by Lady Dagworth, and gently pushed on my way.

Following behind the young girl, we went through room after room. I was trying to match the rooms I was seeing with what I had seen of John's ruined castle the night before, but I was having a hard time aligning the two. Mostly because these rooms were so beautiful and John's were ruined, stark, and sad, even with all the money that he was plowing into it. Some rooms had some wood paneling, while some had stone walls hung with tapestries. Some rooms had chairs and rugs and benches, while others were almost bare except for a bed.

Wodesley Castle had probably been designed after the risk of invasion from the Vikings and France had declined, because there were windows everywhere. Previous to this time, castles used to have only cracks and slits in the walls to shoot out arrows. But these were not modern windows: you could not see clearly out them. They were definitely handmade, with uneven thicknesses so that the world and the light outside was distorted.

Judging from the expanse and décor of Wodesley Castle, the Dagworths were surely one of the great families of England in their time.

Evelyn took me up another circular staircase, but this one had a rope railing that I could hang onto and get up the stairs without fear of falling. We came to a well-lit room containing three desks for writing and a long table in front of a series of mullioned windows: the scriptorium. Usually a scriptorium would only be found in monasteries, where monks copied out texts meticulously, their work lit by candlelight. But some private houses had scriptoriums and used the medieval equivalent of freelance illustrators and writers who were paid for their skills, and supplied with vellum (a thick paper made from animal hides), their carefully hand-crafted inks, probably made from iron gall, or carbon ink made from soot, among other things. I'd have to find out from John how they made their ink.

The room was also a library, with rows of shelves packed with books. I'd never seen an account of a private house that would have contained a library like this one. I immediately went to the shelves but the noise of other people in the room stopped me. Two men were busy arguing over sums at one of the desks. And at the other, writing away on a high, slanted writing table, was John, who was so involved in whatever he was doing that he'd taken no notice that we'd come in. Evelyn was staring at him, slack-jawed, as though he was the biggest rock star in the world.

John was the kind of guy who'd always drawn people in, consciously or not, like a moth to a flame. When I'd met him for the first time, he was holding court in the pub where Jane had taken me to get a drink. He had a great mound of wavy, floppy hair, deep brown eyes, and a sea of admirers, both men and women, hanging on his every word. Upon seeing his little sister Jane, he pulled her into a hug and said, "You all know Baby Jane, don't you? Now Jane, who is this?" he asked of me, and pulled me into his orbit. John was electric. He glowed with energy, and everything about him breathed life and excitement, and never-ending possibilities. That night he was all charm, told riotous stories, and had a way of engaging people from the shyest person there to the grouchiest drunk. I was smitten, and when he offered to walk me home, I pulled Jane aside to ask if that was okay.

I didn't want to weird out my best friend by falling for her brother. But Jane thought it was great. She adored her brother—thought the world of him. And she'd seen me try to make connections with others who weren't right for me. She later told me she'd longed for it to work out.

After I broke up with him, he then went on to write the Young Adult book, *The Training of the Squire*, which received a burst of enthusiasm from reviewers, young people, and a slew of adults. It hit the bestseller lists, foreign rights were sold, and even the movie rights were optioned. I didn't want to read it, but in a weak moment, I picked the book up on the way home from teaching.

The world he described in the book looked very similar to the one we were in now: medieval, a castle, a rich knight. John wrote heartbreaking dialogue, and his plotting kept you turning the page. Although I'd never forgive him for how callous he was toward me in abandoning me for six weeks, a part of my heart glowed when I read that book. I'd wondered, "What if...."

John was in that golden glow at his desk now, even with nobody around him except the two guys working on their big ledger. The maid and I watched him dip his pen into the ink well and scratch away on the vellum, not taking the time to make the manuscript beautiful: he was possessed by the story and seemed keen to get it down. His dark hair hung over his shoulders, and he pushed the strays out of his eyes.

The maid seemed to shake herself from her reverie, likely thinking of the wrath Lady Dagworth would throw her way if she didn't execute her task in the timeliest manner. She cleared her throat and said, "Sir? Lady Hartford is here for you."

A pained look came over his brow, ever so briefly, but I saw it, and it ticked me off. I'm sorry if he didn't get to finish his story. He had a responsibility to me and Harry.

What had been going on with him all these years? How did he work this whole time-travel thing? Who was he stealing from? And who locked him up?

"Ahem," I said, irritated.

"Ah, I see you have recovered most beautifully, Lady Hartford," John said, giving me the nod that the two other men in the room were listening. "I am glad to see you've come out of your room."

I had to pretend that I was a stranger. "Yes, indeed, sir. Thank you so very much for your help with the food. I feel very much stronger now."

Evelyn excused herself to rush back to whatever new tasks Lady Dagworth would throw her way.

"Do you think you can manage a walk around the outside, in the cool air, Lady Hartford? It might be good for your head. And I could show you the castle if you have not seen it already, as we discuss the details of your attack last night. I do not wish to bring back mournful memories, but Lord Dagworth insists that I get the story down for our chronicles."

As much as I wanted to talk to John and ask him a million questions, I didn't want to leave this treasury of books quite yet. Any one of those books tucked discreetly into my dress would help both my solvency and career. Even just to look and take pictures of then of them, if I still had my phone, would be the literary equivalent of discovering a hidden Egyptian tomb. I had been trained for so many years to investigate everything about medieval books, from the thinness of the vellum to the type of ink that was used. But then if I did squirrel a book away in my dress, I would be no better than John—who had been pillaging from these people, and God knows who else—for years. Funding his new decadent lifestyle. That's not who I was, and I didn't think it was who he was either. But I guess the good guy I knew was from the past. Or was that the future, or the recent…?

It hurt my brain to even compute.

John took a firm grip on my elbow and steered me towards the door. A shock of excitement at his touch overcame and distracted me. I was furious with myself.

I'd been alone way too long if a touch on my elbow was enough to make me melt.

I didn't have a cloak, so John gave me his. I usually would protest at this act of gallantry—I was a woman, I was strong—but I took it, because I didn't believe he deserved to be warm.

It was a dull gray winter's day. The sun was completely hidden behind the clouds. In 1344, being cold was a fact of life, not a temporary inconvenience. You were cold from the time you left your bed in the morning, and you were cold when you went to bed at night. In fact, you were lucky if you were warm in bed.

We walked outside onto a second-floor balcony, and I saw the castle in daylight. The inner walls of the castle surrounded the rectangular courtyard, which was paved with large stones. Down below, men on horses watched while others sparred with flat wooden swords. Smoke came up out of a few chimneys, the largest of which was directly opposite where we stood, which must have been the main hall. That building was the oldest with the more dated architecture, while the rest of the buildings attached to it looked almost brand new.

"Okay, now that we're alone—" I said, and with all my pent-up anger, I hauled back my right arm and punched him in the stomach as hard as I could. I met nothing but skin and bones, and oh, did it hurt my knuckles.

John collapsed a little with the blow, but not as much as I would have liked. I wanted him to hurt inside as much as I did. "I'm so furious with you!"

"Ellie," he said, his hand to his stomach, gasping a little, "you being here is *no* accident. Think about it—your curiosity led you here, just as it did me. You were *drawn* here by that labyrinth."

"I wasn't drawn here, you made me follow you!"

"I should have told you sooner about the labyrinth, back when we were dating. You were such a romantic back then—you ate and breathed everything medieval. I was dying to tell you about what I knew for sure about how people spoke, what their manners are like, about the Dagworths, about my life in this world. It was a huge part of me that I kept bottled up. And then when I accidentally got stuck for longer than I wanted, you were too mad at me to even listen…"

I shook my head. "Yes, you should have told me, you blithering idiot. Maybe it could have been a great adventure and you *could* have shown me everything and it would have been amazing. But now it's just a nightmare because I have kids. Your timing," I spitefully laughed at the pun, "your *timing* is terrible."

John looked down into the courtyard. I know both of us were thinking about what life could have been like together, if only he'd trusted me, if only he hadn't lied. Would we still be together? Would I have been the most renowned medieval scholar of my generation, with an inside knowledge of what this world was like that no other historian or English Lit. professor had?

"First off, let me show you exactly where the labyrinth is, and you'll see why you can't go yet."

He took me over to the side of the wall and pointed down.

Two stories below, and down a rocky hill, yet still within the castle walls, I could see the labyrinth, surrounded by a low, stone enclosure. Next to it was a kitchen garden, dormant now at the end of the winter. On the other side of the labyrinth were the stables, and I could see a bunch of men and boys going in and out leading horses, taking off their tack, and brushing them down. Everything was neatly laid out, but busy.

"The Dagworths built this labyrinth," John said. "One of their knights came back from the Crusades a broken man, but when he walked a labyrinth in Spain on his way back to England, he healed, emotionally and spiritually. When he returned, he desired to build a labyrinth here for the Dagworths and wanted to make it accessible to anyone who needed a bit of healing in the middle of their busy daily lives. Living in this day and age isn't easy. The people work hard and get sick easily. Walking the labyrinth helps them."

"Do those people ever take a break?" I indicated the folks below us, milling about the labyrinth. "Do they all go in for lunch at the same time or something? Mid-day prayers?"

"There's never a time during the daylight hours that someone is not nearby. You're going to have to wait until after dark—after dinner."

I'm not a big curser, especially since I had kids, but this situation deserved a good old Anglo-Saxon profanity, and I let one fly. The old ones were the best ones.

"I wish you would relax and enjoy this experience. The Dagworths are good people. You're not in any danger. Here, you look cold," he said, pulling the cloak more tightly around me. It felt intimate, familiar, him looking after me. But our short-lived romance had not been long enough for me to get used to it. My ex, Alex, wasn't nurturing like this—that should have been a clue that he'd bail on being a father.

"John, what have you been doing here all this time? You're their…?"

"Chronicler."

"The keeper of their history?"

"Yes, I write down their stories, and find them books to buy to build their library. When I first came here, I was just a boy, really. But they took me in, looked after me, realized I was smart and could read and write…"

"But what about the times you go missing, when you return to modern life? What do they think about where you go?"

"Well, as I think I told you, often the time moves more quickly here than in our present. So, they think I'm going home to my family, which I actually am, although my parents are dead now and there's just Jane and Guy, and the girls. They know I can only stay part of the year."

"Why would time pass more quickly here than in relation to home?"

"I have no idea. I can't explain thin places either, except I think the people who travel them are meant to, somehow."

"Well, I definitely doubt that, at least in my case. Me being here is an accident."

"Is it? With your background in studying the subject? You don't feel an incredible pull, a sense of connection with this time and place?"

"Well, if that's your hypothesis, then why would you, at 17-years-old and no training in Middle English, come here?"

"Maybe to lay the groundwork for your visit?" He stopped and drummed his fingers on the wall. "I don't know. But all I can tell you is it's so exciting here—things are so… real. Everything is too easy in our world: cars, electricity, hot water boilers, heat, for God's sake. There are no electronic devices here, no distractions. No worthless apps. In our present, nobody seems even capable of talking to each other anymore without checking their phone every twenty seconds. They can't even look each other in the eye. Here, we have real conversations. We listen to each other. The art of the story is admired. Storytellers come from all over to entertain. You can appreciate that, I'm sure, as a lover of story and words. And there's quiet here! No airplanes, no TV, no radio; there is real peace."

It *was* quiet. There was no thrum from cars traveling down the roads, no high-pitched whirring in the sky from airplanes. No buzz from appliances, and furnaces, and air conditioning. All we could hear were the people below and the barnyard sounds of the animals.

"I admit, that is nice. I have an app on my phone that plays bird songs for me, because the street noise is so distracting when I try to work or sleep."

John shook his head. "Ellie, an app? To hear fake birds?"

"Well, it might be a recording…" I stopped, thinking of more problems with his way of life here. "But aren't they *aging* a lot more rapidly than you? Aren't they suspicious of you staying youthful-ish?"

John smiled, looking eager to share, "I tell them it's the well water at my home. So, when I come back from being in modern Wodesley, I always make sure to bring some of my 'special' water for the Dagworths. It hasn't stopped them from aging, but they like to think they look younger than everyone else. Kind of a placebo effect.

"Now," John continued, "considering that you have to wait until nightfall to go back home, what would you like to do? Take a more detailed tour of the castle? See the men practicing their weaponry? Watch what the cooks are making? Go back to the scriptorium? I've got to write up your story for Lady Dagworth."

"Are you going to romance it up?"

John laughed, "A handsome man rescuing a woman with beautiful, long, red hair, enters the castle in the dark of night. He tells his story of an attack upon the innocent lady, who has been betrayed by her servants, and how he came upon her only by accident." He winked, "It's perfect. This story is getting better every minute that I dwell on it."

"Just don't mention me flashing everyone. I want to read it somewhere, though, when you're done, and find it in the British Library. And hey, we need to discuss your nefarious activities with goods you're stealing from these innocent people."

"Ha—it's not that I'm stealing, necessarily, but bartering… They get goods back in exchange."

"Wait—what do you trade them? Please tell me it's something safe like Oreos or rugby tops, not iPads and video games. Not anything that's going to affect the time/space continuum." I knew my *Back to the Future*.

"Well, it has to be something I can fit in my pockets, or something I'm wearing. I've gotten a lot with stretchy tube socks and boxer shorts—"

"Ew!"

"Well, I wasn't wearing them at the time."

I wasn't buying this. "You are not getting jewels and books and armor and—" I gestured to the gown I was wearing—"green silk dresses in exchange for socks? Seriously, what are you exchanging?"

"I'm afraid I'm going to have to reserve that bit of information for another time."

I moaned and rolled my eyes.

He went on. "It's time to focus on what's happening here—today and tomorrow. Today, the Earl of Salisbury is coming, and tomorrow, our two households are traveling together to go to Windsor. King Edward III, one of the finest kings Britain has ever had, is holding a tournament to find the best knights in the land to make up an elite force—it's my guess he's founding the Order of the Garter, although no one knows exactly when he conceived of the idea. The Order is the longest-lasting order of knighthood in history, and the highest honor a knight can get. I've been dying for this day to come, well, since as long as I've been reading up on the history of the times. This is what I've been waiting for—to see how it all unfolds."

"So wait, I thought you were going to take me back?"

"I will, I'll take you to the labyrinth, and instruct you on how to walk it. Then I'll go to Windsor, and be back in 2017 in no time."

"What about the manacles? What about getting beaten up? Who did that to you?"

He rubbed his wrists; the skin was still raw.

"Just a midnight foray I made to a manor house, about twenty miles hence. They don't know me or where I came from, but they weren't happy with my trade. I can't tell you how hard it was to escape that nightmare, but I am thankful I brought my Swiss Army knife with me that at least got me out of my locked room, if not the manacles."

I shook my head, once again happy that I'd had the good sense to break up with him before he shamed us both. "Well, you're a grown up. Not my responsibility—not for a long time. Not ever, really."

As the wind blew my hair, I had a vision of how Sophie's sweet little curls spring around her face with any movement. And how softly she folded herself into my body when she wanted comforting. I thought of the way Abby slept in her bed, her lovey propped under her head like a pillow, and her arms flung back next to her head like a baby.

I started shaking. Jane didn't know them that well—she didn't know what they needed.

Grasping my arms with my hands, I took a few deep breaths. *Keep calm, Ellie. Just a few more hours…*

"Lady Hartford!" I heard my name yelled out from the courtyard down below. We'd been spotted up on the balcony. It was

Lord Dagworth, surrounded by his dogs, and about seven knights. "Come see what your hero Sir Harry is up to."

I squinted down and saw Harry in full armor about to engage in a sword fight.

"How do we get down there?" I whispered to John.

"You're not going to like it," he said.

It was another winding staircase, this time on the outside of the building. No ropes.

CHAPTER ELEVEN

With him ther was his sone, a yong Squier,
A lovere and a lusty bachelor,
With lokkes cruller as they were laid in press
Of twenty yeer of age he was, I gesse.
Of his stature he was of evene lengthe
And wonderly delivere, and of greet strength
The Canterbury Tales by Geoffrey Chaucer

JOHN AND I scurried down the outer stairs of the round tower. Well, scurry is the wrong word for what I did. I *cautiously* went down the stairs, clinging to the wall so I would not trip over my long dress and fall thirty feet onto the stone pavement below. John had gone ahead of me and was nowhere to be seen until I reached the last ten steps. How differently he treated me than Harry, who'd patiently held my hand as I walked down. John stood at the bottom, arms folded, waiting, a cheeky look on his face.

"Slow poke," he said.

"Yeah, yeah," I said. "Sticks and stones may break my bones, and these stairs are designed to do just that."

A group of helmeted knights gathered farther down the courtyard, but I couldn't make out whether Harry was amongst them. I don't know how he had integrated himself into that group so quickly; perhaps men don't need the niceties of language to get along. Besides the knights armed in full fighting gear, three squires in their teens, and two pages, not older than eight.

Lord Dagworth greeted me. "Lady Hartford! Your knight is absolutely extraordinary—how lucky we all were that he did not pass our castle by last night! Harry Dumont simply must come to Windsor with us!" he exclaimed. "With you as well, of course," he said as an afterthought.

"Come where, my lord?" I asked.

"To Windsor, of course. To the tournament. Harry needs to join our group of men from Castle Wodesley. We are sure to win a prize in sword-fighting, and I reckon in jousting as well, if Harry's as good as he says he is on a horse. Bertram," he said to the small page, burdened already with holding extra bits of armor, "go fetch me the destrier, Carlo, with the white spots." The little boy dropped his metal bits in a hurry, making a large crashing sound as they hit the stone pavers, and ran off to the stables in the distance.

"Gentlemen, please remove your helmets for the lady. Lady Hartford, may I introduce to you my knights?"

"I would be much honored, sir." I dropped a subtle curtsey, not sure whether it was appropriate, but it seemed the polite thing to do.

Dagworth walked over to his knights, who didn't look quite as intimidating now that their helmets were off. The first man he walked over to resembled a younger version of Dagworth himself, except extremely tall. He had the same curly hair, the same round cheeks, and ears that stuck out at odd angles. "May I present my second son, Sir Matthew Dagworth. My first son is away fighting for the king, but my second son remains with me."

Matthew bowed.

Next was a man who looked to be in his 30's, with thick, black eyebrows, a slightly balding head of black hair, and a black, pointy beard. He looked exhausted and battle-worn, a few scars visible on his face. "This is Sir Anthony de Lane. He came to us recently from fighting on the front lines in France and Castilla."

Sir Anthony took my hand and kissed it. He was missing two fingers on the hand that held mine. I felt the full wetness of his lips on my skin, as well as his bristly beard, and I tried not to cringe, instead giving him a tight smile. "My lady, your presence at Castle Wodesley inspires us all to fight harder, and faster..." he said, enunciating the words ever so slowly, "until we win the ultimate prize."

"Er, thank you?" I said. I wasn't sure which prize Anthony was referring to, but I had no interest in being alone with him to find out.

Harry was next, and he gave me a big smile, complete with slightly crooked English teeth (had they never gotten orthodontists?). I couldn't help but return it just as broadly. He looked like he was in his element, holding a blunt-edged sword with the tip down, and thoroughly at ease, even in the heavy armor. His twill pants and Irish sweater were gone, replaced by leather pants and a simple blue tunic. I breathed a sigh of relief that he no longer stood out in his modern clothes.

The last knights were introduced, along with a few of the knights-in-training: the squires. I thought we were through, but there was one last knight to be introduced to me. "Ah, I nearly forgot you, my boy," Lord Dagworth said, as he noticed the slight, but very tall young man to his left. "He was our squire for so long, I'm afraid I still think of him that way: Sir Hugh de Rocher."

That was the name of the lead character in John's book that had hit the bestseller list. The pieces all came together now: John had gone back in time and met all these folks and turned them into a story. I'd admired John's imagination when I thought the story was fiction—now I knew it was real.

Hugh now was way older than he'd been in the book, due to the speed with which time passed here, I guessed. The cover illustration had showed him at around fourteen years old; he was asleep, lying down against a rock, with his horse saddled behind him and his sword at his side, completely exhausted after a day spent practicing his skills and running errands for his master. Now, standing here before me, he looked as gentle and pure a knight as he had seemed in that illustration, with dimpled cheeks, full lips, and broad shoulders.

"Sir Hugh!" I gushed. "I've heard so much about you!" Sir Hugh looked puzzled, as did the rest of the men there. I'm sure they wondered how I could possibly know of him, when I had only just arrived.

"Lady, the pleasure is mine," Hugh said formally, and bowed over my hand that I'd offered him.

John felt an explanation was in order to counter my enthusiasm: "Lady Hartford has been hearing the stories of our knights from me, and I told her about how Sir Hugh started out as a squire here."

"Well, well," Dagworth said, "there shall be plenty more stories to get down once we all get to Windsor, by my troth! With this lady and Sir Harry along with us, and of course, you too, Monsieur Stafford, as witness, we shall make quite an impression, quite so!"

I couldn't let Lord Dagworth think that we were going to go with him to Windsor. "My lord, may I have a word?" I asked.

He looked a little taken aback. Perhaps women didn't speak to a high and mighty lord like this, requesting an audience. "Certainly, my lady, certainly!" Lord Dagworth eventually said, recovering from the surprise.

"My lord, I am much grieved to tell you that Sir Harry and I cannot go with you to Windsor. You have been very courteous to us, and we honor you and your gracious wife for that. But I simply must get back to my children, and Sir Harry has agreed to accompany me."

Dagworth tutted me. "Your children, my dear Lady Hartford, can wait. The needs of a child weigh nothing in comparison to the needs of their parents. This is a golden opportunity for you, a lady who is without a formal relation in this country, I hear. You of course have my protection now, but if you find favor with the Earl of Salisbury or even the King, your passage in this country evermore will be one of ease and safety. And may I remind you, dear Lady, that nothing is more important to any of us, no matter what our station in life, than honoring the King with our presence. Now—" he placed a hand on my shoulder—"Lady Hartford, do not be nervous, as you will make a most marvelous impression on the King as my guest, and Sir Harry will dazzle the great court at the tournament."

I started shaking my head, and he put up a hand to stop me. "I will not be dissuaded, and you should recognize how important this is as a woman who has lost everything."

I tried another tactic. "Forgive me, sir, but since I have not been in the English court in so long, I fear that I will let you down with my poor manners and dress." This was no lie. There was no way I could pass myself off as a seasoned courtier. And I just had one dress.

"It could not happen, my lady. Could not happen. You are the most elegant woman to visit us in some time, although the means by which you came were certainly most tragic, but now it seems that you have made a quick recovery…. Well, I know that if Salisbury tells the King that I have not brought you to see him, I will be held personally accountable to him."

I saw Harry and John looking over at me. Harry's face was implacable—like a good poker player in Vegas. John looked amused, his mouth twitching. I think he liked seeing me here, interacting with his friends, forging my way in this strange world.

I hadn't thought of the Dagworths being held responsible to the King if Harry and I failed to go to Windsor. The myth of our dramatic arrival was *New York Post*-style tabloid news, and because the people of the 14th century didn't have the distraction of forty competing stories arriving every minute on their feed, we would be news for a while. However, Salisbury hadn't arrived yet, and so perhaps there would be time to disappear before the king's trusted friend got to the castle. Maybe I could fake an illness and stay in my room and sneak out at midnight to get to the labyrinth....

"Ah, here is Carlo now." A large, black horse, with a white spot on his nose arrived in the courtyard, led by Bertram, who looked as though could be trampled by the massive beast with one misstep. "What do you say, Lady Hartford, isn't he a beauty? I paid a fortune for him from a Spaniard. Harry, why don't you try him out? I'd be interested to hear your thoughts on our prized destrier."

Harry, bulked up with half his armor and some borrowed chain mail, stepped onto a platform and then swung himself easily up on the horse's back. Together, man and horse became nine feet of warrior. The look in Harry's eyes, before he slid the helmet over his head, was all business and anticipation.

With a gentle kick of Harry's left spur into the horse's flank, they were off. Through the courtyard and out the front entrance, they departed the castle grounds, armor clanking and hooves clopping on the stones. There was no awkwardness, no acting. He looked like a real knight. Dagworth said, "Mount up, men! Show Sir Harry the forest, and if you should see any boar while you're out there, spear one for our feast." The rest of the knights took off to fetch their horses.

Dagworth excused himself to go inside and see to the preparations for the Salisburys, leaving me in the company of John once again.

"Do you think Harry is going to be okay?" I asked, trying to follow his disappearing form.

The rest of the men began to ride away. "He's been riding horses since before he could walk. I wouldn't worry. Would take a small army to bring that man down, and the Taliban certainly tried," he said, turning his attention to me. "I think it's high time we got you inside. You look positively blue with cold. Except for your little red nose."

He'd always said I had a cute nose. Was the man I knew back

when I was a grad student gone forever, and replaced with this version of John? Or was he still in there, somehow?

I hadn't even noticed the cold since we had been out among the troop of men, but now that we were on our own standing on the paving stones, one fierce cold gust of wind convinced me that he was right. "Could we go back to the scriptorium? I'm dying to dig into the collection of manuscripts. Have you catalogued them? What's your coolest book?"

John chuckled. "Bookworm—there's a whole castle to explore but you want to shut yourself away with books." He patted me on the head.

I swatted his hand away. "Don't mess up my hair! I don't know what it looks like, but Mary spent a lot of time on it."

"It's pretty, but I prefer it down. You know that."

Eesh. That seemed pretty possessive, and he had no right to … Okay sure, people could have preferences. I grit my teeth and kept my mouth shut.

"Now—" he started to lead the way back inside—"let's swing by the kitchens and get something warm to drink first. There's no tea—that won't be possible to get for another three hundred years. But still, there's usually some hot spiced wine to drink to fortify the old constitution against the harshness of the winter's chill."

We walked back into the castle, through the hall, into the kitchen, and back up to the scriptorium; I was sketching a mental map of the place. I remembered which staircase led to my bedroom. If I needed to make a quick escape, I would need to know as many exit points and hiding places as I could.

CHAPTER TWELVE

Hard is the harte that loveth nought
In May
The Romaunt of the Rose, Geoffrey Chaucer

Back in the library with a mug of mulled wine and some sweet biscuits that John had managed to charm a maid into giving us, I stood with my back to the fire and gazed at all the books. I was like a kid in the candy store.

"Over here is a section I don't touch—Yvonne's nature collection—she's the wife of Hugh, whom you met. You know, the 'squire?'"

"Yes, I met the hero of your book. I guess I can't credit you with coming up with an original story."

"Er, no," John admitted. "I had to fudge that quite a bit in my interviews. Another reason for you to think I'm a thief, then…"

"No, well…" I paused, thinking. "It takes real skill to make anyone's story compelling and readable. I think you write beautifully—you really captured my heart." I stopped. *Heart* was definitely the wrong word, "I mean, captured my imagination. I would have told you that earlier, when the book came out, but—" there was no way I was speaking with him back then.

"You were mad at me? Yes, I know. But I'll take any compliment, whenever it's offered," he said. Then he walked over to the shelves. "You don't know what kind of a treat you are in for. What's your pleasure then? Illuminated with lots of pretty pictures, or verse, with lots of pretty words?"

"Pick me something that's going to knock my socks off."

"Close your eyes, now. Don't peek. I don't want you to know where this is in case you want to steal it later. You know what the minstrels say about redheads?

I shrugged.

"They have debatable moral sensibilities."

I folded my arms over my chest. "Pot. Kettle. Black."

I heard him clear his throat. "Let me defend my questionable honor by saying I would never take from the hand that feeds me," he said. "I do have some morals left."

He placed a book on my lap. "Open your eyes, Ellie," John whispered into my ear. "It's our labyrinth."

I opened my eyes. The book was brown leather, with a stamped title, *Love and Other Turns*, by Anthony de Lane. The book was new, and slim. I opened the cover to see sketches and poems inside. The name of the author sounded familiar, "Is this the man...?"

"With only three fingers on his right hand, and who kissed your hand so rapturously in the courtyard below? Yes."

Each page's first initial was capitalized and decorated down the left-hand side, turning into swirls, patterns, and animals. And the illustrations! There were glorious, miniature paintings on every other page of the book. "When was this made?" I asked.

"Two years ago. Sir Anthony had been reciting his tale since his return from a trip to Spain a few years before—the trip when he lost his fingers. The man has an extraordinary gift. He'd been telling the story in the hall to entertain the family and their friends. Dagworth decided it must be put down on paper to get it preserved and wants to present it to the King at Windsor. He's spent a fortune on the materials, the illuminators, and the scribe. Since Dagworth's star is rising at court, he thought this would be the perfect opportunity to further elevate his standing with this gift."

"I've never seen or heard of a book like this. What's its content?"

"It's about love and death, and how the forces of nature can influence your purpose in life." John shook his head, puzzled. "De Lane is a pretty interesting bloke, if not altogether there." He tapped a finger onto his head. "Spends a lot of time at his labyrinth."

"Does he know about 'The Thin Place?' I mean, he created it after all."

John put up his hands. "I'm damned if he'll even speak to me. The fellow wanders around in a daze when he's not telling his story. It's like he's not really living unless he's sharing the tale. Kind of sad, really."

"Maybe it's because you're not a woman. He certainly seemed on the pervy side when it came to me." I tucked de Lane's book under my arm, and looked at the other volumes on the shelves.

There is nothing better than the smell of musty books. It's as pleasurable as the smell of apple cider donuts in the fall. "I've never heard of this collection of books of Lord Dagworth's."

John ran his fingers along the spines of the books. "You know the dangers of the medieval library—indeed any library. Paper is a precious commodity, and manuscripts were torn from their bindings and reused if they were not deemed essential. Books can be sold, ruined from the weather or fire, stolen, or neglected. Or eaten by mice and insects." He stopped. "I keep hoping, that when I get back, I'll have somehow changed the past, and these books will be found, but when I look up the titles online, they're still not there."

"Perhaps we can save a few?" I asked. "Say, the ten most worthy ones? Would Dagworth notice?"

Save the books, honor the authors. Take some prizes back with me to Jane, where the books could never disappear, where they would be safe in the British Library, and could be reproduced for millions to enjoy. Or at least, the thousands who were medieval nuts like me. This might be a path to paid lectures, to published books. My nervous energy got me up to pace and think.

"Good question," John said. "Dagworth's so busy with his business, he barely has time to make it in here. Maybe just a few missing might be all right…? But then, I don't want to endanger my relationship with Dagworth. He is—"

"What would the implications be for Dagworth if he lost a few books? Would people who could use them in the present and near future not gain the information from them, or the joy? What kind of cost is it to them, even if it's a huge gain for us in the 21st century?"

We went back and forth over the question, but in the end, we came to no conclusion.

I saw movement out of the window. Clouds of dust were rising into the air as a procession came into view. First came four men on horses and full armor. I could see a flag with a coat of arms being held by another man on horseback. And then came a group of men, and a smaller group of women dressed in those pointy hats like they wore in fairy tales. I wondered how those hats stayed on their heads.

The noise of the procession turned from a muffled rumbling into a loud clip-clop as the horses strode onto the cobblestone of the lane leading into Wodesley Castle.

"Yes—the Salisburys are here," said John joining me at the window, gripping my arm lightly. "This is what I've been waiting for." His eyes shone, transfixed by the pomp of their arrival.

If the Salisburys met me, they might well want to take me to Windsor with them. That couldn't happen.

I tucked Anthony's book into a pocket in my dress. It was time to make myself scarce.

CHAPTER THIRTEEN

And the lord of the land rides late and long
Hunting the barren hind over the broad heath.
He had slain such a sum, when the sun sank low,
Of does and other deer, as would dizzy one's wits.
Sir Gawain and the Green Knight

I LEFT THE scriptorium, that beautiful treasure trove of manuscripts that I could have spent weeks in—no, years—if I were not so intent on getting home. Back in my world, ancient manuscripts like that are brought out to you by librarians in carefully wrapped, non-acidic boxes. We each have to put on a pair of white gloves to examine the fragile books so as not to leave any dirt and oils from our fingers that could corrode the paper. And those are rare occasions when you get to actually turn the pages of one. All of the great works have been very carefully digitally scanned so that the books can remain undisturbed for future generations.

My parents are both bankers. Practical people who like to make deals, joke with their colleagues in break room, and above all, make money. They don't get why I spend my time obsessing over an ancient language, interpreting meaning from the poetry and the prose. "How can you make a living doing that?"

The living as a professor isn't one that allows me to go to 4-

star hotels and have a country club membership, but it feeds my curiosity, and my soul.

As I made my way back through the rooms of the castle, for the first time in many years, I thought, what was it about this time that so fascinated me? Was it the chivalry, the romantic stories of quests and unrequited love, the kings and the knights and the ladies? *Yes.* Wasn't it better than analyzing stocks, making margin calls, sitting in stuffy clubs talking about whose deals were bigger, and what celebrity client you had? In a world full of stories about men pursuing women for their boob jobs, and women pursuing men for their bank accounts, I wanted a different world.

At home, that meant my nose had to be in a book to find that world, and my feet planted in front of young adults to explain to them that there was another way to live your life. And it wasn't through building wealth but building a wealth of stories.

Romance, at least in the way fairy-tale way people were dressed and how they acted on the surface (when was the last time anyone kissed my hand. Wait, when was my hand *ever* kissed?), was all around me here.

I came to a rectangular mullioned window, and through the milky glass I could see what appeared to be the kitchen garden. It was too bad I couldn't stay and really explore more. Find out why I was obsessed with this time. See whether it was just a stupid schoolgirl's fixation that had lasted into adulthood and meant nothing beyond that it was fun, or whether there was truly a meaning to it all that I'd never really figured out.

I found a door to the outside and pushed it open. The garden was walled in on two sides by the castle, so it could not support any "full sun" plants within. Perhaps thirty feet wide by twenty feet long, it was a good size; the beds of plants were raised, with stone walkways in between. In the center was a tiny water feature, with a sculpture of a woman seated with small birds near her. Although her face was partially covered by a veil, the statue resembled Lady Dagworth.

A door to the garden opened. It was Anthony de Lane. Even

though I vowed previously not to be alone with him, now that I knew he was the author of an intriguing little book, I was glad to have him to myself.

"Please forgive my intrusion, Lady Hartford. I know my presence with you is neither expected nor desired, but I saw you from my window, and I had to come speak with you."

I quickly extended my hand, and indicated a bench where we could sit together, underneath an arbor of willow branches. Once again, he kissed my hand, although this time it seemed less smarmy. "Sir Anthony, I'm pleased to see you."

"Is this not the most beautiful of places? The people are so friendly, the architecture so beautiful." Anthony looked wistfully off into the distance. "I have traveled quite far—as far as Castilla on the crusades, but I did not make it to Jerusalem.

"I am sure you miss the warmth of the sun in that land."

Anthony took my hand again. "When I returned here, with both my hand and heart torn to shreds and thinking I could no longer go on, Lady Dagworth brought me to this garden. I grew to love it so much that I was inspired to put together a labyrinth similar to the one I'd been to in Castilla, as a thank you to my patroness. Have you had a chance to visit it? I expect you might have—that is where we found you." He looked at me out of the corner of his eye.

"Monsieur Stafford has shown me your beautiful book," I said, skirting the issue. "Does it have to do with the labyrinth? How did you come to know about them?"

He then dodged my question. "I hear that it is your desire to return soon to your home?"

We were not so obliquely avoiding each other's questions.

I tried again. "Do you have much pain in your hand?"

Anthony held out his left hand to show me his injury. As I expected from a man living in the 14th century, it was rough and broad, callused, and with short, somewhat dirty fingernails. Down the left side of his hand ran a thin purple scar where the missing middle, pinky and ring finger used to be. But the healing on the hand looked remarkable, considering the lack of modern medical intervention.

"You have healed full well. How did this wound befall you?" I asked.

"I am too ashamed to speak of it to you—at this moment. Youth, and too much wine made me do some foolish things, for which now I have some very real scars."

"It is a rare person that gets through life without mistakes, and the resultant scars. I too have many scars, although most are on the inside, on my heart. Without error, though, it is very difficult to learn," I said. I often wondered whether I was better off having had my heart broken. Had I become more evolved and more sympathetic to others who didn't have easy lives? Had I achieved more as a result of being on my own?

The light came into Anthony's eyes, and he started to nod, vigorously. "This is a wonderful place for you then, if your heart is scarred. I knew it might be. When I saw you in the labyrinth, I knew it was right that you came."

I remembered the voice right before I'd passed out. It was his. How much had he seen? Maybe us appearing out of nowhere? There was no sense in trying to deny it. "What did you say to us there? I'm afraid I was unwell."

"I asked whether you were here to save her story?"

"Save whose story?"

"I believe that you have come here for a reason."

He knew our secret. He knew we came through the labyrinth, the one that he built. He knew the secrets of the thin place.

He got up and bowed and started to walk away.

"But wait, I have so much to ask you! I need to go home, to go back to my girls."

Anthony continued to walk away, despite my pleas. "Never fear, my lady! We shall speak more!"

What did Anthony know that I didn't?

I left the garden to return to my room, darting back through the kitchens, the hall, and up the tower staircase to my room, clinging to the walls and halls like a mouse not wanting to attract attention. My room was empty, but the fire was still going strong—somebody must have been in recently to tend to it.

I sat down in the wing chair next to the fire and began to look at Anthony de Lane's book. I noticed at the top there was a curving green labyrinth at the head and bottom of each page.

The door swung open. How could I not have heard footsteps coming up the stone steps?

It was Harry, who looked like he'd just run a marathon. Sweaty, stinky, and muddy, he did not have his usual upright and uptight army posture. He was stooped, winced as he walked, and looked pale.

"What on earth happened to you?" I asked, getting up from my cushioned chair and pushing him into it. He felt like one solid mass of muscle, who couldn't be moved unless he was willing. "You look like you've been run over by a truck."

Harry closed his eyes and moved his jaw around, up and down and around, as though he was trying to work out the tension. "I'm all right. Just need a bit of a sit-down for a moment. Is there anything to drink?"

On the dresser there were tankards and a pitcher with a cloth over it. Removing the cloth, I sniffed to see what it was. Beer— perfect for a thirsty man in need of re-invigoration.

Kneeling on the floor in front of Harry, I handed him the drink as I looked into his eyes. "Tell me about your day out. I want to hear everything. And I have news too."

Harry took two or three long swigs of beer and wiped his mouth with the side of his sleeve. He shook his head, "Please, not now. I need to rest." He said this not with the wink he had given to me early in the morning routine, but with a somber resolution.

Five seconds later he was snoring, still covered in mud, still sweaty, with two days' worth of stubble filling in on his face. I hadn't noticed it before, but Harry had two different colored eyelashes—one blond, and one black, and a splatter of mud rested so close to the corner of his eye that it might have fallen in. I reached out to gently swab the mud away with my index finger, thinking that I could get it while he was asleep. As my finger touched the side of his nose, he gently reached up with his hand, moved my hand to his lips, and kissed it, with his eyes still closed.

That was much nicer than Anthony's squelchy kiss, but I was worried. He seemed traumatized. Like he'd seen something horrific.

I got up off the floor to get him a blanket. All of that sweat and mud was going to give him a chill, and I didn't want him to become ill.

With a choice between wool and fur blankets, I decided on fur, and tucked it around him. I wondered about taking off his boots and spurs, but as they were so tight all the way up to his knees, I figured I couldn't get them off without a good deal of tugging that would surely wake him up. So, he remained fully clothed, with a blanket, and a scowl still on his face.

But he'd kissed my hand.

CHAPTER FOURTEEN

"And brought of mighty ale a large quart."
The Miller's Tale, Geoffrey Chaucer

M Y STOMACH GROWLED. The aroma of cooking came up into our tower and taunted me. How many hours had it been since we had that bit of roast beef? The sky grew dark, and I wondered whether they going to ring a giant bell at dinner time to alert everyone, or whether we were supposed to know to just come down.

There were no watches, and no clocks—they wouldn't be invented for another two hundred years. I wondered how people managed to accomplish anything "on time." How could you say: "I'll meet you at 6," or "Let's go to lunch at 11:30," or "Bedtime is 7:30, girls," without a watch? Was it better to live with clocks, or without them?

Nothing could be "set" in time.

A knock at the door disturbed my thoughts—Mary. She came in holding a box with a white ribbon tied around it.

"What's this?"

"I don't know; I found it just now outside the door. I came to tend to you to prepare you for supper," said Mary, with a cheerful smile. She looked a bit more worn down than when I saw her last, and as I reached for the box, I felt her hands were cold and rough. She knew a life that was so much harder than mine. My hands were cold too, but at home I had central heat, washing machines, a dishwasher, running water…

I took the box, and inside was a beautiful piece of dark-blue fabric. As I took out the piece, I realized it was more than just fabric, it was a whole, long and flowing dress.

"Ooh—try it on!" Mary cajoled. She helped me slip out of the dress I was wearing and put the new one on. We didn't need to worry about Harry seeing. Like most men, he could sleep through anything. Whereas I wake at a pin drop.

After I got the dress on, it was impossible for me to know how the dress looked because we had no mirror. "Does it look all right?" I asked Mary.

"Oh yes," she breathed, and I could tell by the excitement in her eyes that it was true. "I would love to have a dress like this to wear one day."

Mary tightened the back and sides of the dress with ties that crisscrossed around the bodice. All dresses I had seen out and about in the castle seemed not to be hemmed to height, but instead puddled on the floor. This made walking a constant battle against tripping over your own hem. Luckily, I was taller than the average woman of the time, and so the puddling was not so significant in this dress.

"Does this belong to Lady Dagworth?"

"No, Madame. I have never seen it before. Indeed, I have never seen cloth of this kind in my life. It seems to capture every bit of light in the room and almost spark like the fire." She turned the fabric from the skirt of the dress in her hands, right and left, and said, "It seems almost like magic."

Who would have given me this dress? Was it John? He knew my size and knew what looked good on me. My brain flicked through the other people I had met… Anthony de Lane? Perhaps it was Lady Dagworth after all? She would have known from Mary that I had come into her home with nothing. But then, how would Mary not have known about the dress?

"Because there are no more rooms in the castle because of

the Earl of Salisbury and his attendants," Mary started, "Lady Dagworth thought that you would want to keep Sir Harry close, due to your recent misfortune. I can make up a pallet for him to sleep on in front of the door. But if you do not wish it, he can sleep in the hall with the rest of the men."

"Oh," I said, blushing, knowing she was going to infer something no matter which option I would choose. "I should prefer it if Sir Harry keeps close by. I am afraid the attack still weighs heavy on me; my brain will not let it go."

"I think you are right and that is wise." She looked down. No more winks from her either. Together we laid out blankets for Harry to sleep on that night.

Before Mary left, I asked her whether she would be at the feast. "Oh yes, Madame. Lady Dagworth has asked that I sit at one of the lower tables and make sure that everyone behaves. Those young squires and pages can get up to a good deal of mischief if they are too excited. I know how to deal with rowdy boys," she said. "But speaking of which, my lady, you need to get Sir Handsome up to dress for dinner." We both gazed at the seemingly vulnerable form of Harry sleeping, but I knew he probably could give some sort of Vulcan death grip in an instant if he sensed danger in his REM sleep. Mary turned to me and smiled. "Unless, that is, you would like me to tend to him?"

"No, no!" I assured her with an embarrassed smile. I wasn't going to have another woman fussing over Harry—I wanted to keep him to myself, even if just for the few hours that we would be stuck in time together. "But do you have time to bring us some hot water?"

"I'll see if I can fetch some from the kitchen, but if not, I'm afraid we wouldn't have time to get any started fresh." She brought me some woven towels from the dresser. "Here, take these, and if I can get back with some hot water, I will. Otherwise, there's a small bowl here, and I'll refresh it later tonight when I can," Mary said, and then she stopped and took a look at me. "But please, do not dirty that beautiful dress. I will be most disappointed if you come down the tower stairs looking any less lovely than you do now."

"Mary." I blushed. I was not used to getting compliments. "You attend to my spirit as well as my dress."

She laughed. "I think Lady Dagworth would have your hide if I were to go back to France with you." Mary left to tend to the rest of her long list of duties while directing me to "come down in a little while."

Did that mean ten minutes, or thirty? I'd been taught to show up not on time ever—but to arrive "fashionably late"—as my mother called it. That way, if your hostess is running behind, that gives her a few more minutes to pull things together.

I guessed it would depend on how fast I could get Harry up and presentable. How could I wake a soldier without getting a knife stuck in my throat? My safest bet was to stay a few feet back and firmly say, "Harry, time to wake up!" in my best mom voice.

Harry jolted back awake and sprang to his feet, ready for action. His eyes were bright and five-espressos-alert. "Where are we going?" his eyes swept the room, perhaps searching for different escape routes.

"Um, just to dinner," I said, trying to tease his tension down. "You are due at a fancy supper."

He rubbed his hands over his face and sighed. "Yeah, I don't really fit in, do I? I seem to remember Matthew said he could loan me some clothes—he's quite tall for his time. But I'd wanted to check on you first, and I guess I fell asleep."

Harry charged off for a few minutes and came back with a bundle of clothes in his arms. "I'm not shy, but I'm rather grimy, and wouldn't mind a proper wash. Wouldn't want to embarrass you as I'm your token knight, right?"

"You're not 'required' to be my knight, 'Sir Harry,'" I said. "It's a free country. Actually, that's not accurate. A monarchy is not a free country. But…"

Harry held up his hands. "So would you mind—"

"Oh yes, sorry," I apologized. "I'll leave you to it."

Now it was my turn to sit outside the door and wait.

CHAPTER FIFTEEN

All this mirth they made until meat was served;
When they had washed them worthily, they went to their seats,
The best seated above, as best it beseemed,
Guenevere the goodly queen gay in the midst
On a dais welldecked and duly arrayed
With costly silk curtains, a canopy over,
Of Toulouse and Turkestan tapestries rich,
All broidered and bordered with the best gems
Ever brought into Britain, with bright pennies to pay.
Fair queen, without a flaw.
Sir Gawain and the Green Knight

THE TORCHES WERE lit so that we could see our way down the spiral staircase when we left our room. Harry, mindful of my fear of circular staircases, walked in front of me while I put one hand on his shoulder, now donned in red silk.

I can't say that the silk tunic and black woolen leggings were a great look on Harry. The silk was stretched near to the breaking point, and Harry had to call me in to help fasten the laces on the back (they weren't quite using buttons yet, but they were getting close to figuring those out). He somewhat resembled a circus performer who suddenly put on weight and outgrew his costume.

Of course, Harry wasn't overweight—it was muscle. I'd seen his bare back. My fingers accidentally grazed his warm skin, and Harry shivered in response.

We got to the Great Hall, transformed; it's amazing what can be done with a drafty stone room when you bring in arrangements of greenery, put tablecloths on roughly hewn tables, and pull out the family's silver bowls, goblets, candlesticks, and urns. Elizabeth Dagworth was a Renaissance hostess before the Renaissance; the Martha Stewart of her time. The effect was enchanting.

I felt like a princess as men took sight of me in this form-fitting sparkly wonder and their jaws dropped open. I wished I could get a picture of me in it as a keepsake—me, who barely got a raised eyebrow in normal life. But all I could tell from my point of view was that it was made up of this gorgeous, glittery and silky material, exposed just enough cleavage to be sexy but not overtly so, and fit my body like a glove. (Spanx, though, would have been welcome).

I remembered Jane's advice from our younger years when we used to "go down the pub" together—"Act like you deserve the attention, no matter how you're feeling on the inside. Just the appearance of self-confidence is incredibly sexy, even if it's only on the outside."

The high table sat on a dais about three feet off the ground, giving those seated a commanding view of the room. The men wore velvet and wool jackets cut long over their hips, tight woolen pants, long suede boots, and ornamental daggers strapped around their waists. The ladies wore their best dresses in different materials and colors—from a yellow silk brocade to a rather violent shade of orange velvet. Quite a few women around the room wore those pointy hats, or veils that covered their hair in cascades of sheer silk. Precious gemstones were on their hands, pearls in their hair and around their throats.

Not having a veil or hat or jewels, I stood out. Lady Dagworth came over to me from the high table and gave me a squeeze. "Wherever did you get that dress? It's astounding!"

"It was left outside my room. Mary found it and brought it to me. You didn't lend it to me?" I asked.

"Dear me, no! If I had a dress like that, I am sorry, Madame, but I would not be giving it to anyone else but me." Lady Dagworth touched my arm and twisted the fabric this way and that; like Mary, it looked as though she had never seen this type of material before. "I cannot abide a mystery. I must know from whence this dress came. Do not worry," she said, with a wink, "I shall be discreet. But I will uncover your benefactor. Whomever it is, he or she has excellent taste, and a fat fortune besides."

She seated me at the table directly to the right of the dais—not elevated, but still a place of honor. I sat between the ridiculously tall heir to the Dagworth fortune, Sir Matthew, who had given Harry his clothes, and Sir Hugh, formerly known as "the squire" from John's book. All the men stood when I came to the table.

I knew I would like chivalry.

The food started flying out from the kitchen. Each course consisted of several dishes. Soup was first, then came the fish course, the stuffed bird course—complete with sculpted cooked birds with feathers on—small game, large game, domesticated animals, then a rather bland pudding, and grace. There was herring, rabbit, quail, chicken, eel, pig, boar, and venison. A great variety of sauces accompanied the meats—one incredible dish was flavored with saffron, almonds, pine nuts, and dates. I had never expected food of this time to be so complex, and to taste so good. I guessed that the time people had spent time abroad fighting in the Crusades and in France gave them ideas about how food was meant to taste.

I soon gave up trying to be polite and taste everything, especially when the eel was presented. I covered it up with vegetables so I wouldn't have to look at that gray snake-like beast. Even touching it with my knife gave me the heebie jeebies.

The wine never stopped coming, but I only took small sips.

Our escape was hopefully coming soon. I knew where Harry was, and John was in the room too… somewhere.

During the course of the dinner, Matthew told me more about the Earl and Countess of Salisbury from Matthew. The Earl of Salisbury, whose name was William Montecute, was a lifelong friend of King Edward III. William's savvy political ways helped free Edward from the corrupt reign of his mother's lover, thus allowing him to rule on his own at the age of eighteen. Ever since, William had been rewarded with land, titles, and riches, and called upon time and time again to serve as the most reliable warrior and diplomat to press Edward's, and England's, advantage in the world. "Politically shrewd he is, with skills that are unmatched in sword-play, horsemanship, and war."

I stole several looks at the Earl up on the dais. A handsome man in his late thirties, salt and pepper hair, and what looked like a few scars on his face.

Matthew knew a little less about Katherine, the Countess of Salisbury. Her parents had both been so famously gorgeous that tales about them regularly made the rounds when troubadours visited the castle. By the look of her, she had only ever known appreciative and lustful glances. Having that kind of beauty must inhabit every pore of your being, whether you dismiss it or use it to its full advantage. King Edward, who served as her ward, married her to William as a reward to his best friend.

I couldn't imagine not having a say in who I would marry. Not that I'd made a good choice for myself with my own free will, but it would be far worse being a part of a political marriage, when not even the most minimal amount of love could be expected.

Minstrels played softly as we ate course after gut-busting course. The Dagworths had spent a fortune entertaining this most important couple. Lord Dagworth, who earlier had seemed so vibrant and excited, looked now as though he could barely stay awake. His head nodded downwards, eyes closing, and it was only the occasional jabs from his wife that kept him going. Lady

Dagworth had great circles under her eyes, but didn't stop moving around the room making sure that everyone was doing his or her job, and that her guests were having a grand time.

As the last platters of fruit came out, the tables in the middle of the room were cleared out of the way, meaning that all who were not at the high table had to stand, and the band started playing livelier tunes.

One rousing tune the band played was the medieval equivalent to an Earth Wind and Fire song when everyone just has to dance. You could simply not stay on the sidelines. Everybody stood up and started clapping along and stomping their feet. When it was done, the Earl of Salisbury rose to his feet and the band put down their instruments. "May I make a request, ladies and gentlemen, of my dear hosts, Lord and Lady Dagworth? I have heard our host proclaim that his wife has the loveliest voice that ever was heard in our fair land. Though it may not be proper for a lady to sing in front of strangers, we are all but friends here, are we not?"

The hall went nuts. Lady Dagworth must have been a popular performer. She bashfully declined, but Salisbury would not have it. Her feigned protests dutifully fulfilled, Lady Dagworth ceased to be the shrinking violet. She strode up to the minstrels and whispered in the leader's ear. The first few notes sounded familiar to me.

"*Heaven, I'm in Heaven,*" she sang, with a voice as strong and clear and sultry as the greatest torch singers.

I clamped my hand over my wide-open jaw—it was the old Irving Berlin song from one of those great Fred Astaire and Ginger Roger movies of the 1930's! There was only one man who could have taught her that song. I looked around the room and found John, grinning from ear to ear. He'd always had a love for classic movies.

I caught his eye and shook my head. "Rascal," I mouthed.

John winked at me.

Now I knew a bit more about what he'd been doing with his

time.

Elizabeth Dagworth swayed her hips to the music, phrasing the words just so, hitting all her notes effortlessly. The audience tapped their toes in time to the music. The beauty of her voice and the men and women in front of me gave me goosebumps. A great entertainer makes time stop, making you forget about every care in the world, and just exist in that moment in time. Lady Dagworth's singing did that for me.

Unfortunately, she only sang that one song. She left her place under the minstrel's gallery to rapturous applause.

The small band of performers then whipped up a completely new sound, and everyone let out a whoop of joy as though hearing an old favorite.

I scooted my way back, to stand against the stone wall of the hall, behind the rows of onlookers enjoying the dancing in the middle of the floor. It was a good place to observe the dynamics.

Harry had been pulled out onto the dance floor by a rather buxom young lady. He was protesting and probably trying to tell her that he was no good at dancing, but she didn't care, and acted quite pleased with herself that she had claimed the first dance with the newly-minted hero of Wodesley Castle.

Mary came up to me with a gentle tap on my arm. She had changed into a pretty red dress. It might have been a hand-me-down from Lady Dagworth. "What are you doing hiding back here? You should be dancing, my lady," she scolded me. "I worked so long on your hair and fitting that dress on you just so, and yet no one can see you back here, holding up the wall!" she teased.

"I'm very happy back here, Mary, but thank you for finding me. You look so pretty in that dress. Are you having a good time?"

"Fair enough, my lady. 'Tis impossible not to miss my husband at such times, truth be told. And I am a bit tired. Lady Dagworth had us all running hither and yon today, and I could do with putting my feet up. But it was a glorious feast, and best of all, the Salisburys seem most pleased with the hospitality."

"Can you retire yet, or do you need to stay to clean up?" I could only imagine how long and busy her day had been.

"Lady Dagworth gives me a few blessings as one of her ladies' maids, and I do get to go to bed when I wish on a night such as this," Mary said, leaning up against the wall in a way that let her rest. Her life wasn't easy, and she didn't get many opportunities for fun. "Madame," said Mary, "let me just say if I were you in that lovely dress, looking so beautiful tonight, I would be out there dancing with all these fine gentlemen and take my pick. Do not waste this opportunity, because soon you'll be back where you came from…" Then she bobbed a curtsey and disappeared into the crowd.

Yes, I would be back where I came from in about one or two more hours, when all the people had exhausted and drunk themselves into a stupor. Back to my little house in Massachusetts, evenings spent reading about times like this. I did need to take advantage. What could it hurt? Looking at Harry, having a good time with his blonde, well why shouldn't I as well? I felt a flash of jealousy looking at that girl, much younger than I, with her classic blond hair and hourglass figure. Was Harry attracted to that sort of look? *Who wouldn't be*, I sighed.

Which one of the men would dance with? There were several, attractive in different ways. Some filled out their tunics with muscles, some had classically handsome profiles, some looked simultaneously goofy and charming. But what was I going to do—tap one on the shoulder? Was that even allowed?

But then a man sidled up beside me, short, dressed in green velvet and a red poufy hat. He took my hand and bowed over it, and in an accent I couldn't quite make out, I believe asked me to dance. I was trying to come up with an excuse that he could understand, when I saw Harry crossing the room to come toward me. I shot him a look that said, "Save me."

"Lady Hartford, Sir, kindly forgive me for interrupting your conversation," he said in his perfect French. "But I have been asked by Lord Dagworth to come and fetch Lady Hartford to introduce her to the Earl and Countess of Salisbury." Harry bowed, tucked my hand around his elbow, and led me away.

"It seems you have quite a fan," said Harry.

"Thank you for sparing me," I said.

"Perhaps he was the only one who could find you in your hideout against the wall. You look far too beautiful to be hiding."

"Why, thank you!" Heat rose to my face. Earlier he'd told me how much he loved the dress and wondered where it came from. I caught him looking at me when he thought I wasn't looking at him. We both pretended that it didn't happen, and the awkwardness soon passed. But I thought that maybe, just maybe, I attracted him. "That pretty blond girl seemed to find *you* rather quickly," I teased.

Harry smiled. "She did, didn't she?"

"I'm sorry you had to leave her. Do you have plans to see her later?" I asked, curious in what he thought of a girl like her.

"Alas, we might be running out of time to meet many other people if our plans go as we hope. But good luck with this crowd." He gestured to the dais. "They seem like the type who are used to getting what they want."

The Earl and the countess loomed above me on their dais. My biggest test yet.

CHAPTER SIXTEEN

"Yet my counsel was of kissing," came her answer then,
"Where favor has been found, freely to claim
As accords with the conduct of courteous knights."
Sir Gawain and the Green Knight

LORD DAGWORTH SHOUTED a hearty hello to Harry and me and waved to us to come to the side of the table. He seemed as happy to see us as though it had been years instead of hours, and as though he'd known us for years instead of just one day.

The Earl of Salisbury, judging by the people gathered around him, gazing at him adoringly, was the equivalent to a rock star. He was slim but well-muscled with his years of fighting experience. All men in the Middle Ages seemed to have trimmed beards, they must have tiny scissors in their sheaths alongside their swords, and perhaps they used the reflection off their swords to see what they were doing? Dressed in a turquoise-colored tunic with nail studs in the sleeves and around the collar, he looked like a combination of royalty and street fighter, with his one wary eye taking in his surroundings, while the other eye remained fixed, perhaps injured in an accident. Several heavy gold necklaces that looked like they would belong on a rapper in South Central Los Angeles ensconced his neck. One had to be confident and well-armed to carry his weight in gold with him.

"My lord," Dagworth addressed Salisbury, "I have forgotten to tell you of the most extraordinary event we had here last evening." Lord Dagworth, dressed in an outer robe of furs over his gold tunic, looked the part of the great host, towering over his more diminutive guest. "We were seated at our tables after a fine meal, when a loud knock came at the door with a cry for help. All of us were taken aback. Who should knock on our door so late at night? I thought it might be a foul trick afoot, but of course we had our outer gates manned, so whomever it was could not have slipped in unapproved. When my men opened the door, who should we see but this man, Sir Harry, and this lady here, swooned in his arms?"

Dagworth then made his formal introductions. "William, Earl of Salisbury, and Katherine, Countess of Salisbury, may I present Lady Eleanor Hartford, and her rescuer, Sir Harry DuMont. Lady Hartford was attacked in the most vicious and foul manner not far from Wodesley Castle and separated from her servants. I had my men out looking for the cruel party responsible early this morn', but all tracks were lost after the night's rain. Sir Harry showed great strength and care in getting Lady Hartford to shelter here at our dear home, and she has recuperated most admirably today under our protection."

I curtseyed as best as I could, and Harry executed a bow with military precision.

The Earl looked me up and down, while saying to Harry, "I commend you, good sir. Well done. We would be without honor if we could not keep our beautiful women safe. For all that is precious in life comes from women."

He continued. "You must both come to Windsor with our party. As my guests. Sir DuMont, you must compete for the prizes at the tournament, and we shall take care of the Lady Hartford until we can contact her family, for surely she is of high noble blood."

Good luck with those best-laid plans, buddy, I thought. *I'm heading straight back to the land of the internet and cell phones, where I can contact my family at any time and don't need a man to help me do it.*

The Earl turned to Dagworth. "Now tell me about these evil-doers in your parts?"

A gentle touch of the hand reached over mine. Countess Katherine. She embodied the kind of beauty that inspired the Trojan wars. Exquisite cheekbones with perfect dimples, wavy, long, blond hair, perfectly shaped eyebrows over violet eyes, a Cupid's bow mouth. I immediately felt dumbstruck and gawky in comparison, like an awkward twelve-year-old who was all arms and legs.

"Come sit by me, Lady Hartford," said the countess in a voice that was a little huskier than I'd anticipated, like she was a smoker, even though tobacco in this part of the world had not yet been discovered. I was expecting a breathy, Marilyn Monroe-type of demeanor, but she pulled a chair over to me without waiting for any helper to do it for her.

I walked over to the chair and heard the men discussing the epidemic of thieves out on the highways. Lord Dagworth said to the Earl, "This fine man, Sir Harry, not only rescues endangered females and shows great courtesy, he also is an excellent swordsman and hunter..."

As I got closer to Katherine, I saw that she was likely in middle age, nearing her mid-40s, with a few lines around her eyes and her forehead, and streaks of gray mixed in with her blond. She took my hand in her bejeweled one and I couldn't help but notice that she sat ramrod-straight, her back not leaning against the cushioned chair. She was a bit smaller than I, as was true for nearly every woman I had met at the castle. "Why are you without the aid and protection of your family? Where is your husband?"

"My husband has died, my lady, and my father as well. I have land in France but was coming to Canterbury to make a pilgrimage for my daughter, who has been sick these last six months. I came to pray for her recovery, as her illness is not responding to any earthly healing," I said.

"But who were you traveling with? Where were they last night when danger overtook you?"

"I was with a party of pilgrims and came to find they were not good people. When the robbers came, they sped away. My horse threw me off my mount. I must have hit my head, as I do not remember anything after that until I awoke here. My maid has gone too. I believe she had fallen for one of the men in the pilgrimage and fancied a future with him instead of remaining to look after me, Countess."

The countess shook her head. "Please, do call me Katherine. The dangers of the open road are great. We women must protect ourselves. I do not like women who rely solely upon their men. It is weak. Women are strong. We give birth. We create life. That is great. My father and mother did teach me so. They taught me to read in two different languages, and ride horses as well or better than any man."

This was a type of woman we never saw portrayed in the literature of the day; of course, we all knew she existed, but men never were interested in telling their tales. Sure, we had Chaucer's *The Wyfe of Bath*, a bawdy woman who extolled her love of sex and money and travel. But this attitude of Katherine's—learning and leading and fighting—was exciting. Whereas Lady Dagworth embodied the 14th century chatelaine with her row of keys and ruling this household with stern but loving guidance, Countess Katherine seemed a woman ahead of her time.

I said, "I love to read as well—it is my passion. The library of Lord Dagworth's is very impressive. Do you get much time to read?"

The countess frowned. "Not as much as I would like. I have the most excellent people assisting me with managing our lands and our people. But still, the earl is often away, and his life and safety are always in my heart, while his duties at home become mine. Only three years ago he was in prison in France. During that time, our castle in Wark was under threat from the Scots. I knew what the earl would do if he were here, so with that as a model, I assembled a band of men to protect it and together we left for the North."

"Oh wow," I said. I would have just called the castle a loss and be satisfied that my head was still on my neck.

"*Wow?* What is this word?" She leaned forward, intrigued.

I blushed. I'd slipped. "Oh, it is short for…" I scrambled for a meaning, "My word."

Katherine raised one brow. "That is a new word for me. I will remember it. I like to broaden my speech. But yes, back to Scotland. William always fights his own battles, and I did not want to entrust others to make the decision of its keeping. Wark sits between England and the Scots, and we could not lose any ground there. But a mistake I did make; our assemblage was not so large as was warranted. When the Scots determined that, they put us under siege. We were there for three weeks, trapped by their maddening bag pipes bleating day and night, and no fresh food. Several of my men were killed when they did seek help. I fought with my sword, and did kill a few men, but not as many as I hoped."

Joan of Arc was the only medieval woman fighter that I'd ever heard of, and she wasn't born until the next century and in another country.

Katherine looked away, as though she were replaying the scenes again in her head. Two goblets of wine were placed in front of us, and she took a long sip.

"I cannot imagine what that must have been like for you," I said.

She sighed. "It is something I do not speak of much, but as you, dear lady, are in difficulties now, I feel I can tell you." She gave my arm a strong squeeze. "The most difficult part of being under siege was that I have young children at home who need their mother. While I thought William could get along without me, I did not like to think of my children being motherless. I had to be strong."

"There is no force greater than a woman who wants to protect her children. I would surely kill ten men or more if my girls were under threat."

The countess raised her glass to me. "To womenfolk."

I clinked her glass—I hoped that was considered good manners, and not weird in this age. Then again, Vikings raised their glasses and said "Skal!" and looked each other deep in the eye, to make sure they weren't about to be stabbed so clinking couldn't be that odd.

The countess nodded her approval. "Mayhaps I need to instruct you on how to handle a sword, or at the very least, a knife. What protection have you?"

"None, except for Sir Harry, whom I barely know," I said, pointing over to him.

Her eyes took in Harry, looking uncomfortable in his too-tight silk shirt. "I see that you have a very handsome rescuer, madame. You are lucky to be alive," said the countess. "But if we have time on our trip, I shall teach you how to fend for yourself."

"I would be most humbled if you would." I knew I wouldn't be there for it, but how cool would it have been to have that lesson? "How did you escape from the Scots?

We were interrupted by servers who brought fresh rounds of cheeses, fruits, and breads, just in case we had grown hungry since the twelve-course meal ended thirty minutes before.

"King Edward himself came with a small army of men and chased off the Scots. Word had gotten to him just in time. It was a joyous relief. We threw a little feast like this one to give our thanks to our King, but only after we got some fresh food in! And speaking of food—eat! You must nourish your body after your assault, and Lady Dagworth has a reputation as one of the finest hostesses in England."

I popped a grape in my mouth. *Where did a fresh grape come from in the middle of January in England?* "What is the King like?" I asked. "I have never had the privilege of seeing him."

Katherine seemed to have no problem tucking into her food. "The King is all that is good and true. His courtesy is beyond all men, although my husband does come close!" The countess looked fondly over at her husband, still engaged in an animated discussion with Dagworth. "I don't know what we would have done in Wark had he not come. He is very handsome, like your Harry, although not as big. And, like Harry," she whispered, bending her head closer to mine, "he does like the ladies." She *tsked*. "Poor Phillipa."

"It's inevitable," I said. "With power seems to come a wandering eye. But of course," I backed up, not wanting to offend, "I'm sure your husband is as faithful as they come."

Wait, what was she saying about Harry? Where was Harry? My eyes roamed the room looking for him. I found him, underneath a bough of greens in an archway, leaning back and smiling as an attractive young woman with a whole lot of cleavage exposed chatted to him. *Damn*. Another silly pang of jealousy went through me again.

"Well, I like to believe so," said Katherine, narrowing her eyes at her husband in an ironic way. "But I had a bit of a time with King Edward up at Wark. He hadn't seen me for a long time, and I'm afraid the victory of freeing us might have made him feel a little… amorous."

I put my hand over my mouth, not knowing whether to laugh or gasp. "What did you do?"

Katherine held up a finger. "I reminded him that he and my husband were friends these past twenty years, that dear William was behind bars in France, and that this was beneath him as both a man, a friend, and a king. He made a very quick exit back to Windsor." She giggled. "In fact, it will be rather awkward to see him again. Unfortunately, the story did make it out amongst the servants. I have been powerless to stop the gossip."

"Couldn't you get out of going to Windsor?"

"No." She shook her head. "My husband and I must be there. King Edward is very excited about this new order he is founding. He wants England to be as it was during the time of Arthur. He wants his order of knights to be the most respected group in the world, and for England to be the shining country on the hill. William is helping him, and as embarrassing as it may be to run into the King again, I have spent too much time away from my husband and want to be with him as much as I can."

Katherine put her finger under my chin. "But what is to become of you, fair damsel? I know you are with good people here at Wodesley Castle, but how will you return to your sweet children?"

I tried to look confident. "Please, Countess, do not worry about me. I have Sir Harry now, who promises he will stay with me until I can get back to my home. He is the very essence of chivalry."

Katherine weighed the argument, and in her eyes, it came up short. "Two people out on the highways filled with danger? You would be safer with a score of men, a lady to keep you company, and a maid to look after you. Let me think on this. I shall consult with William. He may have some good ideas."

"I would rather you do not worry about me. My life is nothing in importance compared with all that the Earl of Salisbury has to worry about."

"My Lady Hartford, worrying about the fate of people, and especially the people of England, is something that William has done all his life. After meeting you, we would not forgive ourselves unless we did something to help." Taking another sip of wine, Katherine leaned back in her seat, and stifled a yawn.

"I fear that I have taken up too much of your time, Countess. I am sure you are very tired from your journey," I said.

Katherine rose out of her chair, and instantly there were two stewards behind her. "You are right, my dear, I am tired. You make delightful company, but I think I need one dance with my husband before we go on to bed. We did have a long day of travel."

The band had been playing the whole night, but nobody from the head table had danced yet.

"William," she called, and then she gestured to the open

floor.

The earl beamed at her. It warmed my heart to see how much they clearly loved each other. They took command of the dance floor, and as the music picked up, other couples joined them. I gazed fuzzily at the scene and reflected how this couple, who had been through wars, imprisonment, sieges, and a rise to power, seemed happy together. There had been so many couples around me in the modern world whose marriages fell apart, some even after forty and fifty years—it had taken away my faith in long-lasting love. I still had nightmares that I was married to Alex.

Perhaps, for a very few, there was happiness. Maybe finding the one for you was a gift from the universe, or God, or whatever you believed. Maybe it was pure chance. Or good karma for a life well-lived in the past.

Maybe it came from persistence. Maybe I'd given up too early.

Speaking of failed romance, John strode over to me. I'd really felt like he was my one shot at happiness back when we were dating—even for years afterward, I missed our rapport and sense of humor we'd shared.

John had dressed for the party plainly in a navy tunic, black pants, and boots. The modest clothes didn't detract, though, from his ability to light up the room. His grin towards me was wide and genuine. I resolved to not let his charms fool me again.

"Madame, I would have the pleasure of dancing this dance with you," he said to me, and bowed.

"It's been a long time since you and I have danced," I said, "and this is no disco in the West End. I have no idea how to do this kind of dancing."

John took my hand and led me out onto the dance floor regardless.

Three dances later, I had figured out what was going on: it was a mixture of square dancing, waltzing, and the minuet. If you made a mistake, it wasn't a big deal, people just laughed it off. I had trickles of sweat running down my back and could feel that my cheeks had turned bright red from the exercise. My hair started to fall out of the elaborate style that Mary had spent so long on.

Then the music slowed. Oh no—the dreaded slow dance, a bust to middle and high school girls everywhere who had crushes on boys who only wanted to dance the fast dances with them.

The singers sang of love: "Do you dream of me, dear lady? Tell me true. Do you dream of me, as I dream of you?"

I looked up into John's eyes, not knowing what to do or even think. I was both uncomfortable with him, and yet we'd known each so intimately. All those thoughts of us together, bodies twisted together, came rushing back to me. He gazed down at me. People dancing close together surrounded us. Women had their heads on their partner's shoulder, the men had their hands creeping down their backs. This wasn't like if I were back in my ex-husband's arms. He and I had completely exhausted all possibilities of staying together. But with John, it was much more akin to, "If only…"

If only he hadn't left me.

If only I had believed him.

If only he'd tried harder to convince me, and not given up so easily.

If only he hadn't turned into a thief.

John pulled me close. I sank into him. I'm not sure whether it was from exhaustion, or because it just felt good.

"Are you having a good time, Ellie?"

Was it proper for Lady Hartford to be dancing three dances with her host family's archivist? I doubted it. But what did it matter? It was almost time to leave.

"You look gorgeous in the dress I gave you," he said. "It looks as though you've been poured into it."

I pushed back from him and felt an ever deeper flush threaten to engulf me. "You! How? Where did it come from?"

"You deserve to look dazzling tonight, Ellie. I have a feeling that with all the work you do—raising those two kids by yourself—you don't get much time to have any fun. You even outshined Countess Salisbury tonight, who is a beauty renowned across the land."

I shook my head, "I don't think anyone could outshine Katherine, though it's nice of you to say that. But the dress?"

"My assistant found it for me from the gallery. There was a girl here who I thought would look super in it, but she passed away by the time I returned. Rather heartbreaking at the time, but there you go—medieval times, and all the joys and sadness that go along with it." John's self-confident beam wavered.

I was unsure what to say. "I'm so sorry." What a tragic story. And a surprise, to say the least. I hadn't heard of him falling in love or having a serious relationship with anyone after me. There was just a series of girls, and Jane rolled her eyes at his "parade of ladettes," that she saw him with. Looking at it his situation now with more informed eyes, it was easy to see why he didn't want to have a serious relationship with someone if he wasn't firmly placed in either land. After all, look what had happened to us.

"It is a beautiful dress. I'm sure she would have loved it. Do you want to talk about her?"

"No, not really," John said. I was acutely aware of his hand on the small of my back, his finger thrumming a beat softly, sometimes wandering out to my hip. "It'd be awkward. Just as I'm sure you wouldn't want to tell me about your marriage."

"Oh, there's no secret there. I simply married the wrong person, and now I'm just trying to make the best of raising two kids by myself. Truly, he's missing out on having a relationship with them. They're my everything. But I try to look forward, not back."

Half the room had cleared out, and the other half was discreetly making out. John took a look around, and said, "Come with me. It's time to gather up your things. I'll leave first; you wait for thirty seconds and then follow me." He winked. Looking around, I didn't see any of the power players left in the room. The Dagworths and the Salisburys had left. Happiness surged through me—*time to go home!*

John waited for me at the staircase that led up to my room. He took two steps up, and then reached for me, grasping me around the waist with his right hand. He put his other hand lightly on my cheek. "I would like to get another memory from tonight," he said before he placed his warm, soft lips on mine. It was just a brush of his mouth at first.

Was it the fact that I hadn't been kissed in a long, long time? Or just the familiarity of it all that made me do it? I pulled his head closer to mine, and kissed him back, harder.

I remembered it all so well: the taste of him, the feeling of his face in my hands, the stubble on his cheeks, the tufts of his hair on the back of his neck. I inhaled the scent of him as I took breaths in-between kisses, and placed my hands on his back, pulling him closer to me.

"Ahem. Sorry to interrupt." John and I broke apart quickly.

It was Harry, and his voice sounded strained. I felt like I'd been caught doing something I shouldn't have. I blushed fiercely, wiping my mouth.

"Ellie was just giving me a goodbye kiss, Harry, or rather, I gave her one. Nothing more. It's time you two were off, right?"

Yes, it was time to stop revisiting the past, and look forward to the future.

CHAPTER SEVENTEEN

"And all these fives met in one man,
Joined to each other, each without end,
Set in five perfect points, Wholly distinct, yet part of one whole
And closed, wherever it end or begin.
And so the pentangle glowed on his shield,
Bright red gold across bright red stripes,
The holy pentangle, as careful scholars Call it."
Sir Gawain and the Green Knight

MY LIPS TINGLED from John's kiss as we made our way up the stairs. But I felt a wave of physical discomfort—my stomach ached, and my head hurt. I couldn't discern why. Was it the ridiculous amounts of food and wine that I was served, or was it because I regretted kissing John?

Or was it because I was upset that Harry had caught us. He knew we'd been an item once, but at the same time, I didn't want this protective, reliable, sweet man to entertain the thought that John and I had gotten back together, because we had not. For me, nothing had changed in how I felt about John. He was a mistake, and I knew it. I had no desire to go down that road again. I enjoyed flirting with Harry. I didn't want it to stop because of John.

John and I had the same passions—books, medieval history,

and he'd even made me look and feel like a princess in this dress, which no man had ever done for me before. But our history together had broken me for a long time.

John took a seat in our room, rather than helping us, and faced the fire in the overstuffed chair. "Do what you need to do." Harry and I shoved our things back in the bags he came with, and then I wondered about my dress.

"John," I said, "do you want me to leave this dress here for you?"

Harry muttered, "Should have known that dress was from you."

"On or off?" I said to John again, trying to move things along.

"Off, if you wouldn't mind. You never know if I'll have another occasion to pull it out for a lady," he said. I felt the sting of that jab, and started tugging at the laces of the dress, trying to blink away a ridiculous tear that came to my eye.

Harry watched me struggle. It was dark in the room except for the glowing embers of the fire. He placed two gentle hands on me. He turned me around to get at the laces on the back of the dress, "Ellie, let me."

Then I was left standing in my shift, freezing from being mostly naked. John eyed me, but I couldn't make out his thoughts. Harry was all business. I hurried, embarrassed, to get the green dress back on me so I wasn't freezing. Harry assisted me again with the ties, his big fingers making quick work of the cotehardie, and John's borrowed cloak swiftly followed around my shoulders. I slipped de Lane's book into the pocket of my dress.

I helped Harry slip off his tunic, and he shimmied out of Matthew's pants, wearing only boxers. Boxers with yellow baby ducks on them. I couldn't help but laugh at the sight of this huge guy in cartoon underwear. "Sexy look, eh?" he said. But in a snap, he was back in 21st century clothes, and we were ready to go.

"John," Harry asked. "Do you want me to bring the armor back with us, or should we leave it for the people you stole it from?"

"I earned it, thank you very much. But yes, please bring it back," said John, tight-lipped.

The torches had all but burned out as we made our way outside by a back door that John led us to. A few people lolled about on chairs, or curled up on the floor, but the band had packed up, and all but the most legless had gone to bed.

The night air was frosty; I pulled the cloak tightly around me. There was no moon visible, so our movements were covered by darkness.

We came down the hill where the labyrinth lay, and once again, I could see the magnificent castle looming up over us, as it had a little more than 24 hours before. So much had happened, but I felt happy knowing that I was leaving it all to get back to my life, where I would come home from work every afternoon to hugs and kisses from my little girls. I had enough experiences with the people, food, architecture, music, and culture in the last day to last this scholar a lifetime of analysis. Not to mention the slender little book from Anthony de Lane.

"Well then, it's time you went in," said John. The three of us stood together awkwardly.

"Are you sure you're not going to come with us?" I asked.

"Come with you where?" said a voice.

I whipped around and peered into the darkness.

"Who's that?" said Harry, in a low voice, looking ready to take someone down.

"Over here," said a man, sniffling. I made out Anthony de Lane, sitting in the middle of the labyrinth.

"What are you doing over there, Sir Anthony?" John asked. "Come out. You'll catch your death of cold. 'Tis a night not fit for man nor beast.'"

If Sir Anthony knew all about how to design the labyrinth, then perhaps he knew about its magical properties. Had he ever used it to go across the Thin Place? He clearly knew about our arrival.

The only thing I grasped for sure was that this man was the only thing standing between me and my babies, and he had to get out of my way. Just then, he stood up in the labyrinth, as though he were guarding it, and began to walk the turns.

"Sir Anthony," I said, "You sound ill. You should not be out in the night air. Please, can we accompany you back inside?"

He ignored my question. "Did you know, Lady Hartford, that there are five circuits around the center? You must walk around the middle five times before you get to where you want to go. Is it not maddening to see your destination so close, and want to skip the steps straight over to the center? Or is the purpose of the walk to contemplate your place in the world, never fixed in one place until the end?"

Anthony de Lane continued, rocking back and forth up onto his toes. "How is it that people get stuck looking at the world the same way? Get up and have the same routine, day after day? That is not what life is about. Life is about seeing *all* that life has to offer, and what God has given to us on Earth to enjoy."

I turned to John, opening my eyes wide at him, trying to see if he knew anything about what Anthony was saying. He shook his head.

"Lady Hartford, before I went on the Crusades, I had never traveled more than fifteen miles away from the village where I was born. I thought I knew everything about life. But my eyes were not fully opened until I was called upon by my king to walk beyond the familiar. Now my mind can't be closed, even though I am back where I started. That's why I built this labyrinth. As I told you, in Castilla I first walked one as a practicing Christian. But then I saw the different views from each point in the ring— this way East to the church, this way West to the castle, this way North to the town square, and this way South to the vineyards. Birds, trees, bees, women, cows, mountains—it made me both dizzy and alive at the same time. I sketched out the path on the dirt each night as I traveled from there to France to the Holy Land and back, trying to capture the essence of the magic. That is how I came up with this design."

My mind was spinning. Why was de Lane telling us all this?

I couldn't keep quiet any longer. "We thought we might have a walk on it before we left for Windsor tomorrow morning. I should like to have the experience that you are talking about. I cannot yet fall asleep tonight. May I please come inside?" I took a step closer to him.

"Lady, you cannot. Not yet. It is not your time."

"What do you mean it is not our time? Why not? I don't understand," I said, my voice coming out unnaturally high, ready to bowl over this runny-nosed, seven-fingered, balding man if that's what it took.

"Five rings mean different things for different people, Lady Hartford. You and Sir Harry have only been in our world for one day." He held up his hands to silence our open mouths. "Do not protest. I know of the power of my labyrinth and know that you are special for being here."

"With all due respect, sir," started Harry, in French, "how can you know anything about us?"

"I recognize the sickness in you, and in Lady Hartford. You are just the same as John of Stafford there. Your hearts are broken, just as mine had been. You do not appreciate the world—you are entombed by your problems. This labyrinth only works for those whose hearts need healing time. Time to appreciate. Time to live. Time to see what exists for you by removing you from your world and into another; then it is easier to see what gifts God has given you.

"On the fifth day, you may come back and enter and see then why your hearts are not whole, and what it is that you are looking for."

I sat down right where I was on the cold gravel, leaned back, and looked up at the stars. Couldn't I just go through therapy instead of traveling 700 years? Why was I chosen?

Harry took over the argument. "Are we not both men of honor, who pride ourselves on our chivalry? Lady Hartford specifically requested that I take her to visit your labyrinth tonight. We cannot deny this lady what she is asking for, sir. It would not be courteous, and I for one as a knight have taken an oath to be courteous."

I thought about the fact that Harry had already taken an oath for Britain as a soldier, how he swore he would be allegiant to the sovereign and her defendants. I was impressed to see how he'd taken up the mantle of the Middle Ages and evoked courtesy now as well.

"I must humbly agree, Sir Harry," Anthony said. "Let the lady try to go in," he said, bowing at the waist.

Try to go in? I raised my eyebrows quizzically at Harry, silently asking him whether it was o.k. He shrugged.

"You're going next, right, Harry?" I asked. He nodded. No hesitation.

This didn't feel right. I was scared. What if I ended up in the wrong time? De Lane's whole explanation had freaked me out: *I am broken. The labyrinth is built for people like me.*

I got up, scraping out the gravel that dug into my palms. Anthony stepped out of the way, and I walked past him onto the chalky outline of the path. "You'll tell me what to do, right, John?"

"Yes, of course, Ellie," he assured me. What was he thinking? Did he want me to go home? Did he want me to have more of an adventure, like he'd had, for years? "Start walking on the path, and then I'll tell you when to turn around."

I put one foot in and immediately I was pitched out again, as though a football player had just thrown me out of the way. *Did de Lane do that?* I landed on my bottom on the frosty grass, outside the path. "What the ...?" I asked, confused and hurt. There was no person in there, and yet some force had thrown me to the ground.

"A thousand apologies, dear lady," Anthony said, as he took one elbow while Harry the other to hoist me back to standing. "I never know how that labyrinth is going to react. It is one of the mysteries of life, I'm afraid, but my suspicions are correct. The labyrinth will most likely not let you in for five days' reflection. You've had but one day here, so you have four more to go. You are in God's time now; *Kairos*, as Mark put it in the Gospels, is the time when God acts."

Four days more to go? *Four days?* This was impossible. It couldn't be. I sank back down to my knees, and tears immediately started to pour down my face.

"Harry," I croaked, "Maybe you should try?" Maybe Harry could break the barrier.

Harry looked down at me and shook his head. "I would not leave you here alone," he said.

"John?" Harry asked.

"Quite happy where I am, thanks all the same," he demurred. "I'm off to Windsor anyway." It looked as though he had known this would happen the whole time by the grin on his face. Or perhaps he was just intrigued with witnessing the magic of this labyrinth.

"I am sorry you could not have your walk this night, my lady" Sir Anthony emphasized the word *walk* as though he knew it was more than that. Those eyes I had seen in the labyrinth when we landed here in the dark were his eyes. "But take this time, it is precious—a gift. I implore you to look all around, from every angle. See what you have not seen before. Life is all around you, and time is precious."

What was this thin place? And why us? Why me?

PART III

CHAPTER EIGHTEEN

"He struck his steed with the spurs and sped on his way
So fast that the flint-fire flashed from the stones.
When they saw him set forth, they were sore aggrieved,
And all sighed softly…"
Sir Gawain and the Green Knight

JOHN LEFT US quickly, mumbling excuses, leaving me alone with Harry back inside the castle. I couldn't believe he'd left yet again. Harry was practically a stranger to me, and John, my former boyfriend, had gone from kissing me in the stairway this very night to deserting me when I was scared and desperate.

I clasped my hand over my mouth trying to suppress heaving, ugly sobs. Harry led me back up the stairs, back to our bedroom that we had left an hour before, so confident in our abilities to go back home. I wrapped my free hand in his engulfing, comforting hand.

"Don't worry, Ellie, we're going to be okay. You'll get back. I'll make sure of it," he kept on whispering to me.

I croaked out a "Thanks Harry," before falling into the bed and pulling the covers up over me as soon as we got into the room.

"Would it make you feel better if I held you?" Harry asked. "I don't want to be weird or anything—I know I'm just a friend of friends—but you're shaking."

I needed someone to hold me. I was scared to death. "Yes."

The bed creaked, and he laid down next to me, pulling me close. His arms felt solid and reassuring. He'd known me back in 2017, even for just twenty-four hours—he knew my reality. "I don't think I can handle this, Harry," I said.

"Sure, you can. Just four more days, and we'll have you back to your girls. I've already calculated it with John's best guess, and that's just one day's time in 2017. Surely Jane and her nanny can occupy them for that short amount of time, right? Jane can entertain anyone and make them not want to be anywhere else."

He was right. Jane did have that gift. She was an excellent mom, and her kids always were occupied by something she'd dreamed up doing, from playing outside to doing "science" experiments, making art, telling and acting out stories, cooking… But surely if she could keep them calm, she'd be frantic not knowing what happened to us?

Harry's solid body wrapped around me, holding my hand, allowed me to slowly relax and my crying lessened. He hummed a quiet tune that I didn't recognize. I tried to remember the relaxation/meditation teacher at university, the one with the cut shoulders and delts, and how she guided us through a meditation to release the tension from first my feet, then my calves…

I succumbed to a fitful sleep, but all too soon I was startled awake by Mary's discreet rapping at the door, "Lady Hartford, Sir DuMont, it is time for us to depart. Do you need assistance?"

Harry's arms startled around me, and then he shook himself awake and immediately hopped out of bed. "We're fine, Mary. Thank you," he said in modern English. I guess she understood him well enough, as we heard her footsteps retreat back down the stairs.

In the early light of day, the fact that we had spent the night together in bed, although fully clothed, left me feeling that we had shared something intimate. He had certainly been amazingly caring and tender with me.

"I think my eyes are really puffy. Are my eyes really puffy?" I asked to get a conversation going.

He turned and looked at me quizzically. "Hmm, a little. Splash some water on your face."

"Okay," I said, and did as directed. The water was so freezing cold, I was amazed it hadn't turned into ice. It shocked me awake. Mopping my face, I turned to him. "Harry, I have to thank you for being nice to me last night. A lot of men would have run away."

Harry shrugged. "Nothing I haven't done before. No worries."

Well, that made me feel special—*not*. Maybe he felt he had to since I was friends with Jane.

I longed for a toothbrush and toothpaste but did the best I could wiping down my teeth with a cloth. As I had never undressed, all I had to do was put on my cloak and riding boots. My dress was crumpled from lying in bed all night—silk does not do well when you sleep on it. But there were no dry cleaners here. Maybe they had an iron?

I had to take a no-excuses-accepted trip away from the security of Wodesley Castle out into the wilds of 14th century England. I had shrugged off the Earl's plans the previous evening because I fully expected to be home by now.

Mary did bring me a gift, though, to help combat the bitter cold: leg warmers. They reminded me of the fashion trend of the 80's, and apparently, they were popular in this earlier time as well. She brought along four pair, two for each leg, that could stretch up my legs or stay bunched up, depending on where I needed them most. I was so grateful to Mary for donating them to me, perhaps even out of her own belongings, I gave her a hug. "Thank you!" I said, another tear coming to my eye, and she seemed stiff, and in shock. She gave me a quick pat and then pushed me away. I felt like I had failed at etiquette again.

So far in this world, from the kindness of strangers, I had received a room, a maid, a dress, attention, flattery, food, and wine. Instead of it being me who was constantly feeding, picking up after, bathing, dressing, entertaining, and transporting others in my role as mother, people were doing all of those duties for me.

The realization made me think of Anthony de Lane's instructions to see the world from different viewpoints. I saw that people who barely knew me cared about me and my comfort, but I didn't understand why. I was not their mother, their daughter, their professor, or their employee. To them I was nothing more than a stranger, a woman on her own who had fallen on hard times. No doubt it was the Judeo-Christian morals of the time, mixed with chivalry, a man-made code to help the weak, be honorable, and courageous.

IN THE GREAT Hall, small loaves of bread were set out on a large, cloth-covered table for each traveler to take. A priest stood by the front door, placing his hand upon every traveler's head and saying a blessing, asking God to protect us and keep us safe. I said a loud "Amen," praying that the world outside the gates of the castle would be as friendly as within.

Outside, the colors of dawn were muted on an overcast day. A light sprinkle of rain came down in a gentle mist. I pulled my cloak over me and raised the hood. Not having ten weather forecasts readily available through radio, television, and smartphone, I guessed it was in the 30's, assuming the typical English forecast of "periods of rain with a chance of sun."

A crowd of people already had gathered in the courtyard. The Dagworths were travelling with about twenty-five people, added to the party of fifty or so with whom the Salisburys had arrived with the day before. The Dagworth party was made up of all of the knights going to participate in the tournament, as well as their squires and pages. I spotted John amongst the men. Some ladies were also accompanying Lady Dagworth, including her daughter Yvonne, her daughters-in-law, and their respective maids.

Mary was tucking herself into a cart containing trunks, along with some of the other household staff.

Lady Dagworth's voice called from somewhere in the sea of bodies: "Is that you, Lady Hartford? With all this mist and darkness, I do not know who is here and who is not!" She appeared from a cluster of hooded women on my right and came up close to take my hands. "*Mon Dieu*, where are your gloves? You are ice cold! Who has a spare pair of gloves or mittens for this girl?"

I heard a woman say, "I do," and soon a little boy came running over with them. I gratefully slipped the knitted wool mittens over my hands.

When she took a look at me, and my undoubtedly red eyes and pale complexion, she said: "Ah, I can see that you are not fond of rising at dawn either, especially after the festivities of the evening a'fore, eh? But look," she said, indicating a small gray horse, "I think that this might make a good mount for you. Calm and gentle is she, and sure not to be spooked by anything on the roads. *Not* that you have anything that you need to be concerned about with this impressive escort, *bien sur!*" she reassured me, turning her approving eyes toward Harry. "Traveling misadventures for you have now come to a conclusive end." *If only that were true*, I thought. She gave me a warm kiss on my cold cheek, and as she did, I realized her scent resembled gingerbread.

A young groom who couldn't have been more than nine handed me the reins of my new horse and informed me of her name, but I didn't really catch it. I thought he said "Brownie," but I'm sure that couldn't have been right, because the horse was gray. I put my hands in front of the horse's nose and let her breathe in my scent. I had last been on a horse in college, when I took a horse-riding class. I got as far as cantering, and then chickened out. Going fast scared me. Being up high scared me. And I had a mean horse assigned to me all semester, which didn't help.

But "Brownie" seemed happy to see me, and nuzzled me, bringing me in for a hug. Our breath swirled together in cloudy white puffs.

"Mount up!" cried the Earl of Salisbury, and everybody from his party got on their horses. "Mount up!" shouted Lord Dagworth, and the rest of us clambered up on our horses.

Sidesaddle, of course. I had never studied the history of horse-riding in the Middle Ages, but all the paintings and tapestries had shown women riding sidesaddle. I guess it looked more elegant and feminine, but it certainly was less safe to ride with your feet just on one side of the horse. It made the horse harder to control, having to rely more on the reins then my legs. The seat on this horse was boxed in, making it near impossible for a rider to fall off, though. I swung my right leg over the left side of the horse, wondering how I was going to ride all day in this position, in the freezing air. Thank goodness for Mary's legwarmers.

The crowd began to move out, with the men in front, the women following behind, and the servants in the carts behind us. The ladies around me were abuzz with excitement at going to court—giggling and talking so quickly that I had a hard time following any conversation. Yvonne, the young wife of Hugh, and the youngest child of the Dagworths; their only daughter, trotted up next to me. I'd met her very briefly last night at the dinner table. She was nice enough to try and draw me out of my sad, not-a-morning person, stuck-in-the-wrong century shell.

Yvonne had dark-auburn hair and hazel eyes. An orange dress peeked out from underneath her gray cloak. To keep warm, she had fur-cuffed gloves, and a fur scarf; of those I was entirely jealous.

After some initial chit-chat about the weather, the journey ahead of us, and the party the night before, I said to Yvonne, "We have a long day's journey ahead. Would you tell me the story of how you and Hugh came to be married?" Marrying for love wasn't common practice in the 14th century, especially for a girl whose parents were in the higher ranks of the feudal system: wealthy, titled, and owning vast tracts of land. I wasn't sure whether to expect a love story out of this girl, or an account of a marriage that joined two powerful families. Either way, it would be a tale I could add to the others I knew to aid me in understanding the time period.

Plus, it would make a good continuation for what happened to the characters in *The Training of the Squire*.

Yvonne's sentences were well-thought out, without any *ums*, *likes*, or *you knows*; she had never been exposed to those crutches.

"I knew Hugh was different from the very moment he first came to our fair Wodesley."

Thankfully I could fill in the necessary background from my many readings of *The Training of a Squire*. Hugh had arrived at the age of thirteen and spent his first four years at Wodesley in intensive drilling exercises of swordsmanship, riding, hunting, hand-to-hand combat, and jousting. But the practice was not only physical. Sir Dagworth drilled into his squires that in addition to standing firm as a knight with physical capabilities to overcome the enemy, they also had to know and reason why they were taking a leadership role. Dagworth was on the lookout for talent and trustworthiness in his squires and was adamant you could not be a great knight without first knowing Latin, Greek, math, and history.

Sometimes Hugh's mischievous sense of humor got in the way of proving himself to his sponsor, such as the time he put three squealing baby pigs in the castle during the evensong prayers. But eventually, as he grew into a young man and saw the importance of the role he had to serve in the tournaments, he calmed down.

"I first noticed his fair green eyes and his wonderful smile. He was usually engaged in either the classroom or out on the field, but when we had feasts at holidays, harvests, birthdays, and the like, I would get a chance to see him. As I was younger, he paid little attention to me."

By the time Yvonne reached the apex of the teenaged-angst years, she was despondent at the lack of having any meaningful interaction with Hugh. "I knew in my heart that he was the one for me, yet he only cared for me in that I was the sole daughter of his benefactor." Despite his seeming disinterest, Yvonne dreamt up ways of trying to run into him. She ran errands for her father to the training stables and to the schoolroom. She took note of Hugh's schedule and tried to find any excuse to be where he was. She took confidence in her lady's maid, Mary—the very one who'd been helping me—whose advice cajoled her to keep up her efforts, even when she was ready to give up.

Her parents became worried she didn't want to go on visits to see other members of their family and didn't want to travel to nearby feasts to meet potential suitors. She couldn't tell her parents that she had found her suitor, because they thought of Hugh as another son.

I could relate to Yvonne's story. Back when I was a gangly, near-sighted, braces-wearing, book-loving redhead with an asymmetrical short haircut who couldn't attract the attention of any boys I liked, I had plenty of resources to soothe my angst. There were teen movies where the nerdy girl wins the popular boy, my best friends were there to talk to on the phone to dissect every move my crushes made, and music helped me either wallow in my sorrows, or give me hope. Adolescent angst is pandered to in the modern age, but there was simply no time for it in the1340's. While 15-year-olds in modern times are just learning to drive and starting to date, girls in 1340 were usually married with kids.

Hugh started going to a few tournaments and proved himself in all parts of his training. Sir Dagworth believed in sending his knights-in-training on mini quests—nothing like a quest for the Holy Grail, but a kind of scavenger hunt that involved several tests of nerve and mettle. When Hugh returned with his bounty (a gold bracelet presented to Lady Dagworth), it was declared that Hugh had passed his tests with flying colors, and it was time to knight him.

It was quite the celebration, Yvonne told me—a special bless-ing and mass at the chapel, followed by a demonstration of

Hugh's horsemanship and sword skills, and his recitation of a tract of law in both Greek and Latin. Sir Dagworth knighted Hugh (at that stage in history, knights could make other knights), tapping him on the shoulder with the sword. Petals flew in the air all around him, thrown by all in attendance.

Yvonne found that she couldn't partake in the feast after, as she hated being reminded of the fact that Hugh barely acknowledged she walked the Earth. She ignored her parents' worried looks when she was not out dancing with the rest of the people her age. Yvonne left for the garden.

She was in love with a man who did not love her. Yvonne, despondent, laid down on the warm grass, looking up at the sunset in the sky, and the flowers and the trees around her. One bee settled down on a flower next to her, extracting pollen in such a precise yet beautiful way, it filled her full of appreciation for all that life was. "I saw in that bee the exact way that God designed it for flowers. I too was made by God, and I too had a purpose. Being miserable about Hugh was not fulfilling that purpose."

She determined that she wanted to study the natural world in depth—the veins on plants and how they fed, the way the limbs jutted out of trees at odd angles, pollination, and butterflies. The world was offering her so much, and her silly infatuation with Hugh had stopped her from seeing all that life had to offer.

"Once I unleashed from moping about Hugh all day long, I found I had more time to think about the world. I devised a system for classifying the plants in our garden, and then I went into the fields and did the same for wildflowers."

Yvonne was an early medieval female Carl Linnaes! Her father gave her a room to keep her records of pressings, specimens, and varieties. I was impressed by the Dagworths—their commitment to their daughter and her uncommon curiosity spoke well of their forward thinking.

"One day, Hugh came into the library. When he came into the room, I think he saw me really for the first time—or, at least, the grown-up me. He asked what I was studying, and I saw he was really captivated and interested in what I had been working on. He sat down beside me, and when he looked into my eyes…" Yvonne paused, searching for the right description, "it was like seeing a firefly show his light for the first time. It quite took my breath away—the spark when he looked at me."

My own heart skipped a beat. Who doesn't love the look when somebody first realizes they are in love?

"Hugh allows me to continue on with my work even though we are married, although things may have to change when I become chatelaine of Hugh's family lands."

Every once in a while, a spark flickered within me, begging me not to give up on love. And hearing the next part of Yvonne's story lit a tiny fire. That one next to the one of the Earl and Countess of Salisbury had laid.

Yvonne's passion for nature had spurred Hugh's interest in her, not her previous hero-worship of him before. I needed to make sure my girls learned that lesson. Never lose your passions, even to one for whom you are passionate.

The horses in front of us stopped. We had been riding for quite some time over gentle hills, past a few villages with small buildings fighting for space near the town green, and alongside fields of dormant vegetation, gray, green, and brown. There had been no sign of the sun since I had arrived in 1344, and I was beginning to doubt its very existence in this century. Certainly, my cold hands and feet were past hope that they would ever be warm again.

Everybody was dismounting, and as I slid onto the ground, my feet were numb. I limped around for a minute or two, and by the time I got the feeling back, the ladies of the party had moved off into the woods for a bathroom break, minus the actual bathrooms. Reluctantly, I followed them. While the privies in the castle were merely holes cut in stones that went down all the way to the ground, it was still better than squatting on the ground with my skirts hiked up, and my Calvin Kleins at my ankles.

That having been done, the muddy field sucked and pulled at my boots until I got to where a bonfire had been set up to warm us all. The servants unpacked a picnic lunch. Blankets unfurled on the cold ground, and a few folding chairs were brought out for Lady Dagworth, the Countess of Salisbury, and their husbands. Sitting down on a gray wool blanket beside Yvonne, we were handed steaming cups of mead, and some more bread with cheese. After scarfing down the bread and cheese, I sipped on the mead. The hot liquid blazed a path of warmth through my body and holding onto the mug revived my freezing hands. I stuck my feet out towards the fire as close as I could without getting burned, and the heat from it began to thaw me.

Yvonne seemed to take the cold, mud, and light rain in stride. After all, she was dressed for the elements. Quickly downing her drink, she was now sketching the scene with some paper and a piece of charcoal she pulled out of a bag. "See that thicket of wood over there, and how the limbs grow together? I wonder how that came to be? Which tree dominated the other and why?" She puzzled over her bit of paper, glancing up now and again as she filled in the details of the woodland scene.

"I see you admire my wife's drawings, Lady Hartford?" Sir Hugh said, standing before us. Husband and wife gazed at each other, and their eyes sparked.

"Yvonne is a brilliant artist, sir, and her knowledge of the natural world is truly impressive. You must be very pleased to have such an accomplished wife," I said.

Yvonne glowed, and Hugh nodded vigorously. "'Tis true, Yvonne is the one with the talent for understanding the world, while I merely don armor and charge about, pretending to be fierce."

I laughed. It hurt my heart to think of him, or any of these men, fighting in actual battles. The 100 Years War was about to begin, and no doubt many of these men would be sacrificed to the cause.

Sir Hugh was undoubtedly more interested in being with his

wife than making chit-chat with me. I excused myself, not wanting to get too far away from the warmth of the bonfire, but I also didn't want to intrude in on strangers' conversations. Everybody seemed so excited about our trip—this might be like going to see the Superbowl if it was held on the lawns of the White House, and your team was playing. Nobody seemed to feel the cold, or the misty rain.

We were getting farther and farther away from the Thin Place. I reassured myself the girls were having a good time with Jane while I was having an awesome time in a muddy field, my bottom sore and chafed from the saddle, my nose so cold it might snap off. Maybe if some sheep showed up it would be a real party…

The men stood about twenty feet away from the fire. In their chain mail they were likely warm enough to not need the extra heat. Helmets off, they huddled. Both Dagworth and Salisbury were in the mix. Harry seemed fixated on what Dagworth was saying.

A small, leafless tree next to me looked sturdy enough to lean against. It was good to stretch my legs. If this trip were up to me, there would be no lingering at this rest stop. Time was money, and we had places to go! Even if I had no desire to get there, I hated inefficiencies. But I was not in control here, and I had nothing to do. So thinking of what Sir Anthony had said at the labyrinth, I followed his advice to look all around me.

To my right I saw horses, men, women, carts, and mules, being slowly rounded up to get back on the road. Turning a quarter step further to the right, Lady Dagworth, apparently the real driver of this outing, was herding people about and ordering them around firmly, all without yelling. She would make an excellent third grade teacher, I thought. Rotating a quarter step again, there were the woods that the other ladies and I had used as our pit stop, and the peculiar trees that Yvonne had started to draw.

One more pivot and I would be through with whatever spiritual guidance Anthony had sent me on. But as I turned, I saw a woman in flames, opening her mouth to scream, about to run past me. My mouth dropped, and I started to scream too.

Her dress was in flames. She must have gotten too close to the fire. She ran from the group in terror, trying to get the fire out, but her speed only gave the flames more oxygen.

As she streaked past me, I knew what I had to do. I tackled her.

Stop, drop, and roll. It had been drilled into my head in elementary school and had never left me. The weight of my body slamming into her back dropped her to the wet grass, the flames coming close to my own dress and skin. I could smell the smoke and singed wool. I rolled the scrawny girl over and whacked at the flames with my cloak to deprive the fire of oxygen. With each hit, the fire seemed to flare up, and then diminish. Each hit I took made me fearful my efforts were futile, that it was too little too late, and she was going to burn to death. Time seemed to stand still as I watched every small fire on her skirt and cloak get extinguished. But at last, the flames were out.

The girl was Angela, who had led me up to the scriptorium to see John the day before. Angela was coughing and crying, in shock not only from her time as a moving flame, but also from me knocking the wind out of her. Her clothes were singed, and I gently pulled her dress up a little to check the skin on her legs. She had some redness on her right calf, but it was not blistered. "It's okay, it's over now," I said in a calm voice, but not calm enough to remember that "okay" was not a word she would know. Mary came running in with what turned out to be a kit of balms and herbs and proceeded to find something that I hoped was medicinal to put on her leg. Another girl, who seemed to be friends with Angela, sat down beside her and pulled her onto her lap.

"Mary—looks like you've come prepared for an emergency," I said, clapping her on the back, my heart still thumping out of my chest. I couldn't stop coughing from the smoke.

"I never go anywhere without my herbs and remedies. Lady Dagworth insists upon it," Mary said, her eyes fixed on Angela's leg. "She never travels without me. My mother taught me well."

Two large hands came under my arms and pulled me to my feet. Harry. "Well done," he said. "That was really…" he paused, searching for words. "That was very brave. Are you hurt at all? Burned?"

"I'm all right, thanks," I said. Besides having a scratchy throat from inhaling the smoke and feeling like I was going to vomit from fright, I was fine. My dress, however, was ruined. Green silk, covered in mud. My cloak half-burned and lying on the ground, smoking. My boots, I now remembered, had been sucked off my feet a few yards back by that deep mud.

"I have never seen such a remarkable act from a lady such as yourself," boomed out Lord Dagworth, his enormous dogs on his heels. That sounded like a back-handed compliment to me, but I took it.

"Indeed, Lord Dagworth," Salisbury said, joining us. "Quite the brave woman. The King will be very heartened to hear how a lady saved a servant's life. Exactly the kind of example of courage and valor that our country should follow."

Salisbury spoke to the assembled crowd. "We near did have a most awful tragedy here, ladies and gentlemen, except for the selfless act of this fine lady. Let us all be reminded of the dangers of fire, and give a cheer for Lady Hartford here, who exemplifies courage."

"Hurrah!" cried the crowd.

"Stafford!" Lord Dagworth called out. I don't know where John had been, but he was at Dagworth's side in an instant. "Make sure you put this in our chronicles." John gave me a brief nod and took off.

I put my head down, once again let down that John didn't seem to give a hoot about me. I took that in for a minute. He was at a crossroads with me, and every time he could choose one that would be beneficial to me, he chose one that worked just for him.

And my cheeks were still burning, embarrassed to be hailed as a hero. I was sure that if I hadn't put Angela's fire out, somebody else would have. I just happened to get to her first. After all, it's what moms do. We pull our babies back from falling on their heads and touching scorching hot burners, we stop our toddlers from running out into the middle of streets, we put helmets on our kids when they ride bikes and buckle them into their car seats, we cut up their food so they don't choke, we pull them out from under the water when they lose their footing in the pool. A thousand times over the course of a childhood moms are keeping little people alive, but nobody ever gives us a public "hurrah." It didn't seem right to get one now.

Katherine of Salisbury came up to me in the middle of my thoughts. "Lady Hartford, I continue to be impressed by your bravery. Every action that you take and story that you share is more remarkable than the first." She took my hand in hers, looking every inch a countess with her hair perfectly done, her face as gorgeous as the night before, and her traveling clothes as sumptuous as her evening wear. "However," she said, as she indicated my ruined clothes and bare feet, "I am afraid the way you look will not make a good impression on the court at Windsor. You are not in the least bit presentable."

I'm sure that was an understatement for all times. Standing next to the dazzling Countess Salisbury in my smoky, muddy dress made me feel like something that the cat dragged in.

"Perhaps I should turn around and head back to Wodesley?" I said, seizing on an opportunity. I could turn this situation into possible gold. "I would not wish to bring shame upon this party." I tried to suppress a grin at the thought of waiting quietly at Wodesley for the four days to be up and requesting Harry to be at my side. *Yes, this could work...*

"No—you misunderstand me. You must come with us to Windsor, of course!" Katherine said. "You need to impress upon the king your situation for the sake of getting you back to France safely. What I was trying to say was that we need to find you clothes that are clean. Where are your things?"

"That's just the problem, my lady. I have only this dress," I sighed.

"What about that dazzling blue dress from last night?"

"It was borrowed." We couldn't go down to the local mall and fix this with a credit card.

"Do not fear—I have more than enough clothes for you. As the Earl is now bound and determined to show you off, you may borrow my clothes and return when you have more made. Follow Claire," she said, gesturing over to a young servant woman. "She will find something appropriate for you, and get you cleaned up. The rest of the party is moving on I see, but we'll have some men accompany you to catch up."

I did not want to be separated from the rest of the group. There was definitely safety in numbers on these dangerous roads. If that was not adequate motivation for getting cleaned up and changed in a hurry, I didn't know what was.

Claire pulled out a navy-blue velvet dress with yellow embroidery, and a plain woolen cloak from one of the numerous chests in one of the wagons. We hustled away from the luggage cart and went back towards the woods, where Claire helped strip me of my sooty and muddy clothes. Mary's poor leg warmers were too muddy to leave on and had to be wrapped up for cleaning later. Thankfully de Lane's book was not burned, and I would keep that safe with me. A clean rag and a small jug of freezing water were produced to help clean my skin, and then I pulled on a new shift over my head, and Claire assisted getting me into the warm dress and cloak. Claire did not comment on my bra and underwear.

Lastly, she pulled out a pair of gloves. With gloves, I was much warmer, or at least as much as could be managed with clothing in 30-degree weather.

We had been hearing the camp leave bit by bit, and when we emerged from the woods, which couldn't have been more than five to ten minutes later, there were only about ten men still left.

Harry, thankfully, was amongst them. The longer I spent with him, the more I knew I could count on him. Even if he wasn't a great conversationalist, he was reliable and trustworthy, and he kept his promise to stand by me. There was a lot to be said for that.

"Where is Angela?" I asked. "How is she doing?"

"I don't think she's too badly hurt, Ellie," he said in French. "The Dagworths sent her back to Wodesley, and she's being attended to. She's more scared and embarrassed than truly hurt."

"Thank God for that," I said. "I was worried I did not act quickly enough. It seemed to take forever to get those flames out." I relived those awful moments in my mind, sure they would haunt my dreams.

"You were really very brave," he said. "And I think you scared the crowd a little, the way you beat back those flames with your cloak so viciously. I don't think these people have ever seen a noble woman move so fast. Especially," he teased, "one of your advanced age."

"Believe me, my heart was in my mouth the whole time. I knew every second her clothes were burning…." I stopped. "But yes," I responded to his barb about my age, "I am *tres ancient* here in 1344. It's a wonder I'm still standing. How many great-grandchildren should I have by now? And speaking of which, what's the plan for catching up to the others?"

"We're meeting about twelve miles more down the road where they are setting up our camp for tonight. Dagworth's son is in charge of our little group. Salisbury wants to get as far as possible today so that we will arrive at Windsor in good time tomorrow."

"Whoa," I said. "Nobody told me anything about camping overnight. What about a nice, cozy, bed and breakfast, or an inn?" Tom was always trying to get me to go camping in the early days of our marriage, but the idea of sleeping outdoors without a lock on the tent to keep out snakes and bears left me cold.

"Stop being such a princess, woman!" Harry rolled his eyes at me. "Do you expect close to one hundred people to squeeze into a medieval inn? Believe me, these Salisburys travel in style. I don't think you'll be too uncomfortable."

"I'm far from a princess, but whatever. Just because I don't like camping doesn't mean—" and I started to go off on a bit of a monologue about how very truly unspoiled I was. This included references to Target, coupon-cutting, and cutting off cable to save $100/month. And worse—holding onto an outdated cell phone that provoked smirks from my colleagues and students. Princesses did not have to worry about cost-cutting. I don't know whether Harry was listening or not, he just nodded every once in a while, with one side of his mouth twitching up in a smile. This got me even more defensive and sent me down the tangent of the awful state of health insurance and medical bills in America.

My horse was brought 'round, and Claire went to ride pillion behind one of the men I did not recognize. Harry offered his hands for me to mount the horse. The poor guy—my boots were muddy, and now his gloved hands were going to muddy. But gallantry was a part of life here—a necessity. At home, chivalry had fallen into a much smaller zone: holding the door for a lady, and the rare instance when somebody would open your car door for you, which was always nice. And then there was the whole debate around whether a man should pay for a woman's dinner on first and subsequent dates. I was of the opinion that if a first date wasn't going well, you should split the check. (I had been on quite a few of those first dates where we split the check.)

But in 1344, women were in a much more perilous position. Women were not armed, and robbers and violence were a constant worry. The clothes women had to wear hobbled them— you could not run fast in long dresses, you were in constant danger of tripping—or catching on fire—and it was hard to mount a horse without getting tangled in the fabric and falling. Women could not live by themselves safely—and this is huge— be economically independent. They were completely dependent on men to take care of them.

To me, that prospect was terrifying. I'd been taught long and hard by my feminist mother that I had to have an amazing career of my own. That I could do anything that I wanted without the assistance of a man. And in many ways, Mom taught me that men were a distraction. They took away from your focus on work. Around men, hormones would mean you'd suddenly want to bake homemade brownies. Make him an awesome chicken dinner. Be by his side to cheer as his team vies for the championship. Nope. It was a slippery slope, Mom said.

Thanks to her, I could change my own tire on my car.

The few birds that were hardy enough to remain in England in the winter chattered away, making their displeasure at our presence in the woods known. Small icicles had begun to form on the end of branches, and the constant drip, dripping of the rain occasionally meant that a giant drop would plonk me on the scalp. I put up the cozy hood on my cloak and felt like a druid.

This ride was one to be endured, and not enjoyed, especially since I had lost the delightful Yvonne as a riding companion. I'm pretty sure Harry wasn't going to tell me his moving love story, ready-made for *The Hallmark Channel*.

The mood over our small group was quiet and purposeful, but not relaxed. We were only ten minutes or so behind the main group, and theoretically could catch them, being smaller and more nimble, but one of those in our party had drawn the short stick and was riding a cantankerous mule who seemed to be forever stalling, halting, and braying its delaying tactics as time passed. *Stupid mule.*

I began to feel myself zoning out, not entirely aware of my surroundings. If I had been driving a car like this, I would have worried about driving off the road, but the horse seemed quite content to ride behind Harry's horse, requiring little attention. I'm at my absolute worst in the early afternoon after a meal—always needing a nap. If I closed my eyes, I reasoned, surely I would stay in my saddle....

CHAPTER NINETEEN

For in telling those tales of the truest of knights,
all the title and text of their works is taken
from how lords hazard their lives for loyal love,
endured for that duty's sake dreadful trials
Sir Gawain and the Green Knight, *line 1126-1997*

MAYBE I DID doze off for a little. When I opened my eyes, the woods we passed looked exactly the same. The monotony of the scenery led me to start daydreaming, and of course the focus of my attention was that man riding on the horse directly in front of me, looking as much a knight as anyone around him. All that I'd learned about Harry DuMont over the brief time I knew him could be fit onto the back of a postcard:

- War veteran.
- Good horseman, and apparently, swordsman.
- Those blue eyes! (Probably gets away with murder.)
- Likes blondes and armor.
- Loyal.
- Sweet.
- Makes Jane laugh.

I decided it was time to flesh out this biography a little more. After all, we had the time.

I ambled my horse over to Harry's. His eyes looked a little red, and he didn't look entirely focused. A little like me before my short nap on horseback. "Anything wrong, Harry?"

Harry shot me a tight-lipped smile and shook his head no. I yawned and slapped my face a few times to try and stay awake, and that made him laugh. I tried again. "Please, Harry, talk to me. Otherwise, I'm going to fall asleep and fall off this horse and ruin the last dress anyone will ever loan me."

"It's your adrenaline leaving your body," he said, finally. "You used up all your energy saving that girl. Classic problem in wartime, when you're being shot at in the morning, but still have the whole day to get through."

"Keep talking, Harry. I don't care about what; just tell me a story."

"I'd rather see you slap yourself again."

"How about I slap you?" I held up my palm in a threatening manner.

Harry laughed.

I persisted. "Come *on*, Harry, tell me something about yourself. We're here, dependent on each other, and I hardly know anything about you except that you speak French like a native, and you were very kind to me last night. And I've convinced you that I'm not a princess, and… Oh, and that you definitely dance like a white man." I laughed, recalling his stiff-legged moves on the dance floor at the feast.

Harry smirked. "Guilty. I would never have been let in the door to audition for *Soul Train*."

Silence ensued. Perhaps in the army they don't talk a lot when they're traveling, or maybe he hadn't been taught the art of conversation. "Okay, I guess I'll have to ask you some *pro forma* questions: What's the last movie you saw, for instance?"

"Oh, hmm, yes," he smiled. "The plot was fairly straightforward. It involved a nurse whose uniform looked somewhat inappropriate, yet so very *right* on her. Her male patient couldn't give himself a sponge bath, but with his nurse's special assistance…"

I shook my head. *Typical man.* "Alrighty then, now I know your discerning taste in movies. Shocker. My tastes lean more to movies that feature a heartsick nun and seven singing children in the Alps."

"That sounds very racy, and kind of creepy. You are an interesting woman…"

"Dude! *The Sound of Music*!? Hello!" And then I realized he was only teasing me. "You got me, Harry. For a guy who doesn't like to talk too much, you can be pretty quick with a barb."

Harry looked straight ahead, his face brightening. "It's what we do in the army. We are well-versed in the art of the barb, or the pun, or the double-entendre. Keeps us laughing in some pretty dark situations."

"Speaking of which," I said, "my bum is so chafed from sliding back and forth on this side-saddle, I'm sure that I rubbed a patch of skin off. How long does it take to grow back skin on your ass?" I asked.

Harry just rolled his eyes, and mouthed, "Princess."

"Don't you even start on that again, or I'll tell you about my battle royale with AT&T."

I shifted my bottom for the nine hundredth time to find a more comfortable position and stretched out my leg that was hooked over the pommel.

"I admire your spirit, Ellie. Life has knocked you down, but you seem to always get back up again." Harry kept his eyes forward, but I could tell he was sad.

"Resilience is the bottom line for me. Without resilience, we have nothing. There are no guarantees for happiness in life, so we have to keep trying, right?"

"Ellie," he said, "I want to let you know I'm duty-bound to get you back safely to your children. So, with you as my responsibility, I have a purpose. This is what I liked about the army. I was helping people get to lead the happy lives they were meant to. Even if I was not meant to."

"What do you mean? What's holding you back from being happy? Have you been cursed or something, doomed to walk uphill with a rock on your back?"

"Something like that. Or maybe it just feels like Sisyphus. It's just I know things will never work out for me. I've been unlucky my whole life."

This was upsetting to hear. On the outside, he looked like he had been incredibly lucky. I wanted to pull him in for a hug, but that was impossible on horseback. "I find that hard to believe. You've been blessed with good looks," I paused, clearing my throat, feeling a little embarrassed at admitting that. "And everyone seems to like you—you've got a whole new band of brothers here. Women throw themselves at your feet!"

"And yet I'm 40, and still unmarried. That tells you something."

I was beginning to want to lose patience. How many good cards had he been dealt that he refused to recognize? "Jane tells me you have a nice farm?"

"Only because my dad dropped dead of a heart attack three years ago—so genetics aren't on my side. Probably won't live past 57. My mother ran off on us when I was seven." He reached down and patted the horse. "The army's really been the only thing that ever made me feel like I was on the right path, and then they made me retire after I got injured. Turned out I recovered fully, but it was too late. I'm sure you couldn't possibly understand how I feel."

I swiped at my nose, runny from the cold. "Look, I don't want to play who's got the saddest story here. That's not what I'm about. As far as I can see we're both in pretty deep shit right now. I've got to just keep going."

"That's another thing, you've got your girls. Nobody would care if I ended up here. No one."

"Oh my God." I lost my patience. "Are you going to start

singing *Nobody likes me, everybody hates me* right now? Because I *will* gallop away and catch up with the Dagworths."

"I'd like to see you try," he goaded.

Damn it if I couldn't call his bluff. "Yeah, well, me too. Except I'm scared of galloping, as you pretty well guessed."

"What, like this?" and he leaned forward over the neck of his horse, got up onto his toes, and yelled, "Yeehaw!" And off they went at full gallop.

Unfortunately, before I could even have a chance to applaud his horsemanship skills, my horse decided to follow, and took off, trying to run beside Harry's horse.

"Help!" I squeaked, with the little amount of breath I had left in me. I don't think anyone could hear that, but the people behind me erupted in laughter, no doubt laughing at me as I careened over on one side trying hard to stick to that horse. I remembered my training to put my heels down to maintain balance, lean over the horse, and gripped her with my knees. Branches scratched at me, and all I could hear was the horse's hooves landing on the hard ground as fast as she could move them. I remembered to pull back on the reins just as we got behind Harry, and yelled, "Whoa!" until finally my horse slowed down.

Harry must have heard me, and he cut the gas to his horse immediately. Of course, his horse immediately responded, like he knew his rider was an expert.

I slid to the ground, shaking, and backed away. Harry jumped down next to me, patting my foaming horse. "Cool down now, girl," he said. "You gave your lady quite a fright, I'm sure."

"Next time you think about pulling something like that, jerk-bag, how about you consider what might happen to the other riders around you?"

"Jerkbag? That's a new one." Harry laughed. "But seriously, I'm sorry. I was just trying to lighten things up after getting so dark back there. I forgot you weren't an experienced rider. I *was* a jerk." He put a hand on my back.

My heart stopped feeling like it was going to burst out of my chest. "Look, if you don't want to talk about why you went dark, that's fine. Everyone is responsible for their own happiness, and I learned a long time ago that you can't force someone to be happy. It's a waste of time."

"You're right—I need to work on it. Probably had a flashback with that girl on fire. Seen too many horrible things that sometimes it just puts me in a foul mood.

"Now," he continued, straightening up, "what I need to do is concentrate on my job, which is to keep your spirits up. I need you to be in top form, and that means having you charm the socks out of the people at Windsor and insure you get us back to Wodesley in three days' time." He helped me back up on my horse again.

I leaned forward to whisper in Brownie's, or whatever her name was, ear. "You better not pull anything like that again, horse."

Harry went on, "Your job, soldier, is to keep chatting with these women, make friends, let Salisbury and Dagworth become your champions, and we will get out of this. I've got at least three back-up plans as that's what I've been trained to do. Part of that training requires me to be quiet, keep my ears open, and assess. I need to keep aware of our surroundings."

"Anthony de Lane would agree with you there. Five rings, five days, four different directions, right? It makes my head spin to think about that labyrinth, literally and figuratively. What do you think that's all about? How can it even exist, and why?"

Harry grimaced. "I honestly have no idea. It's clearly something beyond man's power. When de Lane built it, he must have tapped into something far greater than himself. But he does seem to know a thing or two about how it works. Whether or not he has figured out where you and I came from, I'm not sure."

"He wrote a book about the labyrinth. I've got it wrapped up in my gown. I wish I could ride and read at the same time—it might reveal its secrets."

Harry put a hand up to stop me talking. We reached a cross-roads, and up ahead was a small village. It was so quiet then, with only the noise of our horses' hooves, the birds singing, and a stream burbling alongside the road. As we reached the village, we saw cows and sheep in the pastures. The farm animals seemed smaller than the ones I was used to seeing in modern times.

Then we saw people—the first people we'd seen up close in our whole day's travel through the back roads.

Unlike those who inhabited Wodesley, these people looked like shadows, barely fleshed out. Granted, I was seeing them from the top of a horse, but the five people I saw, two women and three men, were petite, their clothes threadbare. With cloaks, hoods, and little pieces of leather pieced together for shoes, they looked miserably cold and malnourished. I'm not sure how often they saw men in chain mail and brightly-colored tunics, and women like me in a borrowed countess's dress and a fur-lined cloak. One bold little boy ran from behind his mother's skirts and held up his hands. I had no money and felt awful. One of the men with us was beginning to shout at the boy to move on, but I waved at him to stop.

"Harry, do you have any food or something to give him?"

"I have a biscuit that I took from the picnic."

There was no way I needed that biscuit more than this poor boy. "Please, Harry, can you give it to him?"

He nodded, pulled the cookie out of his pocket, and reached down to give it to the boy. The little boy snatched it and ran away, quickly pursued by at least five other kids. I wondered if he would even get a bite of it.

Further along the road, just past some rickety houses made of timber, plaster, and thatched roofs, sat a stooped figure, wearing bells to alert those around that he was near. "A leper," I said to Harry, who may not have known. The man's hood covered his face, so I could not see whether the disease had begun to take its toll.

I was thanking my lucky stars for the advent of modern medicine to cure diseases, just as the most horrific thing I'd ever seen in the flesh appeared in front of me—a corpse, hanging from gallows set up at the western entrance to this small village. It still had some skin left on it, but its eyes had been pecked out, and its belly had been slit from top to bottom, with the poor soul's ribs sticking out. A few threads of clothing still remained on this man. I wondered what crime he had committed, and whether they would ever take him off his rope and stop this public display.

The others in the party knew to avert their eyes, but I was transfixed. It's one thing to read about executions in history and literature, but it's far different seeing it in person. The gruesomeness of it, even the lingering smell, sent shudders through me. I was afraid I would pass out, so I quickly untied my cloak, which had gone from being warmly wonderful to scratchy and constricting and draped it over the neck of the horse. Even out in the chill of winter, I needed as much air as I could breathe in.

Unfortunately, that would not be the last time I would see a corpse hanging alongside the roads we traveled on. There were three more, in various stages of decay and showing different types of torture for punishment.

What crimes did these people commit to deserve such horrific deaths? These corpses, more than anything else, made me realize how much I didn't belong here. Time hung around my neck like a rope on the gallows. I needed to get home.

◆

CHAPTER TWENTY

"Let the boy win his spurs"
Edward III of the Black Prince (his son) at the battle of Crecy,
1345

W HAT LITTLE LIGHT there had been during that cold, damp day was fading rapidly by the time we arrived at our destination—a field about ten miles from Windsor.

An advance team had been sent to set up camp—perhaps as much as a day earlier. A dozen or so brightly striped pavilion-style round tents with turreted tops were placed in the meadow. Three fires were ablaze—one set up to roast meats, another set up with big pots full of food, and the third set with chairs and tables around it to warm the guests.

I slipped off my horse onto my very stiff legs, thankful to be off that blasted saddle and rid of that stupid palfrey, at least for the night. I tried to un-kink my body in a way that didn't look too unladylike. I really wanted to do the yoga poses "cow" and "cat" to get my back to release, but even in 2017 that looks weird outside a yoga studio.

Glorious, wonderful Mary was a welcome sight after the last few miles of scary roadways. "My lady, how do thee fare? I wanted to stay behind to see how you were after we put Angela in a litter back to Wodesley, but Lady Dagworth doesn't like me too far away from her family in case an emergency arises with them falling ill."

"No need to worry, Mary. I am stiff and sore, but that is all. It was a long ride today."

"Come, let me show you where you will be sleeping. Is this not grand? You and I are to be with the ladies. Lord and Lady Dagworth have their own tent, and the Salisburys of course, but the rest of the men and women are all quartered separately."

Mary held open the flap of a tent that was striped red and white, like a candy cane. Inside, the floor was carpeted with straw mats, and five beds had been set up a little off the floor. Yvonne was sitting on one, her boots off, rubbing her toes. She greeted me warmly and proceeded to introduce me to the other women. "This is my sister-in-law Sarah Dagworth, married to my brother Matthew, her sister Theresa, and finally Esther, wife of one of the Earl's Knights, Sir Nigel." The girls were of different shapes and sizes, but all far younger than I, perhaps in their late teens or early twenties. With their assorted serving women, there would be ten in the cozy little tent. The beds were covered with soft-looking blankets and pillows and hanging from the center of the tent was a small candelabra. The Salisburys certainly knew how to travel in style.

"Would you all mind terribly if I got under my covers for a moment? I'm afraid I got very chilled riding out there."

"Of course!" said Sarah Dagworth. "You likely even have time for a nap, if you should desire. We are just gossiping about the men, as usual, and who we think is likely to win the tournaments."

"Please, ladies, do not let me stop you." I crawled under the blankets, and as soon as my head hit the pillow, I was out.

THE SOUND OF fiddles woke me, and I could make out some wind instrument. It was dark in the tent, and I was alone. My companions had gone out to join the party. As snug as I was in my little bed, my empty stomach demanded that I find food, and fast.

"Are you rested? Holding up all right?" asked John, after I was seated next to him at dinner. "I don't know how these lads parade around in armor, day after day." John was dressed simply in a cloak, tunic, and leather pants. "We are eating the most amazing meal tonight, really, considering it's cooked outside," he said. We had roast chicken, boiled potatoes, and freshly made bread. "The Earl surely knows how to travel, having spent so much time on war campaigns in Scotland and France."

Harry was seated at another table—men-only there. But John seemed to be quite happy chatting with the women, which included most of my tent-mates. Our hosts were nearest the fire, in straight-backed chairs with a canopy behind them to keep the chill away.

"If you have any advice for me regarding what I should do with myself at Windsor tomorrow, I wish that you would give it to me now," I said, teeth chattering, inhaling my food. "I can't stay out in this cold much longer."

"Thank you for reminding me, my lady," he replied. "I do actually need to speak to you on a legal matter. Ladies," he said more loudly to the women at our table, "would you mind if I stole Lady Hartford's company from you for the briefest of moments? I need to ask her some more questions for my chronicle." They all murmured their support, and John led me closer to the fire where the spits were now removed. Two chairs were brought over to us.

He stared at me intently in a completely different manner than he had done at the table, where he was convivial but distant. "You look beautiful tonight, Ellie," he said.

I pursed my lips together. Where was this guy's head at? First he kissed me in the staircase, then he treated me like I didn't exist.

"Thanks," I said, crisp and cold, like he'd been to me. I had no intention of returning a compliment back to him. Even if the cold did bring out a charming rosiness to his cheeks.

He continued. "I know you were not a fan of camping back in the day, but this is quite different from the sleeping bags and leaky tent we shared in the Dales, isn't it?"

I couldn't help but laugh, damn him. That had been a truly miserable experience. I'd been eager to please him back then and try all the things that he loved. But after that rainy night camping, when I couldn't sleep on the hard ground and heard every snap of every twig near us and convinced myself that it was a wild animal, I never agreed to go camping again. But this "camping" experience was different. This was *glamping*, that is, glamorous camping.

"Yes, this is far nicer than camping with you." That trip in the Dales did have its share of romance, though. He'd read to me, in his rich, deep voice, and alternately kissed me behind my ears, down my throat…. But I'd long suppressed those happy memories and kept focused on the painful ones. It was the only way I could get through that time after I broke up with him.

"Chaucer was right about the roads, wasn't he?" John said, "And can't you just picture this right out of *Sir Launfel*? All we need is a gold bowl and an exquisite couch for you to lay on for you to 'smote my heart.'"

I had a few questions to settle. "Speaking of 'smoting' hearts, I can't believe you went running off after I got expelled by Sir Anthony from the labyrinth. Harry and I getting home safely is your responsibility. We needed you to help us strategize through this five-day rule, but instead you just left us. And you left me with Harry, and he's almost a stranger to me. You and I used to be really close, but you took off as soon as I started crying."

"Gosh, I'm sorry, Ellie," he said, taking my hand in his. I yanked it away. "I knew we had lost that battle with the labyrinth, so I went on to the next task at hand."

"But did you know about Sir Anthony and his knowledge of the labyrinth, and this whole five-day waiting period?" I thought of how he'd reacted when I'd been tossed out of the labyrinth by whatever magic it possessed. That little grin. He was not being as forthcoming as he should be with me, and it felt like further needle pricks in my skin.

John stiffened. "No, I didn't know about the five days. I've never stayed *less* than five days. Never wanted to—having too much fun."

"Was it so fun when you got placed in manacles you couldn't get out of, and passed out on Jane's floor?"

I rolled my eyes. By his previous calculations, he must have stayed freakin' months when he didn't come home to me. Who does that to his girlfriend? That actually made it ten times worse.

He continued, "I don't want to talk about that now. But let me tell you about the first time when I came back home, I wasn't convinced I would have ever left this place, except I felt guilty about what Mum and Dad might have been going through wondering where I was. And as far as Sir Anthony is concerned, he spends a lot of time out there by himself at that labyrinth. I don't think he's altogether right in the head."

"But why did you run off like that on me at the labyrinth?" I punched him in the arm. "One minute you're kissing me like its old times in the staircase, and the next—you're gone! Leaving me with…"

"Falling into Harry's big strong arms, eh Lady Hartford? I've seen the way you look at him," John said, ice in his voice. "I have to admit, there is much to admire, he is a dear friend of mine and if I were playing for the other team, I'd definitely have a crush on him too. He's always been a hit with the girls, even when we were boys."

"I don't have a crush on him," I protested.

"Then why are you blushing?"

How could he tell in the dark? "Get back to the point, John!" I said, clamping my lips together.

"I'm trying, Ellie, let me tell you: I went off at a sprint be-cause I was worried about *you*—not over your crying. You're a strong woman; I know I don't have to baby you. It was more important for me to look into the laws of the land. Brains are better than brawn, don't you get it?"

I didn't. "I'm not getting what you're saying. What laws were you researching?"

"Over your rights as a 'widow' here in 1344. This is where your background story that you made up on the fly concerns me. As a widow of the gentrified class, the overseeing of your fortune—your land, your title, your wealth, the decision to re-marry—is given to the King. So you, very likely, will be made his ward."

"That's flattering, right, to be made a ward of the king?"

"Flattering, yes, but really, it's just giving him lawful con-trol—you become a pawn on his chessboard. And seeing that your 'land' is in France, that is even more appealing for a King, who devotes his life towards gaining land in France."

The situation was beginning to dawn on me. "Ohhh," I breathed. I ran my hands through my hair, trying to penetrate to my brain: *Think! How can I think my way out of this?* There was no way some man with a crude crown on his head was going to tell me where to go, marry me off to some putrid puddle of a man, merely because it would expand his empire. I was a human being with rights!

But not in 1344.

My voice low, I asked, "So, what are you thinking is going to happen should the King find out about me and my status?"

"Oh, don't think for a second that Salisbury won't be telling him. The most politically astute man in Britain with a prize for his king?"

I could feel my eyes growing wide. "Oh." No wonder the Dagworths and the Salisburys wanted me around—as a woman with land in France, I was like a gift to the King.

"Okay, so *when* he tells him?"

"I fear you will lose your freedom of movement. You might be required to serve as a member of the royal household and be kept there to amuse the King and Queen until your fortune is dispatched to the most advantageous arrangement the King can make."

Fear shot through me again, and the dinner I'd consumed so eagerly before now churned in my stomach.

I was riding towards my own imprisonment.

"So how come you didn't warn me of this before I left Wodesley? I would have been safe there, I should have stayed," I hissed.

"There was nothing that could have been done. You had to come. Salisbury and Dagworth both would have demanded it."

"That's bullshit!" I hissed. "I could have faked a horrible illness. Had a recurrence of my concussion. Run away and hidden in the woods! I can't get stuck away from Wodesley—it's my only way back to my girls." My heart felt like it was beating too fast to be safe. I pulled my hand out of my gloves to check my pulse—was it 200? Harry was not the only one to have early cardiac death in the family.

"Keep calm. Life is not always black and white, and hurtling towards one conclusion only keeps you from seeing other possibilities. Just think of how you got here in the first place—you would never have been able to predict that, now would you? In fact, you wouldn't even entertain the idea back when you were my girlfriend. So don't rush to the conclusion that my worst case will come to fruition. Keep fluid, and alert to possibilities. I want you to be able to enjoy your time at Windsor, but keep in mind the pitfalls that might lay in store for you."

Enjoy? Enjoy? Keep in mind? I would have yelled and howled at him, if we weren't surrounded by others. I needed to put my game face back on. *This whole situation is completely normal...*

John put his hand on mine and gave it a warm squeeze. "Don't worry—you're not dying." He pulled my hand away from my wrist. "With our two minds put together, there's no way we can't succeed. Look at me, after all. I'm having a hell of a time, and I love it here." His eyebrows wriggled, but his smile was tight. He was forcing this light-hearted tone, I could tell.

In fact, there was a bead of sweat on his brow.

THE PARTY BROKE up when a cold mist started to rain down. I thanked my hosts, the Earl and Countess of Salisbury, for the meal and the luxurious accommodations. They were wrapped, arm-in-arm. "Not at all, my dear. Such a lady as you deserves all that we have to share. As does your genial knight, Sir DuMont. We are quite convinced the King will choose to take him as one of his household knights after he sees his skills on the jousting yard," said the Earl.

So now Harry and I were both in line to remain with the King. We had a lot of work to do to get us away from Edwards's orbit.

CHAPTER TWENTY-ONE

And seeing how beautiful she was,
And how dressed, and her face, and her body, and her flesh,
So white, joy swelled in his heart.
Sir Gawain and the Green Knight

THE GIRLS IN my tent sprang out of bed as soon as dawn broke, and their maids immediately set to work. Someone fetched hot water from next to the fire, and another maid brought mulled wine and bread.

I was experiencing the complete opposite of anticipation—I was in dread. My insides felt like a cold and rigid hand had a death grip on my heart and stomach. Mary deftly brushed and arranged my hair, but I could not keep breakfast down for long, and ran outside to vomit. "Nerves," I said, embarrassed, as I re-entered the tent. Mary had her box of herbs out already and prepared a mug of medicinal tea for me. Ginger and peppermint. "You are so good to me," I said to her. "What am I going to do without you when I return back to my everyday life? It will be quite a comedown."

"But surely you have servants in France who treat you as you deserve?" Yvonne had overheard me and interjected.

I thought of my two girls, who liked to brush my hair, and the way they said, "Mommy, it's the color of a sunset," and laid out cheese and crackers and lemonade when we were playing *tea party*. "They are very young, but they are learning. They lack Mary's wisdom for healing, though, and her good advice."

Mary's hand gave me a squeeze on my shoulder, as she gently wove my hair into another complicated hairdo.

THE ROAD WE travelled met up with a larger road that they called a *highway*. While it didn't feature exit and entrance ramps, billboards, and divided lanes, it was certainly wider and better-groomed than the roads we had been on and had more traffic. Many other travelers going to Windsor soon surrounded us.

The Thames ran parallel to the highway, cleaner and brighter than what I had remembered the last time I was in London in the 21st century. Boats floated down the river with small sails, propelled by men pulling on large oars. Everywhere colorful banners floated in the breeze on boats or were held up by men on foot and on horseback. The world was full of color, and for the first time since I had been in 1344, the clouds disappeared, and blue skies stretched over our first views of Windsor Castle.

I had visited Windsor a few times as a tourist, a quaint, touristy town of half-timbered houses, the castle dominating the town as it rises up over it on a hill, visible from miles away. The sheer size of the place could not be gauged either inside or outside, because the views went further than the eye could see on the ground.

The same was true in 1344. There was a much smaller village around the castle, which looked more French than English, due to the Norman invasion a few hundred years' before. Instead of the normal assortment of modern-day shops found in every village in the U.K. like Monsoon, Topshop, and Clarks Shoes, there were signs for Hansen Butcher Shoppe with a picture of a pig, Iron Workes with a picture of a horseshoe, and Stables, which didn't need a picture on its sign. Around the castle lay a shallow, somewhat murky, and smelly moat, which was fed and drained by a canal leading from the river.

Plumes of smoke rose from chimneys escalating over the towers of the castle. Outside the walls, and further away from the river, were the encampments of hundreds, if not thousands, of fellow travelers come to partake in the festivities. Turreted tents were set up on every available piece of land. Voices sang and spoke in accents of all kinds, challenging my abilities to understand what they were saying. The evolving English language influenced by its Viking, German, and French invaders was all around me.

The crowds, the noise, and the smells overwhelmed my senses. It was like all the dreams I'd had as a child about this medieval world had come alive, but not in the way I expected. Now I had a new dream—that I could live in it with no consequences. I had thought being a lady during this time would shield me from the worst experiences, but I realized now that being a woman at any time until the modern era meant you were always at risk. Sure, it wasn't about hard labor for me—yet, but bad things were on the horizon. I wanted to disappear.

To stop the feeling of my heart contracting, I tried to remember bits of old poetry and recall their patterns, made lists of Old English words and their translations, and made an alphabetical list of names found in Arthurian legends. Anything to distract myself.

"Lady Hartford?" A voice penetrated through my exercises, and I shook myself out of it. Sir Hugh was beside me, taking the reins of my horse.

"Let me get you inside, my lady, to meet all the good people who have gathered here today. A set of rooms in the castle has been set aside for our folk. For us, no fellow fair will be forgotten."

We went through the gates of Windsor, away from the throngs.

Inside the high walls was quieter. I breathed a sigh of relief.

There were still masses of people, but they were more orderly. We stopped at a door manned by a guard and dismounted. Sir Hugh assisted me off my horse. I looked around for Yvonne but did not see her.

Wodesley Castle had been beautiful, but nothing could have prepared me for the grandeur of what we walked into. Wide corridors stretched for what might have been football fields, torches lit the way, suspended from walls and ceilings, finely-woven blue and red carpets covered the floors, and the walls had been painted with intricate patterns, broken up by art of exquisite detail and beauty. I would have loved to have stopped and looked more closely at the paintings, but the escort accompanying Sir Hugh walked along at a rapid clip.

To the right and the left of our walk stood guards, spaced evenly-apart every thirty yards or so. They were garbed in tunics of the king's arms—gold lions on a red background and gold *fleur de lys* on a blue background—and stood at attention, with legs apart, one hand on a sword, and the other on a dagger. I wouldn't dare to give them any trouble.

Hugh opened the door to a small, yet sumptuously appointed room. A four-poster bed beckoned to me, draped in silks, bedecked in furs and fine linens, piled high with pillows. Two large wooden armchairs sat directly in front of a roaring fire. I don't know how on earth she had gotten there so quickly, but Mary waited for me, already busy filling a small bath with hot water. I would have hugged her if it were allowed. "Sir Harry's room is through here," said Hugh, and I peeked in and saw an almost-identical room to mine.

"The feast for the women starts in less than one hour, Madame," said Hugh.

"What about you men?" I asked.

"We are grouping where we will gather for the games," said Hugh. *Alliteration. A la Sir Gawain and the Green Knight.* Maybe that was his mental game for keeping calm with the pressure mounting to perform well on behalf of Wodesley Hall. Hugh bowed out of the room, wishing me a good evening.

Mary nudged me, "Lady Hartford, we must get you ready for the Queen and King. We do not want your foreign ways to make an ill-impression on them."

"Foreign ways? What are my foreign ways?"

"The way you carry yourself, the way you talk. The way you treat me. All are different from the way the ladies at Wodesley do things." She paused. "Do not take me to say that I do not prefer your ways to theirs, however." Mary looked at me with a discerning eye. "I'll return in a few minutes, Madame. I need to see about getting you some wine to warm your blood and your complexion. You are much paler than I would like to see."

This was like middle school all over again, where I had to fake it to be cool, but with the added bonus of wearing clothes that I wasn't comfortable in, not speaking the language like a native, and not confident or clear with the etiquette and customs. I'd been caught out, and who knows how many other people had already suspected me and my cobbled together back-story?

Making a beeline for that hot bath, I stripped and eased my way into it. The grime of the muddy roads, the smell of horse, the wet and the chill, were all washed away by the scalding hot water. Swirling around me were rose petals, spices, and herbs— God love that Mary! There also must have been some essential oils too. I ran my fingers up my arms and legs, appreciating my skin's newfound dewiness.

A length of linen laid across the foot of the bath, and because the room was chilly, I draped it further across the length of the bath to keep the heat in, so that just my head poked out, and my legs dangled over the end.

"Lady Hartford, may I come in?" It was Harry, coming from the adjoining door.

Before I had a chance to say much more than, "Harry, wait!" he walked through.

"Wow," he said, taking me as much as he could in all my silhouetted nakedness. "I guess I should have waited longer for an answer, but I can't say I'm sorry."

"Uh, Harry, a little privacy here, please?" I slid deeper under the water, trying to tweak the linen over me with one hand.

He didn't turn around to leave.

"Please," he protested, "don't make me go. You're covered up there, and we need to talk. Where's Mary?"

"She's just gone to fetch me some wine. She thinks I'm too pale." I didn't feel pale any longer. My cheeks flushed red with the way Harry was looking at me. Was this linen see-through, or was he just using his imagination? "Mary might catch you in the room when I'm in the bath," I whispered.

"It's a risk I'm willing to take," he said. He briefly took his eyes off me, and found a stool to sit on, right at the end of my tub where my legs were. He confidently took one of my feet between his hands and started giving me a foot massage.

I could not help groaning with pleasure. Harry's warm hands felt so good on my skin. He used his thumbs to run up the length of my sole, and back down to my heel. Each toe got individual attention as well.

My eyes closed. "You really know how to treat a woman's feet," I said.

"Some say I know what to do with the other parts of a woman as well," he murmured. I half opened one eye to acknowledge the tease, but before I could toss out a comment, he continued, "Oh dear, are these blisters?"

"Um hm. The stirrups must have rubbed my feet the wrong way. But we have no Band-Aids, or plasters as you call them."

"I know what Band-Aids are, you don't have to translate it into English for me. I may not be a PhD, but I do have some knowledge of America." Harry continued to point out various injuries, like, "Oh no, not this little fellow too!" as he continued to do wonders to revive my toes that sent shivers of delight down my spine.

"Is this something you learned in the army? An alternative to using torture to get your way?"

"Maybe." A boyish grin swept over his face, revealing those slightly crooked teeth. Imperfection equals adorable.

I prodded some more, "And what is it that you're trying to get out of me? What did you need to talk to me about?"

"A kiss," he said, meeting my eyes.

My heart quickened. I hadn't dared to hope that he was interested in me, until this very second.

He continued, "I've been wanting to kiss you from the first time I held your hand going up the stairs at John's."

"You saw me and John kiss the other night—I could tell you didn't like it."

"I wouldn't want to get in the middle of anything going on between you two so if there was something going on there—?" He paused.

I didn't say anything because I didn't know how to sum up what I felt about John.

"Oh," he said, half getting up. "You see, I had a feeling you didn't really like him that way anymore. I saw you two talking at the dinner last night at camp, and there seemed to be no love lost. But I must be wrong. I apologize." He made to leave.

"No, stop!" I sat up, clutching the linen to my chest. "Don't go. You are right—there is no love lost. It was lost a long time ago. I don't want you to leave. And I *do* want to hear more about why you want to kiss me." I started to feel a blush forming over my cheeks that wasn't caused by the heat of the bath. "Because, well, I do have a bit of a crush on you, Harry," I said, reaching out to touch his fingers draped over the side of the bath. My fingers were slippery with the oils Mary had put in the bath, and I swirled a little bead of water on the back of his hand. "You've been very sweet and thoughtful to me this whole…trip. And I find you very attractive."

I looked at Harry, waiting for him to say something. "And John?" he finally asked.

"John loves this world more here," I said, pointing out the timbered ceiling, the fire, the bed, "more than he ever did me.

And seeing that releases me from whatever attachment I used to have for him."

He sat back on the stool again and pulled my foot back into his palm. "Ellie." Harry cleared his throat, hesitating. "I think you're incredible, and I don't know if this is a crush or something more. I know I was a sad sack out there on the ride here, but you've injected a brightness into my life I haven't felt in a long time. You in that blue dress. The way you saved that girl. The way you made me laugh on the road when you slapped yourself! I've tried really hard not to fall for you, because of John, because of you being an American, but…"

I was reaching out for his chin to pull him to me, "Wait, what?" I asked, stopping.

"No, it's not because I don't like Americans or anything, but you live so far away, and if I fell for you, hard, then it would make life complicated."

I laughed and gestured to the room around us. "You think *that's* complicated? How about being stuck in the wrong fucking century?"

Harry joined me, and we couldn't stop laughing. Then he put his fingers to his lips, got up and came over closer to me, "I can't kiss you if you're laughing."

He could see me naked through the sheet.

"Are you cold, how is the temperature of the water in this drafty castle?" he asked, and then dipped his hand into the water next to my thighs. "Hmm, getting chilly. Have you had enough of bath time? Do you want me to help you get out?"

The water *was* getting cold. His eyes locked into mine.

"I have a strange feeling you want to see me naked," I teased, testing the situation.

"What kind of a man would I be if I didn't?" he asked rhetorically and raised one eyebrow in a dare.

I could have sent him out of the room with a slap on his wrist for being saucy. I could have asked for a towel. His look burned pure heat into me.

I stood up, water dripping off my naked body.

"Is this what you wanted?" I asked.

He came over to me so fast my head spun like I was falling through time again. But this time his strong arms kept me steady, and I felt his lips on mine.

"I'm getting you wet," I said, through urgent, pent-up kisses as he wrapped his arms and hands around every part of me.

"Doesn't matter," he whispered into my ear, as he scooped me out of the bathtub, and sat me on his lap in front of the fire. He grabbed the linen sheet that had been over the tub and dried me off, wiping off my back, my arms, then running it down my legs, and then slowly over my breasts. "You are so beautiful," he said, in that deep voice that made every part of me light on fire. I kissed him hard, my body alive with being surrounded by this powerfully made man whose arms and hands and lips were consuming me. The feel of his mouth on mine made me hungry for more.

But time was not on our side.

There was a knock on the door. "My lady, may I come in?"

"Damn it!" I whispered. I looked at Harry in despair. I was nowhere near satisfied with that brief encounter.

"Mary, one moment please, I'm just getting out of the bath," I said, as Harry put his palm into his mouth and pretended to bite into it hard in a show of frustration.

I spoke softly into Harry's ear, nibbling on his earlobe. "Let's try this again as soon as we possibly can. Please," I whispered into his ear.

"Don't worry. I'm not far away." He took the sheet, wrapped me in it, and kissed me deeply, one last time. Then he opened the door silently to his room and was gone.

I groaned. I already missed the feeling of him. A part of me that had been put on ice for so long was rapidly defrosting.

CHAPTER TWENTY-TWO

The king kisses the knight, and the queen as well,
And many a comrade came to clasp him in arms…
Sir Gawain and the Green Knight

"MY DEAR, YOU are positively glowing!" exclaimed Lady Dagworth when we met enroute to the reception. "Life in a royal castle does seem to agree with you most beautifully." She was hustling our group of women down the hallway. "It is not allowed for us to be later than the queen. I have heard that Phillipa is a sweet girl, but we do not want to test her good humor."

I was in a foul mood. All I wanted was to be with Harry. As fascinating as a royal feast might be to my hungry brain, my physical side was winning the obsession war.

The Ladies' Feast was held in the Great Hall of the lower bailey, near the castle's chapel. It was much, much larger than the hall at Wodesley. Where the Dagworths could host 100 people, this room looked like it already had 300 people within, with more ladies arriving every minute. An official-looking man took our names, and we were led to our table. The King himself had arranged the seating charts according to rank, we were told.

Not long after we took our seats, horns trumpeted the arrival of the King and Queen. We arose and pressed together for a glimpse of the young couple. I had to stand on my tiptoes to see, but got a good look at King Edward.

Edward was wearing what must have been a heavy gold crown, with roughly-cut large jewels mounted within—sapphires, rubies, emeralds, pearls, and diamonds. He had light brown hair, cut to chin-length, and a trimmed beard that looked carefully maintained, much like the hipster beards of our day. I remembered that he was born in 1312, so that would make him 32. I could not see much of Queen Philippa, as King Edward blocked my view of her. However, I did see that she was small, and slightly plump. I saw a white silk sleeve and an elaborate headdress.

There was a hushed silence as the royal court made its procession through the hall. Not far behind the King came Katherine, Countess of Salisbury, showing her place of importance within the kingdom. The royal procession finished their entrance, with people bowing and curtseying before them, and sat up on a dais built about four feet above the main floor. They probably had an excellent view of the throng of people before them, and their elevation on that stage gave us a very good view of them, which was just as important. There were no TV or newspapers to show the people their rulers, so these appearances were vital to the strength of his monarchy.

The horns blared again with a different kind of tune, after which King Edward stood to address those assembled.

"My lords and ladies of this most noble kingdom, I bid you welcome to the Tournament of Windsor!" There were cheers all around the many tables. "Our feast tonight is to honor the fair women of England. I have asked you here, as you are what inspire our gentlemen, lords, and knights; inspire them to do what is right. This tournament will show us the bravest and most chivalrous of men, and you are what we fight for. Together, we lead as an example, not only to England, but to the rest of the world of what it is to be righteous, what it is to be strong, and what it is to be respectable."

Edward held up his gem-encrusted goblet. "Join with me, ladies, in this feast that has been prepared for you with great care. Eat well, for I know many of you have traveled far to be here. After, it will be time to dance, and to deny the morrow of its day. Let us enjoy this beautiful company."

A line of servants in matching uniforms began to stream in, precise as soldiers on parade. With trays full of food, they weaved and bobbed around the tables and down the aisles of the Hall. I hadn't eaten much in our two days of traveling, and I was starving. Once served and after the blessings, I stuffed my face full of the most eye-popping food I had ever seen, in as ladylike ways as I could manage. I didn't know what a lot of it was, and I probably wouldn't have eaten it had I known, but I was too hungry to ask.

The women around me were behaving with the appropriate dignity to match the setting, and quite unlike their teenage selves from not a few hours before. It was as if they were in a show, and had a part to play, and were terribly nervous about messing it up. Their voices anxiously subdued, they were afraid to get noticed for the wrong reasons—terrible table manners or uncouth behavior—but eager to get noticed for the right—beauty, delicacy, posture, and pretty smiles. Women couldn't get noticed for much else during this era, it seemed.

We made small talk as the courses kept coming. "Lady Dagworth, I never asked you whether you had been to Windsor Castle before?"

"No, I have only been to the Palace of Westminster in London. Such a crowded city." She grimaced. "I am so relieved when I can return to Wodesley. Lord Dagworth often has to go to the city to see to his ships arriving and departing, but I prefer to stay in the country, where my mind is more settled."

"What kind of goods does Lord Dagworth import, my lady? Where do his ships go?"

Lady Dagworth mentioned something about importing wine and Venice and Marseilles, but really, I was nodding a lot because my mind kept drifting back to Harry.

I hadn't been touched like that in years; I'd dismissed the idea that the passionate side of me was important. I rationalized that my work, the girls, and our everyday routines were safe. Were enough.

But desire like that…

A servant came up to me. "The Countess of Salisbury requests that you attend to her, my lady."

I glanced quickly at Lady Dagworth to pardon myself from our conversation, and as I stood, she gave my fingers a light squeeze. Like I was in a nightmare where my feet were encased in cement and the building was on fire, I stumbled forward. Women's faces loomed before me as I passed them, sure everyone was watching me, as if I had gotten into trouble with the principal or something. My breaths came in quick gasps. Somebody grabbed my hand and slipped a scrap of paper into it. I looked up to see that it was John, one of the few men in the room. I guess he had been allowed in to capture the scene for historical purposes.

The paper said: "Prophecy."

Prophecy? What did that mean? Was I a part of a prophecy? Or John? Or did he mean the king? My brain rushed through a series of facts about the time and prophecy.

I remembered that some prophecies had been written during the era predicting political outcomes for kings, kind of like how many people of today follow their horoscopes. The kings embraced these prophets and used them as political tools to give authority to plans they already had in place—like invading France to begin what would be the One Hundred Years War.

I knew the future. At least, I knew it generally. Knowing history came with knowing literature—you had to put everything into the context of the political realities of the world at the time. But nonetheless, I could perhaps prophesize an event that would come true. If that event happened while I was with the king, then perhaps it could give me power over my situation—a bargaining chip.

But what could I use? There were few records of the time, chronicles from people who had heard stories but weren't actually there (I didn't know what was going to happen to John's records), expense sheets for the king, and tax notations. But I did know for sure that Edward was going to found the Order of the Garter because of this tournament.

"*Honi Soi Qui Mal Y Pense*," was written on a plaque at the bottom of my hall in my dorm in London. I had puzzled over it and looked up the story behind it. It is the motto behind the Order of the Garter: "Dishonor to Those Who Think Dishonorably." The order is the world's oldest, and continued on to my day, with the queen and Prince Charles and Prince William all taking part in the annual Garter Day at Windsor.

The story goes that at a ball, and they never determined where or when this ball took place, a woman was dancing with the king when the garter on her leg fell off. Everybody laughed at her embarrassment, but the king picked it up and declared that famous line. Edward III became the exemplar of chivalry.

What was perhaps more intriguing was the actual name of the order: *The Garter*.

History books had pinned the embarrassed dance partner down to three women, and I racked my brain to remember. One was Phillipa, Edward's wife. Another was Joan, who would later be known as the Fair Maid of Kent, and marry Edward's son, The Black Prince. But considering that The Black Prince was still a young boy, this seemed unlikely, as Joan would also have been quite young. The third woman was Katherine, Countess of Salisbury, wife of Edward's dearest friend. I *knew* I'd seen her name before. Why hadn't I connected the two before to this tournament?

I had to think on my feet.

Academics are supposed to be smart, but in my experience, there are different kinds of smart. There are the genius types who are mentally gifted but socially challenged. There are the smarty-pants types who love being the first to weigh-in on a topic, whether or not they know the answer for sure. There are the quick studies who can pick up facts in an instant, who are in contrast with the diligent studiers, who need to review their source material over and over again to test well. There are those who love writing a two-hundred-page long thesis on a topic, versus those who prefer a round-table seminar for proving a point.

I had long been a combination of the above: a quick learner, a debater, and (my brother would argue), a smarty-pants. The quick learning skills came down to genetics, but the debating skills came from my family's dinner ritual. Our family dinners consisted of food turning cold as my father threw out topics for debate, and the rest of us snarled and snapped around the subject like wolves over a fresh kill. My father kept score, and points were earned and distributed for good arguments, counterpoints, and use of both history and current events to back up our arguments.

This family preparation came in handy when I joined the debate team, entered college, and came to start debating my fellow PhD Candidate, Jane Percy at King's College.

But this situation was life and death, not arbitrary points earned over a chicken dinner. If I used my wits in order to keep Harry and me together as a team to return to the labyrinth, it could backfire.

I realized then that even though I'm not one to use my "feminine wiles," they tended to win favor no matter what the era. Mary had done some excellent hairstyling, and I'd had the loan of some pretty spectacular gowns, and perhaps my good 21st century health (clear skin, teeth, sunscreen) helped score some extra looks. I had to use all that I had, because in 14th century England, although there were many tough and strong powerful women (I had met three: Elizabeth Dagworth, Katherine Salisbury, and Yvonne), they still had few legal rights. There was no way around it: with few allies, no relations, and no real land or fortune to legitimize me, I had to tread very carefully.

Chapter Twenty-Three

"Yet my counsel was of kissing," came her answer then,
"Where favor has been found, freely to claim
As accords with the conduct of courteous knights."
Sir Gawain and the Green Knight

Edward III, up close and personal, was a good-looking man. He had been the king since he was fourteen, so for all of his adult life he was used to getting what he wanted, especially after he led a coup against his mother and her lover, Mortimer, when he was 17.

Sitting on a large gilt thrown, with the beautiful Katherine on his left, Queen Phillipa on his right, and a bevy of the richest and the most beautiful women in England around him, Edward looked well-pleased with his position in life.

I bowed my head and curtseyed as I approached the table (I had seen other women do this as I ate my dinner, so I knew the protocol). "The Lady Hartford," announced the man who'd brought me over.

Katherine's face creased into a smile as she took my hand. She turned to the king, "Your Majesty, may I present the Lady of Hartford? She is recently come to your kingdom from France, where she married into an English family who settled there. Eleanor is now a widow and had come to Canterbury to pray for the recovery of her eldest daughter, when most unjustly was robbed and attacked on the roads outside of Wodesley Castle. A gallant knight, who I know the Earl would like to introduce you to at the tournament, rescued her. He brought her to Wodesley Castle, where the Dagworths have been most hospitable in nursing her back to health."

The king looked at me closely, taking in nearly everything about me.

"What part of France are you from?"

"Provence."

"What part of Provence?"

"Lorgues." I'd once read about it in a travel article in "The Telegraph."

"Ah, a beautiful land, I hear. And is the land now in your name?"

"No, I am but a lady, and I have two girls. It has passed to my husband's brother, Eustace." I was thinking on my feet. If I didn't have land of my own, then Edward wouldn't be interested in me.

"Lady Hartford, I do not know of your people, but I am most glad you have come to Windsor. I am deeply sorry that you met with a foul lot of folk on your pilgrimage but be assured that there is no room for evil-doers in my England." He said *England* with four syllables—*En-gal-lond-e* (the nerd side of me couldn't help but note). "They shall be rooted as boar out of woods and be spiked upon the poles of justice; for a fair lady of any part of our society, be she rich or poor, maid or married, *deserven* to ride without danger in our land." He pounded the table for effect with his right hand to emphasize his point, turning some heads in the room.

Edward continued to speak as I stood in front of him, listening like an obedient subject. "That is why we have decided to hold a tournament, to find the mightiest warriors in our country, who are not only fierce to the enemy, but gallant and kind for citizens, ladies, children, and the helpless." Edward had no reticence in expressing his viewpoints, perhaps because he knew that they would be well-met, regardless of their actual merit.

"Your Grace," said Katherine, "I would like to tell you a little more about Lady Hartford, if you will permit me. I know you enjoy a good story, especially one with a hero, or in this case, a heroine." She told the king how I saved the servant from the fire the previous day. Katherine was a good storyteller, filling in lots of details and providing the setting and the dialogue from her perspective. Enchanted with her, Edward's eyes widened, and his lips parted. Queen Phillipa, who was talking to one of the few men in the hall on her right, cast a curious glance every once in a while over in Katherine's direction.

When Katherine came to the point in the story where I tackled the girl and put the flames out with my cloak, the king slammed the table again, this time in delight. He bade me to come closer to him. "Get this lady a chair, and put her right here," he said to the nearest servant who came when he put his hand up. Promptly, a small chair was found, and I was propped between Katherine and the King.

"Lady Hartford, with your hair the color of the precious saffron, and eyes that are liken a pool of water, you do deeds of good for both family and those in danger. Truly, your brave soul and beauty are a rare combination, and one that should be celebrated. From this day on, I declare you as a ward of this court, to assure that you are taken care of during your time in our country. Queen Philippa will be delighted to have you as one of her ladies."

Katherine beamed, and I fell back a little on my chair.

Chicken Nuggets! I rarely swore because I didn't want the girls picking up on it, and I'd gotten so into the habit I couldn't ever utter a real swear, not even in my head. *Chicken Nuggets* had the guttural and emphatic sounds that evoke a good Old English swear word but kept it G-rated.

This was exactly what John had predicted, and even though I didn't have any land, my saving of that poor girl had brought me unwanted attention.

I wanted to bolt out of that room, but I couldn't. I had to keep my head.

Queen Phillipa had turned around at hearing her name called. She appeared to be comfortable with her husband—taking his hand and whispering a private joke into his ear. Then she looked at me, smiling. "Has our dear King found me a new lady? These are wonderful words. What is the lady's name?"

The King tried to remember. Katherine leaned over, and said: "Your Majesty, would you allow me to present Lady Eleanor of Hartford? She is remarkable."

"Wearing a remarkable dress too, I see." Indeed, I was back in the shimmery blue number of John's. He'd packed it for me once we knew we were all coming to Windsor and sent it over to Mary. "No wonder you have so captured the attention of the King!" I didn't know if this was a compliment or a barb, but the look on the Queen's face wasn't all that sincere, and I didn't blame her. She was being saddled with a woman she didn't know.

"May I offer my gratitude for your gracious hospitality upon this magnificent occasion," I said. "This feast reminds me of how it would be in King Arthur's Day, with the knights making merriment before proving their skills to the King."

Phillipa immediately lost interest in the conversation and turned back to her partner. I guess she wasn't a fan of either literature or of Arthur. But I still had Edward's attention; he was smiling. "Are you an admirer of the tales of King Arthur?" he asked.

My hands shook. I'd been memorizing the kings and queens of England since I was a little girl, studying their portraits in a book I had. Reading their mini-biographies, and later, reading the first-person accounts of their lives, and even some of their letters. I needed to answer his question: "Indeed, I have been since I was a little girl and found books on him in our small library at home."

"You have a library, lady?"

"Only a very small one, but my father believes in the power of stories and education to encourage people to live a good and honorable life."

"A wise man, your father," said the king. He took a drink from his golden goblet.

"Yes, he is. I owe him much. I see that you encourage and entertain with your tournament and your feasts. All around us there is much excitement to see these knights compete. How did you decide to have the tournament?"

I fished around, wondering what I could grab at with some inkling of his background, his history, the literature, and the world in which he lived. I needed to keep the conversation going long enough for me to wow him with some tiny bit of fortune-telling. I didn't want to be one of his pieces on his chessboard. I wanted to be one of the players. The player who won her own destiny back home. My mind was ready to be focused, aimed, and fired at the target.

"I dreamed that I should hold a tournament at Christmas," he said, leaning back, looking proud as he surveyed the scene. "I saw all of it happening as it is now—the snow on the ground, the feast for the ladies. I knew it had to be in January, and that it could not wait. I also saw a round table…"

Dreams—yes, I could run with dreams if he followed them.

"Your majesty, are you to build a table round for your knights, as King Arthur did? That would be most inspiring to young and old to see our king following in the footsteps of Arthur himself." He was about to speak when I kept going, "But let me tell you that I had a dream at Christmas as well. It was at a ball, and a king and a lady were dancing, and to her great despair, the garter on her leg came off in front of the whole court. But do you know what the king did to stop the laughter? He held up her garter and declared that no one should tease her: *"Honi soi qui mal y pense!"* he said. It was the most chivalrous scene I had ever seen, even if it was just a dream."

"Honi soi qui mal y pense? Dishonor to those who think dis-honorably," he translated into English. The king laughed it off, and said, "Well lady, let us hope that no woman loses her garter

tonight!"

The queen then discreetly interrupted, introducing another subject who needed or attracted their attention, and I was summarily dismissed.

I had just returned to my seat and tucking into some sort of custardy pudding to drown my sorrows in dessert, when the ear-splitting sound of trumpets nearly startled me off my seat. We were directed to make our way out of the hall to another part of the castle for the ball.

Outside we were accompanied by a band of flutes, tambourines, and some sort of guitar, while torchbearers lined the way. Entering the ballroom, we saw that the men had preceded us, and lined the outside of the massive, long room, which seem to stretch the length of a football field. The men let out cheers at our arrival.

I'm sure the whole place has been renovated countless times since the reign of Edward III, so what was there in 1344 probably doesn't exist in 2017. At this time, it was a stunning room of cream, red, and gold embellishments, with those curious stacks of blocks overlapping each other that were used in place of paintings, mirrors, or murals. The hand-drawn wallpaper was complemented by intricately crafted tapestries, depicting scenes of castles, knights, hunting, coronations, and village life. In addition, billowing from the tops of the high ceilings, were banners of the king's coat of arms.

Now that all the women and men were together, we were numbering somewhere over 500, and the room began to heat up, helped by an enormous number of candles on the walls, and candelabras suspended from the ceiling. Still, there were pockets where the lighting was dim, and though there were numerous servants to substitute candles that had burned out, they couldn't keep up. I didn't know how I was going to find anyone I knew, as I'd lost the Dagworth ladies on my frosty scurry up the hill. I was hoping to find Harry.

The first person I saw was Yvonne, as she was standing next

to the tallest man in the room, her husband Hugh. Squeezing my way past silks and furs, sheathed swords and intricately embroidered tunics, the glitterati of the kingdom. They stood stiffly in their finest, trying to look as though they belonged. Yvonne was taking it all in with an innocent joy.

Hugh circled back to his wife again to take her for a dance. They slipped off into the larger circle of dancers, Hugh tall and slight, and Yvonne, tiny and spry. He was a joker, and she was studious. It looked like such a mismatch, but it was working for them.

Surrounded by pageantry, and the sights, sounds, and smells of the Middle Ages, I remembered Anthony de Lane's advice. This was what I'd studied all my life but never hoped, of course, to experience. Now was my chance for Day Three. So, I stood still, and then turned 90 degrees four times. First, I saw the dais, on which the king and queen were now sitting. They both looked happy with the scene before them, and a line of admirers had queued up next to them, hoping for an audience.

Another turn to the right and I saw nothing but strangers. A large group of men gathered in a circle, jovially arguing about something. Purses opened, and gold coins changed hands. Perhaps this was a betting pool for tomorrow's tournament.

Pivoting another turn to my right, a group of women, also huddled in a circle, laughing. Their guffaws and hands over their mouths as they giggled, reminded me of girls at high school, gossiping.

I turned the final time, and there he was, almost at my side, reaching out for me. Harry.

◆

CHAPTER TWENTY-FOUR

"Wel coude he sitte on hors, and faire ride;
He coude songes make, and wel endite,
Juste and eek daunce, and wel portraye and write.
Prologue, The Canterbury Tales, Geoffrey Chaucer

"THEY WERE STUFFING us like fatted calves, ready for the sacrifice," I told Harry. "I honestly don't know how these women stay so skinny. I have yet to see a personal trainer, a treadmill, or a Pilates class since I've been here," I joked.

"Maybe they are burning calories from shivering in this cold," said Harry.

"Well, whatever, it's working for them." I smiled.

I noticed Harry was shifting his eyes, surveying the room, ever vigilant.

I nudged him in the side to get his attention. "Hey, maybe I'll start a new diet fad when we get back home. I'll call it: *Medieval Women Don't Get Fat,* and people will love it because they can eat as much as they want. Unfortunately, the food that comes with the plan will consist of roasted hedgehog on a spit and stuffed peacock, along with a mandate that you must turn off the central heating in your house."

Harry turned back to me, eyes shining. This felt right. He'd seen me at my worst, crying and hungry, and still liked me. "How about, *Lose Your Fork, Lose Your Fat?*" he said. "You can give up that professor's career and live off the royalties from all the franchises."

Pleased by his sharing my humor, I asked him how his feast was.

"Well," he said, "for a men-only event, everyone was on his best behavior, which is not the way I'm used to seeing that kind of scenario play out. There were prayers, lots of pleases and thank you's, and plenty of talk about the best way *not* to be killed tomorrow."

"Well, I'll follow their lead and use some pleases," I said. "*Please* tell me you're not going to compete tomorrow?"

He shook his head and plastered a smile on his face. "No."

I groaned. "Harry, for God's sake—these men have all been practicing this since they were my girls' age. You've only been doing it for a few *days*. As much as I respect your career as a soldier, I just don't see how you won't end up a pile of pulverized bones." My hands found their way onto his chest, trying to drive my point straight to his heart.

"'Pulverized bones?' You have got quite a way with words, lady," Harry said, a real smile blazing across his face. His gaze had made me melt a little before, but now that I know that he felt the same about me, it lit me up inside. I tried to remember again why we were at this stupid ball, and not back in my room, ripping each other's clothes off.

"I take notes from the greats," I acknowledged, "The Pearl Poet, Chaucer, Malory, and even as modern a revolutionary as Will Shakespeare. But seriously, I was kind of hoping you'd stick around, just being my bodyguard? Protect me from all this riff raff?" I joked, pointing to all the bejeweled people in fur and silk around us. "I feel much better when we stick together."

"I'm with you, believe me," he said, drawing his lips into a thin line. "I think about you all the time—want to be with you all the time—but I can't figure out a way to get out of this. I don't really have much of a choice but to compete. Both Dagworth and

Salisbury are all over me about proving myself to the king. What an honor this is, not letting them down, or the King down, etcetera, etcetera. Beyond coughing up a lung tomorrow, I don't see how I can possibly get out of it." He put his hand over mine, still placed over his heart. "Thanks to modern medicine and nutrition, I guess, I'm pretty big for a man around here. That gives me an advantage on the jousting court, or whatever it is they call it."

The wine continued to make me bold. I leaned into him and whispered, "Look, Sir DuMont, I don't know what we started this afternoon, but I certainly intend to see it towards its natural conclusion, whatever that may be. I'm not really sure what your *modus operandi* is with women…"

He shook his head. "I don't have one, Ellie," he protested.

"Come on…" I prodded.

"I'm here already with the pick of women. You're different. In fact, you're *very* different." Harry meant to compliment me I'm sure, but that label—*different*— happened to be the same one my ex-husband had called me. Back then, it wasn't a compliment, it was one of his reasons for not wanting to be with me.

"Yes, I am different." I started off with all the things Tom used to complain about me. "I spend too much time with my nose stuffed in old papers and books. I'm a smarty-pants. I don't get my nails done, and I don't spend a lot of time on my appearance. Oh yes, and I'm not at all typically pretty. I don't have blond hair, and my skin will forever be extremely pale instead of a golden tan." Thinking of all the teasing and odd looks I experienced over the years at being "different" got me steamed.

Harry shushed me with two fingers that tilted my chin up towards him, pulling me close to his lips. He breathed, "There has never been a woman more fascinating to me than you, Ellie. You're the sexiest, bravest, most intriguing women I've ever met."

Wow. That tore my defense-system right down. I desperately wanted to kiss him right there in the middle of the ball. But the damned convention of the times forbade it. All I could do was say, "For God's sake, Harry, don't get killed tomorrow. I don't know what I'd do without you, in more ways than one."

Harry took my hand off his heart and took a step back from me. "Do you know what matchmakers advise people to do on their first date? They tell them to see a scary movie, or do something adventurous like bungee jumping, because it raises the adrenaline and forms a bond between two people." He smiled. "Well, let's consider this trip one very long, adventurous first date. I personally can't wait for the second, or the third. But maybe we'll make it a bit more tame. Maybe dinner at an overpriced French restaurant and a movie?"

That was the best proposition I'd heard in a long time.

A loud voice interrupted our conversation. "Lady Hartford, Sir DuMont, what a pleasure to see you." John stood before us, and whether or not he noticed a change in the atmosphere between Harry and me, he did not register it in his demeanor. "I understand from the countess that Lady Hartford here made a good impression in front of the king. Dear, did you take my advice and prophesize? Do tell!"

"Please don't call me 'dear,'" I said, my lips smiling but my teeth clenched. "Dear" is what my parents called each other when they were ticked off with each other. "To answer your question, yes, I did make a prophecy, which might come true now, or three years in the future. About the garter. History doesn't tell us for sure, and who knows whether it will score me any points."

The room suddenly seemed noticeably quieter as I spoke, and the people around us turned in one direction as the music became easier to hear.

"What's happening?" I asked Harry, who, being the tallest amongst us, had the best view of the room.

"The king is dancing with the countess."

John nudged Harry in the ribs. "It's good to be the king, eh Harry? Having the most beautiful women in the kingdom at your disposal. There's rumor aplenty on a dalliance or two he's had with that Katherine—the wife of his very best friend."

I wonder if there was a double *entendre* there. John and Harry were friends, and now Harry and I were together, at least for this night.

I elbowed John in the stomach, and whispered in his ear, "Katherine told me that story, and said nothing ever happened. Besides, Salisbury is right here in the room—you don't make the moves on your best friend's wife in front of him and the whole of the nobility."

Everybody was quietly gossiping, just as we had been. There were lots of raised eyebrows, whispering, and giggles, but I could barely even glimpse the couple to make my own appraisal of the situation. This wouldn't do with me not being able to see. All my years of living in London and hustling my way into and out of the Tube trains at rush hour taught me how to slide into places without pissing anybody off. So, I sidled, and slid, and gently nudged my way up to near the front of the circle that had formed around the king and his dancing partner.

The pressure on King Edward III to dance well would be far greater than that of a groom on his ceremonial first dance with his bride. The ruler of the realm, the representative of a nation, and some believed God's chosen leader of his people should not look like a doofus when he danced. If he were to appear weak, off-beat, ill-mannered, or assumed any number of unappealing attributes, his power would lessen, and word would spread.

But King Edward did himself proud. Young, handsome, tall, with broad hands, he held and maneuvered Katherine with grace and dexterity. He looked like he was truly enjoying himself, similar to a great actor who was performing his role to perfection.

Whereas the king was in his element, Katherine was decidedly bothered by something. It soon became apparent what that was. It looked as though she had to sneeze, or run to the bathroom, or had an urgent call to make....

Or could it be that her stockings were falling down? Could it be that John had timed this whole crazy trip perfectly, for me to see the mystery of the Order of the Garter unveiled right before my very eyes? *Score one for my prophetic skills!*

You had to feel for Katherine. There is not a woman alive who hasn't had a fashion disaster—leaving the ladies' room with her dress tucked into her underpants, not realizing that her top was see-through, or grabbing two mismatched shoes for a college formal. Yes, those things all happened to me. There have been women at the Oscars who tripped on their trains in front of a billion people, and women interviewed on important news shows who unknowingly had a false eyelash tear away and appear spider-like to the unprepared viewer.

This was perhaps the only time in the history of fashion disasters, to my knowledge, that an embarrassing moment became a rallying cry for bravery, civility, and honor.

I still hated to see the exact moment of this monumentally historic fashion fail, though, just as I hated to see people publicly humiliated anywhere at any time.

Katherine's stocking was tripping her up, perhaps around her shoe, and three steps to the right later, there was the golden garter lying on the floor that had come untied from around her leg.

Should people have ignored it, and let them dance on? Perhaps that would have been the polite thing to do, but that might have aligned itself with the worldview that it's okay to leave your best friend with a piece of spinach on her teeth after lunch as she heads back to work, because you didn't want to embarrass her.

I was going to have to be the one to alert the king, who was blithely dancing with this perfect woman, too busy making eye contact with his subjects around the room that he was unaware that his partner was in distress.

Maybe I should have sat back and let the scenario play out the way history had intended it to, but nobody else was speaking up. I was going to instigate history, for better or worse.

I quickly ran down a list of options for interrupting a king at his own ball to point out that he was missing out on his partner's distress but came out with nothing verbal that wouldn't throw me in the dungeon, like "Yo, King!" like they'd yell out at a Boston Red Sox game. There was the option of a loud achoo that might cause him to turn and look at me, but he might decide to have good manners and ignore me.

The band was behind me, and I made a split-second decision to create a physical distraction, rather than a verbal cue. This would take the attention away from Katherine just long enough for her to alert the king. I shimmied my way over to the mandolins, pretended to stumble, and then fell over the music stands and caused several of the instruments to miss their note. I ended up on the floor. I can't lie: it hurt. People laughed, and I apologized as I got up and picked up music stands. In the meanwhile, the king had been alerted by his partner.

"*Honi soi qui mal y pense!*" I heard King Edward III say, as he held up the golden garter in his hand and looked directly at me on the other side of the room. Nobody dared to laugh any more, either at me, or at Katherine.

CHAPTER TWENTY-FIVE

*"Alas," said Sir Gawain, "that ever I should endure to see this
woeful day." So Sir Gawain turned him and wept heartily, and
so he went into his chamber.*

Le Morte D'Arthur, Sir Thomas Mallory, 1470

"YOU DOVE HEADFIRST into an orchestra of minstrels. I wish I had my iPhone on me—that video would have gone viral," Harry said.

John gave me a discreet handshake. "I don't recognize you, but I am proud."

I railed at that internally. He had no right to be proud of me, like I was his.

I was still hurting, feeling bruised up and down my legs and arms where the instruments, music stands, and pointy-toed shoes had raked through my flesh. It was a bold and unusual move for me to fake a distraction, but I considered it necessary, not only for my friend Katherine, but for the sake of history. And yes, for the sake of elevating my new status as a prophet.

The party was over—it was pretty much over when the king had held up the garter, made his pronouncement, and then encouraged his knights to do the same in order to be "stronge and firme" for the jousting competition, which was now only eight hours away from starting.

It was midnight in Windsor Castle, and I was alone in my room with Harry. I knew he needed sleep as well, but he persuaded me to spend time together with the line, "If I die tomorrow, I want to at least have spent one night in your arms." With a line like that, how could I resist?

To be honest, I didn't need a line. At all. I'd been dying all night to pick up where we'd left off.

I'd politely asked Mary to leave; she was supposed to be sleeping on a pallet on the floor. Harry volunteered his room for her and his own comfy bed and vowed that he would not disturb her. Mary gave some rote protest that must have come with her ladies' maid training, but it was more with a wink and a nod than anything really sincere.

I wanted to make this memorable for Harry, and for me. We could either attack each other in a torrent of passion, or take things nice and slow, as we had started to earlier. The bath was no longer at our disposal, but there was still a nice fire.

"I never got a chance to dance with you at the ball," said Harry. He bowed and reached for my hand.

I placed my head on his chest and entwined my arms around his waist. He put his hands on my hips and pulled me close. The top of my head didn't make it to his shoulders. There was no awkwardness to this slow dance. There were no pent-up hurts and misunderstandings. This was brand new. *God, he smelled so good.* When I got home, *when*, I was going to find this scent he was wearing and bathe in it.

I accidentally stepped on his boot, a little stiff in my swaying. It'd been a long time since I'd been with somebody new. I was intimidated by him. By his past. By all the girls he'd likely been with before. A mom with stretch marks and love handles couldn't measure up, I worried.

"More than a *wom-a-a-a-n…*" Harry started to croon.

Okay, this *BeeGees* song was my new favorite. I laughed at his high falsetto. "That Maurice Gibb sure knew how to write a song," I joked.

"That would be Maurice, Robin, and Barry. Team effort." He lifted my chin to stare down into my eyes. "'We can make forever just a minute at a time.' Genius. Like you."

He had an ear for lyrics that was impressive. Smart too. *Damn.* I was going to burst into flames, possibly, or my knees were going to give way and I would puddle into a pond, like the Wicked Witch of the West.

He leaned back over me again, his voice softly singing in my ear, his breath hot on my face. Screw it, I thought. It was time to take this dance party up a notch.

I pushed him gently up against a tapestry hanging on the wall and kissed his lips. He closed his eyes. Then I moved my kisses down to his neck and he let out a moan. I stood on my tiptoes to gently bite his earlobe, and he leaned down to kiss me back.

"Taking over, are you?" Harry murmured. "I'm not so sure about that." He spun me around, and with one arm around my waist, and the other on my back, started untying and unraveling the one-size-fits-all dress I was wearing, while at the same time moving his lips over my newly exposed neck and back, and sending shivers down my bare skin. I arched my back and leaned back against him, grinding my body against his.

All at once the final tie that held my dress up was undone, and the fabric fell to the floor. Harry tugged the white shift over my head, and I was naked except for my boots. "This is a look I could get used to," Harry said, looking me up and down. "Cowgirl? Naughty dressage competitor?"

"Something like that," I said, quaking a little in the cold, wondering where to put my hands. "Or, how about a very chilly, time-traveling professor?"

"Ooh, yes, I think I saw that in a sexy film once." Then, with the firelight the only thing in the room illuminating us, he helped me step away from my puddled dress. His warm hands brushed his hand lightly over my breasts. He moved his free hand around one hip and down along my thighs, and then….

I moaned. My needs and desires were expertly met. I felt free and bold for the first time in a long time.

"It's not fair for me to be the only one naked," I said, my voice insistent, but quiet, aware that Mary was on the other side of the door. But before I could even finish my sentence, Harry too was bare, and we were skin on skin, his desire for me fully evident. Those muscles just around the hips—I wish I knew what they were called, because every man should work to have them— were magnificent, and his skin glistened by the dancing light of the fire. I pictured those arms, that back, those shoulders, at work on the farm, pitching hay easily. I imagined him showering after, the soap running down his chest. "You're beautiful," I said. "I honestly don't think you're real. Maybe this is a dream, and I'll wake up, like Dorothy."

He opened his mouth to speak but didn't say a word. Instead, he shook his head. I reached out for him. I wanted him to fill the void that had been empty for too long.

With my arms around his neck, he laid me on the bed. I no longer cared about anything—no Mary with her ears pressed against the wall, no love handle worries, no exes—nothing except getting more and more of him wrapped up in me, around me. Coupled together, we were lost in each other, staring into each other's eyes, communicating with words and our bodies the exquisite pleasure we both were feeling.

Afterwards, both of us breathless, Harry slowly raised himself up into a stretch above me. Sitting back on his heels, he stretched his body out for me like a living sculpture, I admired every inch. He was a man who truly had the ability to make me—at least for one hour—forget what year it was.

⇥⟫⟪⇤

THE CLATTER IN the hallway the next morning began early—it's hard to stay quiet if you are in chain mail and armor. I was spooned into Harry's body, the heat from him keeping me warm enough that I only had a sheet of linen on top of me.

"Good morning, sexy," he said. "That was an incredibly hot night."

"Yes, it was," I smiled and stretched, and turned to face him, and shielded my mouth from him.

Despite my morning breath, he kissed me. "I would so love to stay with you like this, Ellie, but if I don't get away from you and that siren call of yours, I'm going to miss suiting up with our team from Wodesley. I don't want them tracking me down and finding us *en flagrante.*"

He slid out of bed, and I enjoyed watching his naked body as he padded around to collect his clothes. He was so exquisitely crafted, it was as if the gods had had a hand in his design. But there was one man-made imprint—a long scar that wrapped around his middle, starting from his ribs and going close to his spine. I was tempted to ask him about it, but I didn't want to bring down the happy mood that we were both in for our remaining minutes together. Once he'd gotten reasonably clothed, he came back to the bed, leaned over me, and kissed me lightly, his lips just grazing my upper lip, saying as he finished, "We'll have to do that again, very, very soon." Then he tapped on the door to his room. Mary appeared at my door, the picture of discretion, already dressed and with a bowl of hot water ready for me to start my own preparations for the day.

"Thank you, Mary," I said, as he closed the door to his room, "for letting Harry and me be together last night."

"It's my job to look after you and make my lady happy," she said. "You've had a rough go of it, I know. Why should a woman not enjoy the company of a man as fine as Sir Harry to help ease her through the dark of night?"

As I was getting dressed, we heard loud voices coming from Harry's room, and I recognized the voice of Dagworth, who was probably coming to pick Harry up for the tournament.

Moments later, a knock at our connecting door came; Harry had come to say goodbye. Dagworth accompanied him into the room and looked in. Harry said, "Lady, may I wear a token from you to compete in your honor?" Harry was dressed in the colors of Wodesley—blue and gray, and his armor, with some chain mail added from somebody's collection.

I didn't know what to give him. I knew from my readings that ladies usually gave an extra sleeve (as sleeves can be laced on and off) or a scarf. I didn't have a garter, but I did have the necklace around my neck.

I garbled together something to say: "Please take this token with my, my…" I hesitated. Would "best wishes" sound too formal and distant? Would "love" seem like it was coming too early? I found what I hoped was the right word: "With my deepest affection and desire for your safe return." This gathered an "Aw" from all three present in the room, and Harry kissed my hand with a tenderness that took my breath away.

I unclasped my necklace and handed it to him. He tucked it into the chain mail, and I could see the three letters sticking out—for me, Sophie, and Abby—from between the metal pieces near his heart. With a bow, the two men swept out of the room.

"Mary, let's get a move on. I don't want to miss a thing," I said.

It was Day 4. I had to plan our escape.

THERE'S A HUGE disconnect in what men were asked to do in medieval times: be courteous with gracious manners while being a killing machine when called upon. Support and protect women and children, and ride as fast as you can with a lance attached to your body to try and unseat another man riding as fast as *he* can at you, from the opposite direction. Recite love poetry to a lady and pierce another man's heart with your sword. I suppose this has been true throughout history, that men are sometimes required to do unspeakable things in the name of glory, honor, king, country, or defense, and then have to snap back to a world that wants to see only the civility in the man, and not the raw animal courage or the stink of fear.

So, while we in modern America and England—or any country, really—have our sports stars who are titans on the field, and regularly known to get in trouble off of it, the men in this 14th century tournament were required to be titans on the field and exemplars of the best of human behavior. They were the demigods among mortals.

The trappings of this medieval disconnect were particularly profound in this setting: flags flapping on the field in the courtyard of the castle, the carefully constructed viewing platform for the king and his court, resplendent in jewels and fur, and the powerful horses arrayed with colorful mantles, pawing at the ground, and occasionally bucking or rearing in anticipation or annoyance, steam roiling out of their flared nostrils as if they were dragons.

Amidst all this pomp and grandeur, blood would be spilled in the name of the king. The participants, some as young as 16, and some as old as the Earl of Salisbury, were as yet shielded from the viewers' eyes. I couldn't imagine the nerves that they must be feeling, because I was beside myself with worry—and I was only an observer on the sidelines.

I sat with many of the ladies from the Salisbury/Wodesley party in the grandstand, the second row from the front, about twenty people away from the King and Queen. I didn't know where John was—getting behind-the-scenes interviews with the contestants, perhaps, like a sports reporter before the big game? It had snowed overnight, and apart from the tracks that were made by the people walking in, everything looked pristine and fresh. The sky was a bright blue, the sun low in the winter's horizon, and the air crisp and cold. Snow glistened on the branches of the trees surrounding the fields, weighing them down.

The tournament was down the hill from the upper castle— where Great Windsor Park is now. At the top was the royal enclosure and a turreted compound. On the other side of the field was the standing-room-only crowd who had camped outside the castle walls to watch this show of shows.

The ceremonies began with a parade of the entrants. Each knight had a standard bearer march in front of him with his flag, and together they made a circle around the field. In the middle of the field was a double-sided log fence where the jousting was to take place. The top posts of the fence went up as high as a horse's shoulders. The length of this fence was about seventy-five feet long, and not very wide.

A man dressed in a long, silver-embroidered coat came out to announce the rules of the competition. I did a quick head count and estimated there were 100 knights present. The successive rounds would have winners against winners, until there were ten knights remaining. Each of these knights would then be judged on horsemanship skills, sword skills, and have an interview with the king. Seven would be chosen from this group to join the Order of Knights, and the rest of the were to be filled with the king's own picks.

Once I saw the first joust, I knew we would be there for a while. After trumpets sounded, both knights got an introduction similar to a boxing match ("In this corner…"), a triumphant ride around the field to attract applause and support, and a bow to the ladies and the king in the stands. Each knight seemed to come with his own cheering section. And then came the crazy twenty-second "sport" where two horses and two men rode full speed towards each other on opposite sides of the fence with a twelve-foot-long lance pointed at the other's chest. It happened so fast that I wished we had a modern "instant replay" on the big-screen in slow-motion, because I couldn't tell sometimes what happened. Sometimes there was a clear winner because he was able to knock his opponent off his horse, but other times it looked like both knights got hit, but both were able to stay on. The judge in front of the strike zone seemed to figure it out, though, a winner was declared, there was cheering, and the knights left the field.

One match took what seemed to be about ten minutes total, and there were approximately forty-eight more to go.

If that rate was kept, that meant we had an incredible twelve hours of competition to watch. There weren't enough hours of daylight in the winter for all this to happen, and I knew I wouldn't be able to bear it in the cold without moving, even with the fur robes that were provided to keep our legs warm.

I had yet to be contacted by any member of the king's party about the fact that my prophecy had come true, or that I was to be a ward. Hoping they might forget about me if they didn't see me, I tried to keep a low profile. Mary had found me a hat to keep my head warm, and it did a good job of covering up my red hair, which I asked if she could pin up.

The Earl of Salisbury came out as the next contestant. The crowd went wild, knowing his reputation earned by years of winning at previous tournaments, and on battlefields for the king. His opponent was Matthew Dagworth, Lord Dagworth's eldest son.

The Countess of Salisbury was cheering loudly for one who was supposed to be refined and dignified. She had a huge smile on her face, and looked eagerly at her husband, trying to catch his eye. She must have, because the earl walked his horse over to the enclosure, bowed to his king, and then came up to where the countess was sitting just behind me. "Countess Katherine, may I have a token?" He took his helmet off, and I could see his matted hair already shiny with sweat, despite the cold. His eyes seemed to pierce right through his wife. "My lord," said Katherine, "I pray thee wear this garter with my greatest love. I hope it brings thee glory in the highest."

As she held out her scarf for him to tie around his sleeve, he took her bared hand with his gloved one and kissed it, closing his eyes and seeming to inhale the scent of her skin. And then, dropping it gently back, he bowed again, whirled his horse around, and left for the end of the field.

Matthew remained at his end of the field the whole time,

perhaps wisely not wishing to take away any of the spectacle from the king's best friend. I wondered whether he was nervous, facing certain defeat from this renowned warrior, but if he was, it was impossible to tell because of the ridiculously large helmet covering his face.

They rode towards each other. Matthew badly mis-aimed his strike, and Salisbury wasn't able to deflect it. The earl's neck seemed to snap backwards. My hand flew to my mouth before I screamed out loud, as did many others, although the countess stayed silent, her hand cupped over her mouth in horror. The earl crumpled sideways on his horse, which continued running down the field with Salisbury's body half-falling off. His squires and others on the field ran after it to stop him from being further injured.

When they finally caught the horse, and took Salisbury off, a cheer went up as he raised his hand! One of the men put his head down close to him and relayed a message whispered from the earl. "He says, 'Do Not Fear. This is not the end of Salisbury!'" I saw Countess Salisbury sway and fall back into her seat, her lady's maid catching her head and cradling her on her shoulder. They half-carried the earl off the field, his legs trying to work, but not exactly holding him up. The countess got up to go after her husband.

If this was any indication of how the day was going to go, I was going to need a bottle of Tums; my stomach was in turmoil. It was sure to be an endlessly emotional day of seeing people almost get killed every few minutes. Rider after rider came and did his best, but only one prevailed, while the other was either knocked off his horse, or slammed. Only a few times did both men miss, and they were simultaneously eliminated.

To stay warm, I took breaks walking around the enclosure, as I noticed other ladies were doing. While the lap furs and mittens and scarves all helped, I wondered why the king had to have this tournament on the coldest, bone-chillingest day of the year? This was no good for his people. They could all catch the flu here and he'd wipe out half his nobles.

And what was he thinking of me, if anything? Did he remember how I prophesized something that came true? If so, perhaps I could turn that whole vision thing into a power play, and make demands, like getting out of Windsor and returning to Wodesley. *Today*.

To stay warm, I visualized green grass and trees in blossom. I pictured pina coladas on the beach, with Harry rubbing SPF 50 sunscreen onto my back.

Another blast of trumpets shocked me out of my daydream, and the emcee called Harry's name. I saw young Bertram run in after him, and then climb over the fence in the middle to watch the festivities. For a boy so young and so far away from home, he didn't appear nervous or homesick—launching himself up and down pogo style to do something with his energy. During the journey out, I'd noticed Bertram was never far away from his knight.

Harry, while strong, and excellent on horseback, didn't have years of specific jousting training to back him up. I felt some serious, almost prophetic (the king would want to know) premonition that this was going to end badly.

Blood had already been spilled on the snowy ground.

Unable to bite my gloved nails, I twisted my hands, and bunched my skirt up into knots. I remembered that scar around his ribs that stretched around to his back, his perfectly proportioned but vulnerable body underneath all that armor, the way he looked as he rose above my outstretched body. As long as I live, I will never forget that sight.

Yvonne, sitting beside me now, dug her nails into me. I realized that Hugh was up as the opponent for Harry. It seemed ridiculous that two working on the same team should be up against each other, but I wasn't familiar with the particularities of medieval elimination contests.

Neither Yvonne nor I could speak. I wasn't entirely sure I wanted to be holding her hand if her husband killed Harry, but then, I didn't think I could be watching this potential slaughter without holding onto somebody.

The knights dipped their heads to each other in a sign of respect, and then rode off to the opposite ends of the field. The announcer raised his flag when they had put their helmets down, shouted: *"Allez!"* and lowered his flag to signal them to go. Harry's horse got off to the faster start, digging into the ground and shooting off as though it was the Kentucky Derby. Hugh's horse was slower, but larger, and as the horses worked up to their top speed, they seemed to rattle the entire field with the pounding of their hooves. The knights lowered their lances at each other, and in that brief split-second that they galloped past each other, contact was made, and both men were hit.

Harry tilted over sideways as his lance broke apart on Hugh's chest. He managed to right himself and not fall off his horse. Hugh, however, was stopped by the impact on his chest and thrown off his horse. I saw Hugh lying on the ground; time seemed to stop as I waited for him to show some sign of life. I reached my arms around Yvonne, who turned pale and then slumped against the woman next to her. The seconds passed: one, two, three, four, five…. And still, no movement.

Even if I knew little about medicine, I knew more than the people there. I jumped out of my seat, scooted past the women directly in front of me, lifted my skirts up enough to get my legs over the side of the enclosure, whistled at the guard underneath, and gestured to him that he catch me as I jumped down, about eight feet to the ground.

With a thump, I landed heavily in his arms, and then dragged myself through the mud and snow. When at last I reached him, Harry was there; he had removed Hugh's helmet. Hugh was deathly white, and as I fell to my knees beside him, I didn't see any movement. I ripped off my gloves and slid two fingers to Hugh's neck to check for a pulse. I could find none. The sweet hero from the *Tale of the Squire* had died right here in front of me. The impact of the lance must have stopped his heart.

"Get this off of him!" I yelled to Harry and Bertram to get the metal plate off Hugh's chest. The three of us worked to unfurl the straps on his chest plate. My cold fingers seemed too clumsy to get the job done, or it could have been that they were shaking wildly. Urgent time was passing as oxygen was not getting to Hugh's brain. I thought of the baseball players I'd read about who had been hit hard by a ball to the chest, hard enough to stop their hearts like a jolt of electricity. If this is what happened to Hugh, there was a chance I could get his heart going.

At last, we got the chest plate off, and instantly I straddled him, my palms on his sternum, pounding a rhythm back into his body. One, two, three, four, one, two, three, four.

"What are you doing, lady? Stop doing whatever it is that you are doing!" I heard.

One, two, three, four. One, two, three four, One, two three four.

The only other sounds I heard in my brain was the sleet now hitting the roof of the royal box, the sound of Yvonne wailing, and the metal on the armored knights around me. I heard Lord Dagworth's voice, shouting something into the wind.

One, two, three, four.

"Remember. To the tune of *Stayin' Alive* by the BeeGees," Harry whispered in my ear.

"Lady, please stop," said Bertram, tugging on me, tears running down his face. I shook my head, and he buried himself into Harry's chest.

"There lad, let the lady work. She knows what she's doing," Harry said to Bertram. To me, he said, "Keep going, Ellie. You're doing it right. Let me know if you get tired."

One, two, three four.

Then, there was movement in Hugh's face, and a weak cough arose from his throat. With his eyes closed, he turned over on his side and wretched a dry heave, allowing air into his lungs. The crowd behind us erupted in cheers.

"Welcome back," I said. I climbed off of him, realizing a little late that probably no one had ever seen a woman straddle a man before in public, let alone beat on his chest.

His reply came back in a whisper, "Did I win?" He smiled, and then passed out.

I checked to make sure his pulse was still going, placing my head on his chest to hear the sweet rhythmic thumping. A group of men had gathered around him, and lifted him carefully up, carrying him inside the castle with Yvonne, now recovered enough to be by his side to hold his hand.

And then, I looked around at the stadium full of people, staring at me as if I were a pariah.

CHAPTER TWENTY-SIX

"Wel coude he sitte on hors, and faire ride;
He coude songes make, and wel endite,
Juste and eek daunce, and wel portraye and write.
Prologue, The Canterbury Tales, Geoffrey Chaucer

E NTERING INTO HUGH'S world in John's novel, *The Tale of the Squire*, so many years before, I'd never imagined that I would be the one to actually save the young man's life.

He was now settled in his room, propped up on many pillows, eyes closed, but a healthy glow in his cheeks. Mary was with him, right alongside Yvonne. They debated between the two of them the remedies that Hugh needed to recover his strength after that awful shock to his heart, both acknowledging that they each had his well-being foremost in their minds. Yvonne was receptive to ideas that Mary had, and Mary was eager to hear Yvonne's theories. I stood at the back of the room; as the adrenaline slowly left my body, only my hands still quaked. I tried to quiet it by holding them together.

Lord Dagworth came up behind me. "He's a fine lad, our Hugh. I do not know what we would have done if he'd died out there on the field. I'm not quite sure what you did to bring him back to us, my dear lady, but our family is forever in your debt." He reached out to take my hand in his and bowed over it.

"Dear Lord Dagworth," I said, patting his hands, "with all that your family has done for me, showing me such great hospitality and care, I could only help but view you as my own family. I had to do what I could to save him."

"I won't ask where your knowledge comes from, my lady, but I do, with grateful heart, appreciate that you have it." Dagworth left me and went to stand beside his daughter.

John entered the room, looking all business as his eyes searched the room, and then seeing me, walked over. "Lady Hartford, may I see you out in the hallway please?"

I nodded and excused myself.

"Well, you're both a genius and a fool," he said.

"A fool? What have I done?"

"Saved Hugh," said John. "Do you know you're the center of everyone's gossip now, girl? They think you practice some sort of dark arts in being able to bring a still heart back to beating. You having red hair simply does not help the case. I've heard the word 'witch' being volleyed about like a shuttlecock in badminton."

"Maybe it's a good thing they're scared of me. They wouldn't want to keep me around then, right?" I was hopeful. "Why are you so angry?"

He didn't answer at first. He rubbed the back of his neck and scratched his fingers through his stubble. "Damn it, Ellie, you're ruining everything," he said. He suddenly looked shocked. As though he'd said something he had not wanted to say.

"What? What am I ruining? I saved Hugh. You didn't want me to save Hugh? What am I ruining?" I asked again.

"I had wanted you to be successful with the king. Everything was going so well. Salisbury likes you, the countess, the Dagworths. You even prophesized what I thought you might about the garter. We were running on all cylinders! Until Hugh got hurt. Of course, I love Hugh like a younger brother, so…"

I shook my head, hoping I was not hearing what I really was hearing. "You *did* bring me back to 1344 on purpose. You've been using me, manipulating me, this whole time? And Harry?" My voice dropped to as low as it could possibly go. I wanted to kill him. How could he?

"Now Ellie, hold on, let me explain," he said.

"You goddamn selfish son-of-a-bitch." I went to slap him, but he caught my arm. I wrested my wrist away from him. "What am I, a money-maker to you? Aren't you rich enough already at home? How many cars does a man need that you steal a mom away from her babies? I thought I knew you, once, a long time ago. I thought you were a good man." I was in shock. John may have left me all that time ago, but he didn't ruin my life. He ruined our relationship. This was far different. He separated me from my family in a way that might never be rectified if I couldn't get out of this place.

John took a step away from me, knowing I wanted to strike back out at him. "Now Ellie, I just thought that bringing you here might be good for you. Jane told me about your circumstances, and how you basically have no life—just work, and parenting, and work, and more parenting. I thought you could use an adventure."

"You're trying to get me to believe that this was some selfless act—just for my entertainment, right? That's bullshit. Then, why are you saying I've 'ruined' things?"

"Well…" He looked hesitant, as if he was going to try to keep up the act. Then he shook his head and shrugged. "Do you know how long I've been coming here, and playing on the "B" Team? Dagworth and his family are sweet and all that, but I've been wanting to meet King Edward and be at Windsor always. I've been reading up on him, strategizing, and staking things out, but I've never been able to get this close to him. But thanks to you and your story, and Harry, you two have opened doors for me that never would have been opened as a mere scribe. You're like the dream team in this world—Handsome Harry and Lady Hartford, with her dazzling American—well, French—smile and beauty."

"But wouldn't you have come along with Dagworth anyway?"

"No. I'd asked him, and he'd said no, it was too costly. He said they'd tell me all about it when they got back."

"Why didn't you become a knight yourself? Why not just travel to Windsor on your own? Jesus, John. To resort to this? Kidnapping!"

"Well, I can't be a knight. First of all, I'm not that strong. Picking up a sword for me has always been a challenge and gotten worse since I've been coming here. Maybe it's a side effect of time travel, but physically I'm just not that strong anymore. I get winded sometimes, even going up the stairs. Second, you can't just knock on the door and get invited into Windsor—you have to get invited by a friend with power. So, I knew Salisbury was coming, and…"

"Why bring me into all of this?"

"Because you were meant to be the king's ward, remember? That would keep me here, too, if I played my cards right. I knew what would happen to you when you came through the thin place, that Harry would probably fare better than you and 'rescue' you. The fact that he invented the part about finding you on the road was pure genius. Your story went viral, even without the aid of the internet. I knew you'd be okay because, for starters, we don't have many women who look like you in this day and age. You're healthy, with beautiful hair, you've got clear skin, a decent rack—"

"Oh my God. I was just a piece of meat for you to purvey? This gets worse and worse."

"No of course not. You're also an expert on the language, well-versed in the general history, and a truly nice person. That meant that everyone would like you and want the best for you. And that's exactly what happened."

"What about Jane? Did you want her to come too?"

"Don't be ridiculous—she'd beat the holy hell out of me. I put an old alarm clock in the girls' bedroom and knew that they wouldn't know how to turn it off because they'd never seen one before. I had the timer set perfectly."

I grabbed him by his throat. His eyes widened, but he didn't try to pull away. Maybe he couldn't. I had a tight grip. "So how long did you intend for this whole charade to play out? Indefinitely? Keep me away from my children always? Just so you could play a little role in a fantasy life? You're pathetic."

"No, not forever," he said, pulling my hands off him. He didn't seem that weak to me. "Thank goodness for de Lane helping me out that night—first, putting the manacles on me to make you curious, and second, for using his strange skills to keep you from going home. I want you here just long enough for the king to see my true talents, and how he couldn't possibly live without me. I want to go back home and show Jane that I've made it into the history books. I'll finally outshine my sister."

I had not only been in love with a man who would abandon me, I had been dating a sociopath. How had my judgment been so wrong about him? Had he gotten worse over time, or was I such a stupid young adult I missed all the warning signs? Or, chose to ignore them and hoped that my gut feelings were wrong?

"Well, thank God, it looks like maybe I've figured my own way out. I can't believe I even trusted you at all. I'm such a dumbass. I hope you get found out for the fraud and thief that you are. What you've done to me is so wicked, I can't even believe it. And poor Harry's still out there competing! In a ridiculous amount of danger. He's like, your oldest friend."

"Don't use the word, 'like,' you sound common."

I shoved him out of my way. "Ugh! I *am* common. I can't even bear the sight of you anymore, Stafford, just get the hell out of my life." I went to check on Hugh.

I was relieved to find him sitting up and laughing now. Yvonne turned to beckon me over to his bedside.

"We owe you so much, Lady Hartford. I am forever in your debt for saving my dear husband's life." She threw her arms around me and sobbed.

Hugh reached out to pat her back. "There, there, wife. You cannot be rid of me so easily. I am simply too good and handsome to die so young."

Yvonne and I both laughed through our tears, as Hugh's humor broke through what had been a somber mood. Dagworth came over. "How are you feeling now, lad? You gave us a fright, full of dread."

"I'm ready to get back out there and fight again, sir. Who is at the top?"

Dagworth's face turned beet red, and he coughed, swallowed hard, and coughed again. I put my hand on his arm.

"What is your distress sir?"

"It's Salisbury," he said. "His soul has departed this Earth." He crossed himself.

"No, that can't be true," I said. "He was fine a few minutes ago."

"God rest his soul," Hugh said, crossing himself, saying a quick prayer.

Dagworth shook his head. "I have seen it oft' times myself. The body does rally for one last time, and then the wounds prove too great. He was a gentleman amongst gentlemen, a lord amongst lords. A good friend." He put his hand over his face, and he started to cry.

I thought of the man, full of life this morning, on the road the day before with the Dagworths, dying so young through a bad twist of fate. "I can't believe it. Poor Katherine.

"Oh my gosh." I suddenly realized Harry would be still in the match, since he would have moved on to the next round. "I have to go back out there. Forgive me!"

MY ARRIVAL BACK in the royal enclosure got people buzzing. Big time. What on earth did they think of me? A heroine, or a witch?

Or some crazed woman who likes to climb on top of dead men and pound on their chests? The king knew me as a prophet, but also witnessed the scene when I saved Hugh. I hoped he wanted to get rid of me—I was too strange a woman, surely, to be around his wife. Hopefully not too strange to go on living though, right? On the other hand, maybe he did value me as a prophet, and would overlook the possible witchery. But I needed to get Harry and get him back to Wodesley. This jousting was far too dangerous.

I didn't know a soul out there, as all the women I knew were with the Dagworths or the Salisburys. My heart hurt so badly for Katherine.

I tried to find a place at the back, to the side, where few could see me. But the buzz had gotten around, and within moments, I saw the king turn his head to look at me. He gestured over to one of his men and directed him to do something. That man then began walking toward me.

I quickly got up out of my seat and scrambled out of the enclosure, trying to blend into the throngs of people who were in the standing-room-only spots. Luckily I didn't have one of those cone-shaped hats that would have given me away on the ground.

The knights still left in the competition, I guessed, were probably on the other side of the courtyard, where I had seen them ride. I needed to find Harry. In one day, Hugh's heart had been stopped and the Earl of Salisbury had died. As strong and able a man as I believed Harry to be, the higher up the ladder he got in the tournament, the meaner the competition.

Slipping around the corner of the castle, I saw the security team guarding against interlopers who might gawk at or bother the contestants. They were as big and broad as a brick wall and while John had surrendered me to my fate, Harry and I were a team.

I approached the nearest guard, dressed in livery. He had a long sword unsheathed and pointed to the ground.

"Good sir," I said, giving him my best American smile courtesy of fluoride, orthodontia, and real toothbrushes, "may I please pass? I must see my man, Sir Henry DuMont, on a most urgent matter."

The man looked at me, puzzled. Then he eyed me up and down, perhaps dwelling a little too long on my "decent rack," smiled back at me with his crooked, yellowing teeth and bowed, stepping aside to let me past without saying a word.

I hurried through the disorganized scene of horses, pages, and knights. There were landmines of horse droppings everywhere, and I carefully weaved my skirts and boots around them. There was a whole lot of testosterone in the air as well, complete with swearing, joking, and leers.

I should have come with a man, or Mary. Perhaps they thought I was something other than a lady, maybe a groupie who came to give a favor in return for a brush (or grope) with a jousting superstar. I began to feel distinctly threatened, like a woman at a drunken frat party. These men were fighting in a life-or-death contest, and my presence proved a welcome distraction.

"Hello, lady! Care to take a load off on my lap?" a man cat-called. I kept my head down. Rule #1 of self-defense: do not engage.

"Ho hey, milord, she can take a load off of you!" another joked.

"Mademoiselle, I have something that I'd like to show you, that 'tis sure to impress."

I kept walking, lifting my head up now and again to see if I was any closer to Harry, if he was even here.

Rough hands clamped down on my arms, stopping me. Then a scratchy face with beer breath came to rub against my cheek, and declared, "Care for a dance?" With one hand clamping my arms together, I felt the man's other hand try to lift my skirts. I squirmed and tried to get away. I remembered the self-defense instructor at college lecturing a small group gathered after a rash of muggings, "Men are stronger than you; you can't outmuscle them, but you can go for their most vulnerable parts." My hands were no longer an option, but I had my feet.

I kicked back with my foot and attempted to land it somewhere on the man that I could not see. I felt something metal. I had just kicked armor. My self-defense techniques would never work against somebody wearing armor.

"Nigel, you got a feisty one there. And dressed so fancy. I wonder if she's a lady?"

"No 'lady' would come into the staging area," the other man argued.

"I am a lady!" I yelled. "Unhand me, I am a ward of the King, and he would no doubt have your head for the way you're treating me. Harry!" I yelled.

The arms around me released, perhaps scared by what I said.

"Lady Eleanor!" It was Harry, thank God, sword out, ready for action, on the back of his horse. Bernard came running along behind him. *"Qu'est-ce qui se passe ici? Montrez-moi l'homme qui vous a traité crapuleux."*

"Sir DuMont, *ce n'est pas le temps pour une lutte.* No more fighting!" I reached to get on his horse, and he pulled me up the rest of the way, so that I was sitting in front of him. He steered us away from the creeps.

"Ellie." Harry tapped me on the back of my head with his chain mail gloved hands. That hurt. "Where's your brain? Why did you think coming back here was a good idea? The only men left, besides me, are complete mercenaries. All the gentleman knights were defeated hours ago; these guys are animals."

"I needed to come see you, but I can see now that was a mistake. It's like Mad Max back here." A delayed shiver of fear and adrenaline shot through me. "Hugh nearly died, and Salisbury's dead. I feared you might be next, and oh, the best thing? This whole thing—the labyrinth, the clothes for us—John set it all up to get us to come, so we could take him to Windsor. His whole drunken scheme—the manacles—it was all an act."

Harry was silent, at first, then admitted, "I was afraid that might be the case…"

"What! You suspected it the whole time?"

"Well, yes, and you did too, initially. But you bought into his storyline, and I thought you might be better off if you spent less of your time angry with him, and more of your time working on being smart and figuring your way through this whole thing."

"But he's been undermining me, Harry. Told me to tell a prophecy to the king—"

"And what did that get you?"

"Then he wanted me for his wife's lady-in-waiting? To be in his court and not get away?"

"Is that better than being accused of being a sorceress? A witch?"

I paused, considering his argument. "Well, yeah, I guess." I didn't like to lose an argument. "But still, I couldn't let Hugh just die out there."

"I agree. And if you didn't give him heart compressions first, I would have done it."

I suddenly realized where we were, and how it looked to everyone around us. Not proper. Besides, the pommel of the saddle was digging into my lady parts in the most awful way. "I need to get off this horse. As romantic as this looks in those pre-Raphaelite paintings, your armor is digging into my hips."

Harry grabbed me under the arms as I slid off the horse so I wouldn't land with a thump. "Just think of what it's like inside this get-up," he said. "It's rubbing my skin raw. I'd get down too, but it's really hard to get back on again with all my gear."

I stood next to the horse and said softly, "How about you ditch that armor, and we make a break for it. We could be back for day five."

Harry shook his head. "No, we can't go it alone. We need the Dagworths to go back with us. It's too dangerous to travel by ourselves, and I don't want to end up on one of those gallows we passed in every village. A good mission is founded on teamwork, and we need a bigger team. It must be thirty miles back to Wodesley."

"So, you're saying you can't just point this horse's nose out of here and make our escape right now?"

"One horse couldn't carry us back that far. We have no food, no blankets. You would freeze to death. You barely made it here with a tent and a bunch of ladies' maids!"

"Don't start on that 'princess' thing again. You had your own moments of despair and self-pity too. Let me work on the Dagworths. And in the meanwhile, could you just try to fake getting hit out there." I mimicked soccer players who ham up an injury for the referee. "And get yourself out of this tournament? You've gotten way further than anyone expected you to...." I looked up at him, hopefully.

Harry shrugged. "I'm not a great faker, but I'll do what I can. But please, take care of yourself. I can't be with you everywhere you go at the moment, and what happened back there—" Harry gestured back to the zone of misogynists and would-be rapists— "scared the hell out of me." He leaned down and slipped me a knife. There was a pocket in my surcoat I put it into. "And try to get the Dagworths to send one of their men with you."

"Come here." I yanked his arm down to me. "Give me a kiss." He did as he was told, beautifully. "Hm," I said, "that was a great kiss, but you stink."

"Apologies, princess. We have an issue with our kits lacking deodorant."

"I'll make a complaint to your commanding officer. Or whomever it is that stocks army stuff?"

Harry grimaced. I guess I'd gotten it wrong. I hated getting things wrong.

I continued, "But I'm getting you and I home, and then all I'll have to complain about is ordinary mom stuff again, like toys and clothes left on the floor, and food on the counter. And entitled undergraduates.

"That's the spirit," Harry said. "Go forth and conquer."

I smiled, "And you go forth and fall on your ass!" I slapped my bottom.

Harry stopped, suddenly serious, and reached down to put a heavily-armored hand on my shoulder. "Ellie, if anything should happen—if there's any emergency, we meet back at the labyrinth, no matter what. Promise me."

"No," I said, "I won't leave here without you." My lips pursed tight. I wouldn't do it.

"If you must, you will. I'll meet you there. I promise." He gave my shoulder a squeeze and turned his horse away.

CHAPTER TWENTY-SEVEN

"A tale is but half told when only one person tells it."
The Saga of Grettir the Strong

As I walked back to the castle, a smaller person emerged, walking stiffly in full armor. Helmet. Chain mail. Shoulder plates. Belt with a sword. Leg plates. I really didn't want to get harassed again, so I kept my head down and put my hand on my knife that I'd put in my pocket.

"Lady Hartford?" asked a woman's voice. From inside the armor.

What?

I stumbled to a stop. "Yes…?"

She lifted up her helmet. "It's me, Katherine Salisbury," she said, her eyes rimmed with red, a single tear running down her cheek.

What was she doing in armor? "Oh, Countess." I reached out to her, but there was nowhere I could touch where she could feel me. "I am so terribly sorry about your husband. It is a true tragedy. I only knew him for two days, but I could see how he adored you."

She gulped, looking as though she was just about holding herself together. "I must redeem him. I must take on this fight for him and win the tournament."

"You can't be serious?" I asked. If I were she, I'd be weeping in bed, maybe even unable to even let go of the cold body of my dead husband.

"I'm jousting for the Salisburys. I do not want my husband to be remembered for this. I want *us* to go down in history for the right reasons—our story cannot end here on this day. The Earl won many wars, he was a true gentle knight, good to his people, the favorite of his king. I will joust and take his place. The first woman knight of the first Order of the Garter. William taught me enough to do this."

This was madness. She was in no shape to fight anyone, and not just because of the shock she'd had—she wasn't thinking straight. Would she be able to do what she needed to do in that split second on the field if her eyes were blurred by tears?

"I'm afraid you too will be hurt terribly," I said. I'd just seen the giants behind us who were the ones left standing to fight. In no way could she topple one of those hulks. Unless she got her lance just in the right position at just the right moment—only then could she overcome a bigger man. "You have to hit your opponent just at the right moment."

She stood up straighter. "My lady, I've been watching tournees my whole life. I know just where to strike whomever it may be that I come across. I am determined. If I go down, I shall die on the same field as my dear husband, and that is not a terrible thing. We will be together in Heaven."

"But your children?"

"They will know what I've done is right. They shall hear the stories. You shall tell them, won't you?"

Oh my God. What an awful task to take on. I needed to go back to Wodesley, to my own children. I didn't even know where the Salisbury children were.

I couldn't deny her request, though, when she was about to take on this fearsome role. If it came to it, and I prayed that it would not, I would figure out a solution.

"Countess, of course I shall tell your children of your bravery and resolve. I'd beg you to reconsider, but I see that your mind is made up."

She reached for my gloved hands, which she took in her armored ones.

"Thank you for being a good friend. I think if we had lived closer to one another, perhaps, we could be the dearest of companions."

I nodded my head, sniffing again to try to restrain the tears from falling fast and furious. The roof of my mouth was burning, like it does when I'm desperately trying not to release the ugly cry.

She turned and walked into the lion's den.

CHAPTER TWENTY-EIGHT

*"What is better than wisdom? Woman. And what is better
than a good woman? Nothing."*
Geoffrey Chaucer

I HAD TO bear witness to her fight.

One of the king's guards was on the lookout for me. He had a kind voice for a henchman. "Lady Hartford, would you kindly accompany me to see His Majesty?"

Edward III and his wife sat in carved golden chairs in the viewing stands, cushioned in red velvet, with a perfect view at the center point where two knights clashed head on. The equivalent of boxed seats on the fifty-yard line at an American football game.

"Ah, I knew they would find you!" the king boomed over the cheering crowds. People turned around to look at me. Some looked away quickly, as though just looking at me was dangerous or immoral. The king took this in and narrowed his eyes. "Are you enjoying yourself, Lady Hartford?" he asked, as he gestured to the person sitting next to him to let me have his seat.

"But of course! This is such a day of delights, and I am honored to be seated next to you, sire." I hoped "sire" was the correct term of address. God knows I'd probably read three dissertations on *Manner of Address in the Medieval Court as Depicted in English Literature,* but a woman's brain could only retain so much.

Especially under stress.

I was in his lair. He had all of these people to do his bidding, this enormous fortress, this town, this whole country served him. His problem was how to get them to continue to pay their taxes and be enthusiastic about supporting his war efforts. *My* problem was how could I go back to being an unnoticed woman in a big world? I wanted to slip back into the shadows, but I felt as though a gigantic spotlight was on me. I shivered.

"Cold?"

"No, I'm fine."

He shook his head. "You are an unusual woman, Lady Hartford," he said. "Most of the ladies of the court would have demanded a blanket by now, but you have been here for some time, silently suffering from this fearsome chill." He snapped his fingers and directed somebody to fetch me a fur. "I am most intrigued by you. You saved a life, you have the gift of prophecy, and you do not complain. We desire to know your secrets."

"Sire," I said, gathering my thoughts, "first, may I express my deepest condolences over the loss of the Earl of Salisbury. I had but the briefest of interactions with him over the past three days, but he was a noble man, and I am sure your majesty is in deep mourning for his loss."

His eyes clouded over. He had seen much loss in life in battle already, but this was his childhood friend, his protector, his ally. "Yes, Lady Hartford, we are most deeply grieved. Salisbury was the finest man we knew," his voice choked, "and it is a great loss to our country. Still, our work here at this tournament is important. We must see who our strongest and sharpest men are." He cleared his throat. "If only you could have saved dear Salisbury as well as the young Dagworth boy. Where did you learn your healing arts?"

"I have seen a healer who came far from the East pound on a chest in such a way with a man whose heart did stop. The man was revived. I could not help but try this method with Sir Hugh. And you asked of my gift for prophecy; well, it was merely a dream I had. Everyone dreams, it's just that perhaps I remembered this one. Quite a coincidence!"

"And the cold?" he asked.

"I think it is because I can only think of how my sweet daughters are doing, and I worry for them so. It is with every desire in my heart that I return to them immediately."

"Women are often attached to their children, even noble ladies such as yourself. My own mother," he said, stopping short. His mother's reputation was that she'd been both good and power hungry—a true dichotomy. He continued, "My own mother did not like to be far away from me when I was a young boy. I think sometimes it is good to have separation from our parents."

"If I may offer a different opinion, sire, I think that may be true for boys who are raised by their mothers, but I know a woman's place is with her daughters, for they must teach them everything. I am sure that our beautiful Queen does love her children so."

Edward III would eventually have fourteen children by the woman sitting by his side. She was likely pregnant right now. Giving birth in the 1340s was truly dangerous; so many women and children died. Although my doctor left it unspoken, it's clear that I would have died without c-sections, and so would have my girls.

"Our truth," the king said, "is that we must think of country first, family second. Today the mothers of these men who come before us to compete—" he gestured across the field—"have sacrificed their sons to their country in the hopes that they will win for their king and country on the battlefield. These competitions show me who the bravest men in our land are, and who can be spared to stay at home and take care of the land and our people. Your knight, Sir DuMont, has proven himself proudly."

"He saved my life by a miraculous chance on the road, and is a good warrior as well, or at least, Lord Dagworth tells me so."

Horns blared, announcing the next entrants, and in rode

Countess Salisbury, wearing her family's colors, flag flying ahead of her.

The king stood up, his face suddenly red and fierce. He roared, "Who is that wearing Salisbury's colors?"

Katherine steered her horse over to the King's stand, raised her helmet so that we could see her face. The crowd gasped. She dipped her head. "It is I, Your Majesty—" she placed her hand over her heart—"Katherine, Countess of Salisbury, here to represent my husband, your friend, The Earl of Salisbury."

Edward was not having it. "Get down off this horse now, Countess. We are in mourning. This is no time for jest. We are choosing knights for the Order of the Garter. You cannot be a knight—there are strong men who compete to be amongst my round table."

She pulled up her horse even more tightly to grandstand, getting up as close to him as she could. She spoke in a low voice, but I could hear. "You did not say anything of a *man* being a knight. Why can not a woman be a knight as well? You know that William taught me well—"

"I have always thought he was a fool to teach you—"

"It made us happy," she said. "For fourteen years, we were happy. Please, Majesty, let me pay him tribute in this way. And if I am a great soldier, it may be your kingdom will be known for not only your male warriors, but its female ones as well. You and I have talked about Boadicea, Queen of the Celts, the Warrior Queen, driving off the Romans in her chariot?"

I remembered this from my studies, from the writings of Thomas Jerome Baker. I could recite it by rote and almost see the page in front of my eyes: *"What is deemed as his-story is often determined by those who survived to write it. In other words, history is written by the victors...Now, with the help of the Roman historian Tacitus, I shall tell you Queen Boudicca's story, her-story..."*

"We have a queen, we do not need another," he said, looking defensively at his own wife.

"I would not dare to suggest that, Your Majesty. Merely that this land has been renowned for its great female warriors. Let us see whether I can be one as well." Katherine's voice broke, and a tear ran down her cheek.

I could barely breathe. She was so brave, so calm, and so persuasive. I said a prayer that she would convince him. "Let her try, please, let her try."

It was hard to see what the king's reaction was from behind. He had a decision to make, and this was an opportunity for him to show his wisdom and diplomacy. I couldn't imagine what was going on in his head. I stole a look at Queen Isabella, and she had a combination of horror and fascination on her face. Surely, they too were friends as well if their husbands—with all the easiness or awkwardness that might go with that.

"Salisbury," the king announced, loud enough for all to hear, "you may do battle."

CHAPTER TWENTY-NINE

By God! if women hadde written stories,
As clerkes han withinne hire oratories,
They wolde han writen of men moore wikkednesse
Than all the mark of Adam may redresse.
Wife of Bath prologue, Canterbury Tales, Geoffrey Chaucer

THE KING STAYED near the field, off his throne. I took advantage to get up from my seat and move closer to the exit. I had made a promise to Katherine and was not going to leave until I knew whether or not I had a duty to fulfill. If she survived and she became a knight I'd certainly never heard anything about it in history books, which made me worry that this was all going to go very badly.

When the two fighting knights came out again, it wasn't the Dagworths' flag that the other rider marched out with, so I knew she was competing against Harry. I wouldn't know who to root for if that were the case. But that meant whomever she was fighting was one of those awful bullies I'd met back behind the enclosure.

I found an empty spot quite a few seats away from the king. Two people came over to me: John and Yvonne.

"The Countess is jousting in honor of her husband," I said.

"The news is all over the castle. Hugh begged me to come

watch and report back to him with my own eyes." Yvonne had a small sketchbook with her and a piece of charcoal and was rapidly drawing out the scene.

"I hope that means that he is well-recovered?" I asked.

"With thanks to you and the Almighty," said Yvonne, squeezing my waist, and leaning her head over my shoulder. I gave her a squeeze back.

"She hasn't got a hope in hell," John said, shaking his head.

My hackles got up. I believed she had a chance—for truly, what did we know about her? Could you assume that just because she was a genteel lady that she could not fight as well as any man? Did a person need sheer brute strength in order to win?

"Regardless, you should be taking notes as chronicler. I have never read of this scene—the people need to know it."

John tapped his head. "I'm committing it to memory. As soon as I leave here I shall write down everything that happened today."

"Good," I said. "Does that include you being a conniving and cold-hearted asshole?" And then I had a thought. "Wait, how many years again have you worked in chronicling?"

"About twenty, in 21st century time," he said in my ear.

So that Yvonne could not hear us, I said very softly, "And have you ever found your writings in our time—in the future? At libraries, collections…" I prodded.

John squirmed, "No."

"Why do you think that is?"

"I'm not sure why and it's driving me to distraction," he whispered. "Like I don't even exist here. It could be because the Dagworth's house doesn't last too much longer—I haven't been able to pinpoint it down to the exact time, but it quickly starts to degenerate. It's entirely possible that all his books and histories were destroyed or moved."

"Have you thought to suggest to Lord Dagworth that he move his collection to a safer place?"

"Yes, in the future I will do that, but I am not sure what he would make of such a suggestion now."

The trumpets sounded, and the horses came back in and lined up, taking places at opposite ends of the field in what was now a very familiar position to me.

I didn't think I'd be able to watch, but I could not keep my eyes away from what was unfolding. The two horses and their riders ran together at full-speed, lowering their heavy lances, and aiming at their hearts.

Bam!

The two fighters met in the middle, lances crashing against the other's armor. Each person jolted at the blow, and even though the countess was sent flying back in her saddle, she managed to stay on. Her opponent, however, fell to the side of his horse. She had aimed her lance perfectly and scored.

The crowd erupted into cheers, and Edward actually leapt over the balustrade and landed athletically onto the field to get to the countess to congratulate her.

"Lords and ladies," he said, taking the countess's hand in his own. "I am proud to introduce to you the first member of the Order of the Garter, Katherine, Countess of Salisbury." Everyone was yelling and clapping, including the man whom Katherine had unseated. "The rest of the contest will continue tomorrow. I have seen enough today to cheer our whole kingdom that we and we alone have the best fighters in all the world. May those who seek to do us harm shake in their boots at the notion of taking any one of us on."

Edward and Katherine, who'd dismounted, walked into the castle together. But before leaving, she turned to take one last look around, found my eyes, and smiled. I gave her two big thumbs up. I'm not sure she would know what that meant, but I hope it came through with my smile.

With the king gone, and the queen getting up to go, that left the rest of us permission to go inside, get warm, and for me to disappear.

HUGH'S ROOM WAS in chaos when I knocked. People madly dashed about, gathering things and stuffing them into the traveling cases.

"Hello?" I said, to anyone who would slow down to speak with me.

Lady Dagworth noticed me first. "Oh, Lady Hartford, I am so glad to see you. We must leave, now! Go back to your room and gather your things."

My heart leapt. My plans came together without me needing to do anything. "What about Hugh?" I asked.

"Oh, he is as strong as a bull. He's already dressed in his traveling clothes and gone to get the servants and the horses and carts. Eleanor, I am so sorry to drag you away from Windsor in all the excitement, but we really mustn't stay any longer. Our family has been asked to leave, by the express orders of the Queen."

"The Queen?" I asked. "Why? What's happened?"

"The Earl of Salisbury's death is what happened, and my own dear son Matthew the one who gave him his fatal blow. Of course, it was all fairly done in the tournament and there was no foul work afoot. And yet we are all blamed for killing the favorite of the king's, not to mention Queen Phillipa's. I fancy she had a soft spot in her heart for him, just as the king has one for the countess, as we saw last night. A tangled web, you see? Matthew is now *persona non grata*, and we are all tainted. I certainly hope this does not damage my dear Dagworth's business and future relations with the king; may this all blow over like a storm once time has passed."

"I was just sitting next to the king and Phillipa—they didn't say a thing to me!"

"Well, you certainly have come up in the world since you were found abandoned outside our manor," she said. She was not jealous, she seemed happy for me. I don't think she knew about this whole "ward" thing, and I certainly was not going to let them know, or else they wouldn't take me.

The Dagworth's beautiful Wodesley castle would, not far in the future, be ruined. I'd wandered around the remains of it with my girls; the tumbled stones, covered with moss, made an atmospheric backdrop for the girls' fairy tale stories. Was this accidental death of Salisbury the start of the Dagworths' downfall? Although my visit hadn't caused this turn of events for the Dagworths, I felt responsible for them, and wished I could help.

Harry and I had been lucky to end up with the Dagworths and not a more vicious bunch. Theoretically, John was responsible for that. But I would still never get over my anger for what he'd done.

I went back out into the hallway to gather my few possessions from my room, when a beautifully dressed lady stopped me. "Are you the Lady Hartford?" she asked.

The woman was a tiny little thing, she couldn't have been more than four-foot-eight inches tall. She wore an ivory silk gown with green metallic threading woven throughout, and her hair was wrapped into a headdress made of emerald-striped fabric.

She introduced herself, "I am Lady Hastings. I hope that you were not full of worry that your belongings were taken away— we simply moved them to the side of the castle where the Ladies of the Court reside. I do hope you like your new room. I found this book in your things, though, and intrigued, I have taken a look at it."

I felt a pit in my stomach, but I knew I still had a chance to get away. After all, this was a tiny lady, and I was a much bigger woman. She was going down if she was the one thing standing between me and a ride back to Wodesley.

"What a delight to make your acquaintance," I said, lying through my teeth, "and thank you for seeing to my move. But you know the dear family who rescued me is leaving now, and I do wish that I had a chance to bid them goodbye before I take my place here in the household. Would you give me a moment? Oh, and I am happy to let you have this book, but I do need it now." I took Sir Anthony's book back from her.

"I would be happy to accompany you," Lady Hastings said. "I will fetch a wrap if we are going outside. It is such a bitter day."

"Oh yes, please do. I would not want you to be cold. I will meet you right back here," I said.

"You do not wish to come with me?"

Ugh! This woman was hard to shake! "All this traveling back and forth has really worn me down. Would you mind if I just sat down here to wait?" I pointed to a bench that was in the long hallway.

"*Bien sur!*" she said and hurried away.

As soon as she got around the corner, I immediately went the other way, out the only door I knew to the outside. I hoped the Dagworths were already outside and ready to go in thirty seconds or less, because little Lady Busybody would know exactly where to look for me.

I went running out to the courtyard and down the stone-paved drive. The castle was so impossibly large that it took forever to get away from it. I broke into a sweat worrying that I wouldn't know where to find them. If worse came to worst, I would just dash out the front gate, and hope that I would catch the party leaving along the road. I could not be in Windsor anymore. They wanted to keep me and never let me go, with my never-before-seen skills. Maybe John further whispered in somebody's ear that I was worth holding on to.

That miserable bastard.

The Dagworth coat of arms!—I saw it on a standard that a man was holding all the way down at the bottom of the castle grounds. I picked up my skirts and sprinted as carefully as I could down the icy paving stones.

I spotted Yvonne near a group of others, and ran up to her, my breath coming in gasps. "Hide me!" I implored. "They want to keep me here forever as ward to the King, but I can't stay. I've got to get back to my children."

"Lady Hartford! What say you?" asked Yvonne, who put her hand on my arm as I panted and looked around. "Why would you want to run away from that great honor?"

"Please, just trust me. I need to get away from here, and they will come looking for me." I hopped up into a cart and pulled a blanket over my body. "If a small woman in an ivory and green dress comes, say you haven't seen me anywhere. Please!"

"Shh, Eleanor, she comes now. Keep still."

Five minutes later, the wagons were rolling away, and I could hear the clip clop of the horses in front of the carts with the Dagworth family, presumably, on them.

I hadn't had the time to find Harry. My heart sank. I had let the other half of my team down—he was stuck on his own, with his passable French and deplorable Middle English, as a possible recruit for the king's army. Would he try to find us immediately? Maybe he'd catch up to our carts? Maybe he'd find John? There was the possibility that he was with the Dagworths' group, but I didn't know for sure.

Without John and the Dagworth party, Harry would know no one.

The rocky, unpaved road, the stale air underneath the blanket, and my guilty conscience bore a hole through my stomach. The bile rose in my throat, and a vice-like grip of tension in my temples made the misery that much worse.

Every step was getting me closer to my girls, but farther away from the man who was possibly the only man, in any time, with whom I could see myself falling in love.

✦◇✦

CHAPTER THIRTY

The lyfe be short, the craft so longe to lerne.
Parliament of Foules, Geoffrey Chaucer

THERE WAS A lot less fanfare on the way back to Wodesley than there had been going to Windsor. There were no Salisburys setting up their tents in a field already secured. As we left close to sunset, we didn't get more than five miles away from Windsor before we had to stop for the night. I was praying the whole time that we were not being pursued by guards from the castle looking for me. I hoped it took them a long time to search the castle before they figured out I wasn't there, and by then it would have been too late to go out.

Lord and Lady Dagworth didn't interrogate me much when I emerged from my hiding place in the wagon. Gathered around a small, smoky fire, they were so very upset about losing the favor of the king and feeling responsible for Salisbury's death. I promised them that I would be leaving Wodesley just as soon as I could and would bother them no more. Of course, they insisted I could stay, but I think there was an element of fear that they were harboring a runaway, which could further damage their already-stained reputation.

John sat on a small stone, mouth set in a straight line. He used a stick as a dagger to poke holes in the ground. "I knew the earl was going to die, I just didn't think it was going to be Matthew who took him down."

"You knew?"

"Yes, that made it into the history books that he died at Windsor in the tournament."

There were so many repercussions about what he'd told me, but I had more pressing matters. I pushed him in his side. "You need to go back and get Harry. Bring him back to Wodesley. He doesn't know anyone there anymore and he speaks only French to the people who seem to know it, since he knows little Middle English. I feel terrible I didn't have time to get him before we left. He's one of your best friends."

John laughed. "Your crush on him is very sweet. Very thirteen-year-old girl. But you have to realize that man shot his way out of an army compound invaded by the Taliban. They were sitting ducks. Harry got some sort of medal from one of the minor royals for his bravery. And you're asking me, weak as a lamb, and quite frankly, finding it a little hard to breathe, to go and rescue that one, who is as strong as an ox? He'll be just fine."

Frustrated, I turned away from John and found another seat in front of the fire, hugging my knees to my chest, and sank my head down. I had visions of Harry looking for us, finding our empty rooms, yelling my name, his face crumpling as he realized we had gone. *Maybe I could go back, sneak into the castle…?*

Sneak into Windsor Castle? That was madness. I remembered what he said to me: "…if anything should happen… we meet back at the labyrinth, no matter what. Promise me." The only way around this was through it—me staying the course I was on and hoping to God that Harry could follow as soon as he could.

After a dinner of bread and wine that I could not choke down, I realized that I hadn't done my looking in four directions for Day Four. It was a cloudless night, and the moon was waxing, but still quite bright in the sky. So many stars—the entire Milky Way was visible. To the East was the rising moon, to the South were the stars, to the West were the stars, and to the North there was a thatch of trees blocking my view of the sky.

I turned East again and looked up at the moon and prayed that Harry would be okay and catch up to us, somehow.

We rolled out blankets on the frosty fields, under the stars, near the fire. But every branch that snapped, every horse that moved in the night, I thought might have been the king's men coming to drag me back to Windsor.

Sleep. When was the last time I'd even slept? It was days since I grabbed anything more than fitful minutes here and there. I desperately needed eye drops. I needed a sleeping pill. I needed a freaking mattress with a proper pillow and central heating.

Forget it—I couldn't sleep. I needed to do something so that I wouldn't go nuts. I nudged Yvonne awake and asked if I could borrow her sketchbook and whatever type of writing implement she had. Her eyes barely opened as she scrunched up her eyebrows in a half frown, and then pointed to the satchel next to her and quickly fell back asleep. In the satchel, I found her sketch of the tournament field. I hoped she wouldn't mind, but I wrote Katherine's Order of the Garter story on the back of it. In my best, medieval cursive.

And then I left a note on the side of the illustration. "Yvonne, please make sure people know her story. It's important. Please take care of this. Lady Hartford, January 1344."

WE STARTED OUT before sunrise, putting out fires, rolling up our blankets, saddling horses, making discreet trips to the forest for a rest stop. Lord Dagworth hoped we could complete the rest of the journey in just one day. I had no clean clothes to change into, as what little borrowed clothes I had were packed up and sent to my "room" in Windsor. "Don't worry, Lady, we'll get you fixed up back at Wodesley," Mary said, giving my hair a quick brush. We left it down long. It was too cold for Mary to do anything with it, and wearing it long kept my head warm.

I felt like I should hide again in the cart, but Yvonne told me that the riders on horses were going ahead of the carts and would be back at the castle first, so if the king's men were in search of me, they would catch up to the carts first. So, I got up on the horse that had brought me to Windsor.

The ride was grueling, but I was encouraged as we kept getting farther and farther away from Windsor without anyone in pursuit, although I still wished one lone rider would come, wearing my necklace. I took over his role in his absence and came up with varying plans if any of the king's soldiers came up to us. I'd gallop off into the forest or throw myself off the horse and into a ditch where they could not find me, or scramble behind a stone wall. Every new vista we took in, I came up with an exit strategy.

It was twilight when Wodesley finally came into view. Relief coursed through me at the cheery sight of the castle with smoke pluming out of the chimneys, torches lighting the entrance. We clopped into the courtyard, and I slid my stiff body off the horse, as a young groomsman took it.

I looked around for John, and upon seeing him, motioned him over. "We must get Anthony de Lane. I can't wait another second."

"Hold on," John said. "I've got quite the haul that I want to bring back with me. More treasures for my collection. You get de Lane, I'll get a bag together, and I'll meet you in a moment at the labyrinth."

There was no time for goodbyes with the Dagworths and Mary. I felt like the long journey back to Wodesley was all about that. One of the serving girls led me to de Lane, who was in the scriptorium, writing on a piece of vellum. Hunched over the desk and wearing a black coat and black leather trousers, he did not look up from his work when we came in.

I walked up to him and gently placed my hand on his wrist so that I would not startle him. "I'm back, Sir Anthony. It's Lady Hartford. It's Day Five. I'm ready to walk the labyrinth again. Can we make haste? There may be men wanting to take me back to Windsor."

He stretched out his arms and moved his neck from side to

side; he looked stiff from writing at his table, but not surprised to see me.

"Forgive me, sir," I said. "I do not mean to rush you. I do hope your cold is better. But I fear there are men after me who mean to take me back to Windsor immediately," I underlined that point again, "and I must get back to the labyrinth, quickly."

I rushed to the window to look out, and saw in the diminishing light, a trail of dust rising up from the road beyond the castle, and the flash of flags.

Sir Anthony de Lane finally looked up at me. "I understand that sometimes life throws in some complications to make your journey all the more meaningful. I hope that you have been observant on your days here. Tell me what you have seen as we walk to the labyrinth."

He held on to my arm, perhaps to steady me as we set off. Perhaps I was jittery, after all it had been days since I had been this close to getting home, and I didn't want victory snatched away at the last second.

We proceeded quickly through the castle, out some back stairs, and down to the labyrinth garden.

John was there waiting, with a cloth bag stretched full. I didn't want to judge him for what he was bringing and whether he should have been bringing it. I was not the time travel police at the moment. He had to face his own conscience.

"We are missing one, are we not?" De Lane observed.

"Yes—our Harry," I gulped. "He was still at Windsor when we had to leave. I'm sure he's doing his very best to come right now, but we can't take any chances that I miss this opportunity. When he comes back, please tell him what happened, and that I can't wait to see him?"

"Of course, my lady," he said, soothingly. "I shall assist him."

The guy was like a Zen master. Nothing seemed to upset or rush him. "Now tell me, before you go, what you observed."

I started, thinking back, trying to remember everything like the good student I have always tried to be. "On Day One, I wasn't aware of my assignment yet. I just noticed how kind everyone was to me, and couldn't understand why…"

"On Day Two, I saw the bustle of a journey, Lady Dagworth in charge, the woods, and then a woman on fire. If I hadn't been looking…"

"You *were* looking," said Anthony.

"On Day Three—" I wracked my brain—"I saw the King and Queen, men in groups, women laughing, and then sweet Harry." I couldn't think about Harry for too long, without losing it, missing him in the empty space next to me. And then picturing him back at Windsor; could he be wounded, sick?

"On Day Four, I noticed the night sky, and how well I could see all the stars, and the moon, and how black it was in the trees.

"Today is Day Five, and I haven't had the chance to look around until now." I gathered my thoughts—fast. I thought I could hear shouts in the courtyard. Surely, they would not look in the labyrinth? I spoke quickly, "I see that to the East is the Castle, where people I respect live and were so hospitable to me. The South is the labyrinth, which shows me that there are great mysteries in life that I have no understanding of, and that makes me a little crazy, because I want to know everything and don't like it when I don't know how to explain something. These two things—the castle and the labyrinth—they live side by side with regular people—the known and the unknown. The West is the open road, where travel, dangers, and adventures wait, and the North is the castle wall."

"Of all those images, Lady Hartford, what sticks with you? What speaks truth to you?" de Lane asked.

I thought about this. I felt like Sir Anthony was trying to drill a lesson into me that I was just not seeing. But I needed more than anything to get this right. This wasn't just about a perfect score or grade.

"I just don't know what answer you're looking for from me," I said, with probably more than a hint of desperation. "I want to give you the right answer." My heart was racing. Horses whinnied up in the courtyard.

Sir Anthony smiled, patient. "Think of your heart in relation to these points. Do you know why the labyrinth let you through, and Harry, and even that scoundrel John Stafford over there? It was your hearts. They were damaged, and closed, and walled up, very much like that wall over there. See how it's your North? But yet to the East, West, and South are love, mystery, and adventure. You were pointed only one way, too focused on the wall and your obstacles to change direction."

I looked over at John, "Do you think that's true for you? You don't seem to even care about love. Not anymore. Maybe not ever."

John shrugged. He too was annoyingly cool, not seeming to sweat that we were being quizzed while there might have been soldiers looking for me just yards away. "I've never had much luck with my heart. After you broke up with me, Ellie, for a very valid reason, I have never felt right being serious with anyone. How could I commit, when I want to spend part of my time here with people I love, and part of my time back in the present, also with people I love? That's why," he said slowly, "this may be my last visit."

"Really?" I asked. "But you love it here. You seem like you are in your element here, whereas you have a harder time at home."

De Lane looked on, interested.

"It's not because I don't love it, but I fear that all this 'traveling' is taking a toll on my body. Remember when I fell over in the labyrinth getting here?"

I nodded.

"I think it's my heart. Anthony called it when he said it was broken. I suspect it really, truly is."

I gasped. "Jesus, John! You've got to get that looked at!"

"I'm short of breath, and I've got pain, I'm weak—far weaker than I've ever been. I'm a little worried."

"Oh, John," I said. "We'll get you help."

I turned back to de Lane. "Are you still looking for something from me?"

He nodded, silent.

"Well, I'd have to agree with John that my heart has been opened. I did not expect that I could trust another man again, and while I haven't known Harry for that long, I hope to know him better," I paused. There had to be more than just a crush on a guy. "Thinking about it, if I hadn't taken the time to look in four directions, I would have missed out on saving somebody's life, or helping somebody. I was missing things that were there. They've always been there, but I've been so self-absorbed, so immersed in my own little world, that I haven't seen them. I did enjoy the adventures when I wasn't worrying about getting back here. It felt good to help people, to make a difference. And," I said, hoping I'd said enough, and inching towards the maze, "if I could just get on that labyrinth path, I'll be able to enjoy them further upon reflection."

De Lane nodded. "You may go through now." He put his hand on my shoulder. "And do not worry. I have seen the way Harry DuMont looks at you, even from the first moment you arrived. He will do anything to follow you."

"Thank you!" I said. A weight came off my shoulders. I gave de Lane a hug. I didn't know where his powers or perception came from, but he'd helped give me a new lease on life. I had his beautiful book in my cloak's pocket, and I intended to figure this whole thing out.

I heard voices coming closer. It was time to go. John stepped onto the path, and I followed his movements up and down the paths. I was thinking about my girls, thinking about the day when I'd left, all while walking left and right, and up and down the path. I tried not to be fearful, but calm and relaxed. The sound of shouts got louder and louder, but then it morphed into the scream of a jet engine. Then pain shot up through my leg, and once again, I was falling.

PART IV

CHAPTER THIRTY-ONE

Be ye that holden this tale a folye,
As of a fox, or of a cok and hen,
Taketh the moralite, good men;
For Seint Paul seith, that al that written is,
To our doctrine it is ywrite, ywis,
Taketh the fruyt, and lat the chaf be stille.
The Nun's Priest's Tale by Geoffrey Chaucer

THE COLD FROST on the ground seeped through my clothes. I felt that first, before the screaming in my ears stopped. My head was still spinning, but the rotations got slower and slower, until they finally stopped. I opened my eyes.

Wodesley Manor, dark, but lit with electricity and Wodesley Castle, in ruins behind it. I was back, but how much time had passed? I saw a form on the path. It was John. I crawled over to him, still feeling very woozy, but adrenaline surged through me.

"Are you okay?" I asked. I rolled him over, and his eyes were closed. I felt for breathing, a pulse, and they were there. I slapped his cheeks, lightly. What if his heart had given out? "John! John! You're back! We made it!" Seconds later, his eyes shuttered open, and he focused on me.

"Lady Eleanor?"

"Just plain old Ellie now, John. Do you think you can get up?"

"Meat's in my pocket. Get it please."

I dug around in his jacket pocket, and there were two strips of roast beef, covered in lint and dirt. I felt so dizzy I didn't care, and I handed him a strip as I choked one down.

When he finished, he rolled onto his hands and knees, and with assistance from me, was able to stand and not fall over. His big bag of belongings was next to him.

I didn't feel nearly as bad as the first time, perhaps because I was not so scared. I was surging with adrenaline, eager to see my girls, and let Jane know we were okay.

"Let's get inside. Lord, I hope this is still January 2017."

We trudged up the hill to the main house, stopping from time to time to let John catch his breath. The front door was unlocked.

We walked down the hallway, still weaving a bit. There was no noise of little girls playing, so it must have been late. I saw a light from Jane's study, "Jane?"

I don't think she heard me at first. She was sitting in her arm-chair, staring at the fire, her chin in her hand. "Jane?"

She turned towards us, standing in the door, and flew out of her seat, dropping to her knees in front of me, breaking down into sobs. "Ellie, thank God!" She grabbed me around the waist, crying. "I've been so worried!"

I got down on my knees too and folded her into my arms. "It's okay, Jane, I'm back. I'm all right. How long were we gone?"

"About twenty-four hours."

John collapsed onto a chair, looking gray and taking shallow breaths.

"I'm so sorry, Jane. Are the girls okay? What did you tell them?"

Jane gushed out a big breath, her voice shaking. "I told them that you had gone off with John and Harry for a little while, and that you couldn't call, but would text. I didn't know how long you would be gone if John took you to wherever he took you?" She looked at John, eyebrows raised and looking angry. Then she turned back to me, "Your smartphone was on the stairs. I made up an excuse to ask the girls your code, and of course they knew it, so then I pretended to be you and sent them texts from 'you.'"

"Thank you Jane, so much. The only thought keeping me sane was that you would take good care of them. Are they asleep?"

"Yes, they're having a 'sleepover' with my girls in their room." I wanted to go up and kiss them immediately, but I knew Jane needed an explanation.

"Jane, sit down, please. You need to know about John." She turned to look at him, and her eyes narrowed in concern at his gray and shrunken figure. I continued, "He really does time travel. We just spent five days back in the year 1344."

"My God!" she said, her eyes growing large.

"I know, it's hard to take in."

"But five days? You were only gone one?"

"Time travels faster back then—I'm not sure why or how. I'm hoping this book will help us." I pulled out Sir Anthony de Lane's book on the labyrinth, and Jane started to examine its pages, careful not to damage the manuscript.

"This is crazy. The vellum is brand new and shows no sign of weathering or age."

"I've got plenty more here, Jane," said John, pulling open the bag at his feet. There were books, a small tapestry, a religious painting, and a ring.

"Jesus, John, what *didn't* you take?" I asked.

John then pulled out the little sketch Yvonne made, with my story about Katherine of Salisbury written on the back. "Yvonne gave me this, just before I left."

"No, no, no!" I said, sitting down. "I wanted her to have proof that what we saw happened. Without it, Katherine's story might just fade away. Shakespeare's sister, all over again."

John grabbed me by the arm. "Um, first," he said, "would you mind calling an ambulance? I think it's time for some modern medicine." His words grew more and more faint.

Jane and I sprang into action. She called 999, and I laid John out on the floor, knees up, in case he was on the verge of fainting. It was clear by his super-white skin, and his blue-ing lips, that he was not getting enough oxygen.

"How long's it going to take?" I asked Jane.

"The village's first responders are on their way. Not long now." Jane got down next to her brother and took his hand in hers. "I'm sorry John, I'm sorry I didn't believe you. I guess I thought you were trying to tease me again."

"It's okay, Jane." John patted her hand. "It is pretty hard to believe. But it's so magical."

John could be dying and was in pain, but there was a large part of me that wanted Jane to know the real truth. Here and now. "Jane, he pulled off the whole act—manacles, the dinner, the revelation, and all, to get me and Harry back in time. So don't go too sweet on him thinking he's some kind of saint who you did wrong. It was a horrible, selfish thing to do, and all because he wanted to meet the king."

Jane glared at John, and then said, "Wait, where *is* Harry? I'd assumed he went with you because his car is still here, but why isn't he with you two?"

Well, that's when I broke down. Everything was so overwhelming, the relief in being back and knowing that the girls were fine; John looking terribly ill, and Harry being missing. Guilt that had been tamped down by the fear of separation from my children suddenly welled to the surface. I had left a man behind. And that man was the sweetest, kindest, most loyal man who had ever been in my life. He was alone, in 1344. My sternum felt like it was being crushed as I thought about Harry and the danger he was in. There was nothing I could do now to help him. I finally choked out, "He's not with us. We hope he's not far behind."

The EMTs and an ambulance came, and they got John on oxygen and hooked up to a cardiac monitor. Jane climbed in the ambulance with him and promised to let me know what was happening.

I tiptoed upstairs. The girls were all lying on the floor, some in, some out of the sleeping bags, some lying sidewise. Sophie was out of her teddy bear sleeping bag, wearing only her shortie pajamas; she'd probably gotten hot. I checked her feet, and she was cold, so I put her feet back under the cover. I kissed each of their cheeks, inhaled Sophie and Abby's sweet, familiar scent of the ridiculously expensive organic baby shampoo I'd been guilted into buying. I couldn't wait until they got up in the morning so I could smother them in hugs and kisses. They wouldn't ever know why I was being so affectionate and what had gone on, but it would haunt me forever.

I took a long, hot shower, and got updates from Jane on my phone, which she'd given back to me before she left. John's lab tests revealed a severe iron deficiency anemia, and it had caused his heart to struggle. They were hoping that once they raised the iron levels in his blood that his heart could start to repair itself, but it was early days. At least he was getting the help he needed at long last.

I crawled into my bed, with its high thread count sheets, a firm mattress, warm and fluffy duvet and flannel covers, and started to do research on my phone. Research on iron deficiency, research on Katherine of Salisbury, King Edward III, the Order of the Garter. And then, I put in the search bar: Harry DuMont. Nothing came up.

I woke up later with the phone still in my hand. I put it on the side-table, rolled over and fell asleep again.

CHAPTER THIRTY-TWO

And theron heeng a brooch of gold ful sheene
On which ther was written a crowned "A"
And after, Amor vincit Omnia."
Canterbury Tales, Geoffrey Chaucer

T HE NEXT DAY the Three Musketeers, along with their two best little friends, were back together again. I could see them, touch them, breathe them in, stroke their hair, and hear their sweet little voices as much as I wanted to now. I would not be separated from them again, except for ordinary things—school and playdates, and the occasional night out with my friends. But those would be routine partings, the stuff of everyday life.

When she saw me, Sophie almost immediately began whining that she was hungry, and said she'd been so sad without me that she could barely eat. "Don't listen to a word she says," protested Jane's nanny. "She's been eating faster than I can bring her food. I honestly don't know how such a skinny child can possibly eat so much!"

Abigail wanted to show me her journal, where she'd been busy with to-do lists of the things we were going to do in London, the trip she'd been promised. She'd drawn pictures of the sights, accompanied by historical facts about each one. She was definitely my little girl. When I could set the girls in front of a TV show for thirty minutes after lunch, I ventured out to the labyrinth, and sat on a bench, staring at it. I was willing Harry to appear, as if my mind could pull him back in front of my very eyes.

But of course, I had no such skills, and the labyrinth remained empty. I thought over and over again: *Should I just go back? Should I get a party of men together—Hugh, Matthew, Sir Dagworth—and bring him home from Windsor?* But it was too dangerous—not just for me, but for the Dagworth party. They were not welcomed there anymore.

Two days later, John was released to the care of Jane, booked for weekly visits with a cardiologist, and handed a huge list of instructions for pills and medicines. Sophie and Abby came with me to see him up to his guest room in Jane's section of the house, around the corner from mine. Each took a hand to guide him up the stairs, very slowly. "Careful, Mr. John," Abby said.

"Please, just call me John," he said. "No need to be so formal. It's 20—?"

"It's 2017," I finished. "Yes, Abby, it's okay. You can call him just John. Just like you do Jane. They're brother and sister, after all."

Sophie said, "John isn't as pretty as Jane, though."

"Sophie! Be nice," Abby said, never one to waste an opportunity to correct her sister's errant ways and set her straight.

"I'll leave you all to it," I said, turning to go to my room. "John, I'm glad it looks like you're going to be okay."

John called after me, "Ellie, wait," he said. He still looked gaunt and tired, but a hint of color was back in his cheeks.

"Yes?"

"You were right—I was horribly selfish, and I did a terrible thing. I'm sorry. You belong with these girls—it makes my heart happy to see you with them. They truly are marvelous creatures."

I could only nod, choked up for a second. A mother's heart is pulled in twenty thousand directions a day, from boredom to rage, from tedium to the best conversations you'll ever have, from sheer panic over illnesses to sheer wonder at the amazing way they are turning out. I wouldn't have wanted to miss any of it.

But I was also thankful, so thankful, for a chance to see beyond our world. To see the bravery and the pageantry and the music and the dancing. To be reminded of our tenuous hold on mortality and savagery. And more amazingly, to understand that time was not linear, and that there were places where all laws of time could be broken.

"Thank you, John, for the adventure. You were wrong to take me, but I shall never forget it."

"Shall we go through some of those books I brought back tomorrow?" he asked.

"I'd love to," I said.

⇻⟫⟫⫷⫷⇷

THE GIRLS INSISTED on sleeping with me that night. I was in the middle, so neither girl had any more of me than the other. Abby snored slightly, and Sophie kicked at me in her dreams, maybe scoring soccer goals, maybe kicking at alligators. When I made extra sure they were fast asleep, I untangled myself from their limbs, and snuck out of the bedroom. I went to sit in front of the labyrinth again. If I had any superpowers at all, I was going to try to utilize them to get him back. I concentrated hard on the memories of the long and dangerous roads he must return on, as well as all the guards at Windsor, and his thuggish competitors.

Nothing happened. I wrapped the blanket I'd taken to keep warm tighter around me.

I remembered how Elizabeth Dagworth sang, *Night and Day*, in the castle. I so desperately wanted to know what happened to them all. They were so utterly charming, hosts who'd cared so much for me in the short time I was with them when their plates were already full. Yvonne and Hugh and their love for each other, Sir Matthew and his astonishing skills, dear Mary and how she'd simultaneously pampered me and told me what to do for my own good.

Jane had assisted me in my research looking for any signs of the Dagworth family, and she had found no historical records of them after 1349. There was no mention of Sir Harry DuMont either. And no mention of Katherine being an original Knight of the Order of the Garter.

We would have to dig deeper. Not all information was online. We'd have to figure out what records hadn't gone digital yet. Perhaps I could even find out what happened to Sir Hugh and Yvonne, and John could write the sequel to *The Tale of the Squire*.

But tomorrow, the girls and I were going to catch a train into London and see all the places I'd told them about for so long. We were going to go on the London Eye, and see Buckingham Palace, and walk through my favorite place, The National Gallery.

It was time to make some new memories with my girls.

WE HAD A half day of touring around London, walking through St. James's Park and seeing Buckingham Palace and Big Ben and Parliament, and enjoying a filling afternoon tea at Fortnum & Mason's of sandwiches and sweets. My exhausted girls had to be carried in from Jane's car at bedtime. I slid them under the covers, this time in their own room, and tucked their lovies up under their arms and cheeks so they would know where they were and that they were safe.

I looked out my bedroom window, and the moon was out, and it reminded me of the night John and I came through. I went down to the labyrinth again. I'd felt terribly guilty the whole day enjoying my time in London knowing that Harry was still trapped. I felt selfish and sick about it. Jane took a look at me heading to the door and nodded her approval. "Go do what you have to do. I'll be here in case the girls need me."

I wrapped a scarf around my neck and pulled a hat on my head and walked down the garden path. *Clank.* It was a familiar, metallic-sounding clank. I ran. The moonlight flooded the turf-lined path, and there, in a heap, was a man in armor, right in the center. My heart began to thump nearly out of my chest.

"Harry!" I yelled.

"Don't come out here." He turned over on his back, panting. "You know what happened the last time."

It took a few agonizing minutes of him rolling onto his side, then rolling onto his other side, before he was able to get up and get out of the center. It was so hard for me not to rush out there in a fit of impatience. At last, he came over to where I was standing. Then he fell over again onto the cold ground.

I kneeled over him, taking his head on my lap, stroking his forehead, taming his eyebrows, trying gently to make his head stop its dizzying internal whirl. "Are you all right? Are you hurt? Oh my God, I've been so worried!" I hugged him around his armor, which he probably couldn't feel. It wasn't comfortable, but I had to hold onto him.

"Are you mad?" I asked. "I'm so sorry for having to leave you. I had to take my chance when I could, they were after me, the King wanted me to be his ward, and—" I took a breath. "Oh, there's so much to tell you, and I want to hear all about what happened to you. But first, I really want to kiss you," I continued. "Can I? Would that be all right? Or are you too angry?"

"I was afraid you would talk so much you would never get around to it," he replied at last, so softly.

I kissed his sweet lips, his beard rough against my skin. I couldn't stop. I kissed his eyes, his cheeks, his neck.

"Okay, calm down there, Lady Hartford," he said, clearing his throat. "How about you help me up? I know I need some beef, and then a hot shower. I know I stink to high Heaven."

"I hadn't noticed," I lied. "But tell me, how did you get back to Wodesley? What took you so long?"

"It's a long story. But to sum it up in an executive briefing, Edward III is a really, really stubborn man. Explains a lot about our history. Even though I ended up faking an injury and keeling over in the least injurious way I could think of, he still wanted me. But thank goodness for Sir Anthony de Lane. He is a real romantic. He snuck me out and helped get me back. It just took a little while. In fact, de Lane wanted me to give you this...."

Harry pulled out a small, rectangular object, wrapped up in a piece of linen. I knew instantly it was a book. I unwrapped it, and saw it was another book of de Lane's. The one he must have been working on in the scriptorium.

"He told me he wanted you to take care of his story and learn more about what he was trying to do. He actually was pretty ill when I left. Perhaps he thought he was running out of time."

My first impressions of de Lane had been all wrong. He wasn't creepy, he was brilliant, and romantic, and had some sort of key to the universe that no one else had.

"I'm very honored that he entrusted me with this." I had to know more. "But what about the Dagworths? Did they get into any more trouble because of the Earl of Salisbury's death? And what about Katherine? Why can't I find anything about her being in The Order of the Garter?"

Harry shook his head. "When I got back to Wodesley, the Dagworths were packing up to leave England. Turns out old Dagworth had another property in Tuscany. Castello Worthi. I think we need to look it up. They wanted to lay low for a little while, until the King and Phillipa got over the Earl's accident." Harry ran a hand through his hair. "Maybe Castle Wodesley was abandoned by the family, and perhaps fell into disrepair, inhabited by vagrants maybe? Any number of things could have happened. But hopefully, they continued to thrive in the wine business, and enjoyed the warmer climes of Tuscany. *La dolce vita.*"

"And what about Katherine Salisbury?"

"Well, that was interesting." He stopped, and swayed, then steadied himself and started walking again. "A lot of the men started raising a fuss that a woman had been elected to the Order. It got very political. I could see Edward struggling to figure out what to do. In the end, Katherine said that she did not want the position, which I think was a lie, but she could probably see what an issue it was becoming for Edward. Plus, I think Phillipa might have given her a word or two.

"Damn it all!" I kicked the grass. "Just think how different the world would have been if she had been able to do it, and people had found out about it. Now all the proof we have is a sketch Yvonne made and the story I wrote on the back of a piece of vellum. It won't even carbon date… I don't think. Hmm." I started to think about whether that was true or not. It wouldn't have aged 700 years in time travel. Or would the vellum and the ink be traceable to an older time?

Jane and John were going to be so excited to see Harry, and I couldn't wait to get him inside the house. But first, I had one more question to ask. "Hey, did de Lane ask you any questions to get into the labyrinth? He did for me. I felt like I was giving my oral thesis all over again."

"Yes," he hesitated, suddenly shy. Then he said softly, "I said that in every direction I looked, I saw you. You were my east, my south, my west, and my north. You astounded me with your bravery and genius in survival. And your big heart. I realize it was rash of me to think that just because a person doesn't work as a soldier or in human rights, or whatever, that… it doesn't make you a good person. In fact, I think you're quite marvelous." He stopped.

I looked into his eyes, anticipating a relationship ending "but." There was always a "but." An excuse. A reason to pull away. To leave.

"I'm a little embarrassed to tell you that, though, since we haven't even been on our second date yet," he said, looking deep into my eyes. "So would you like to go out with me, Lady Eleanor?"

A warm glow enveloped me. I wanted to cry out of sheer happiness. Harry was back, he didn't hate me, and he still wanted to "date" me.

Whatever doubts I might have had before, I knew now that Harry felt the same for me as I did for him.

"Oh yes!" I exclaimed. I gave him a hug. Again, ouch. Armor hurts. I began to unlace the back to get him out of it as I pushed him up the hill. "How about a nice, boring, French restaurant, with French onion soup, ratatouille, and *crème caramel*? No swords, no balls, no lances, no heraldry. Just two ordinary folks, out to spend an outrageous amount of money on a very mediocre meal. Sound good?"

"Heavenly," he said, leaning on me to get him up the hill. "Just promise me I don't have to carry you into the restaurant."

"No heavy lifting for you—I've had my steak. Now let's get you one. I have some interesting plans for you, but I can't take advantage of a man in your weakened state."

"Very chivalrous of you, Ellie."

"You pay me no higher compliment."

Under the moonlight, we walked past the walls of the ruined castle, and into the lights of the very modern Wodesley Manor.

The End

Acknowledgements

I first started this book when my girls were Sophie and Abby's ages in the book. Now they are respectively in college and newly-graduated from college! Without the support of my initial writers' group of Judy Goldman and Charla Muller, the book would never have been finished. They convinced me that Ellie needed to be stronger, more self-confident, and I am forever thankful for them cheering me on to the finish line.

To Carrie Pestritto, the agent who took me on, and spent so many hours with me on three different drafts. And yet publishers said my book fell between genres, so they passed. My thanks to you, Carrie, for all your great ideas.

To my new writer's group of Lisa Williams Kline and Emily Pearce, I will be forever grateful for your encouragement and friendship. You both deserve to be members of my Order of the Garter!

To my editor, Cynthia Blackburn. You made me laugh in your editorial notes with your enthusiasm and humor, and your suggestions were excellent. You are a true delight to work with!

To my daughters, Georgia and Lucy. Thank you for being understanding of my need to disappear into my room and write for the majority of your childhoods! You are my greatest joy and accomplishment in this world, and I treasure being your mom.

To my parents for encouraging me, always being just a phone call away. And thank you to my mom for fostering a lifetime love of books.

To Rosemary Thorpe for helping me with some key facts and helping me find what looked close to Wodesley Castle. The best ex-mother-in-law a woman can have!

To all my beta readers and friends for their feedback on all these different drafts: Kalie Koivisto, Karen Alley, Carin Siegfried, Jessica Daitch, and Kimmery Martin. You all are talented and insightful readers, and I appreciate the time you took in your very busy lives spent with my characters. To Kitty Rabinow for cheering me on and helping with the research for the series.

To the original inspiration for my Jane, my professors Jane Roberts and Janet Bately at King's. Thank you for encouraging me to continue my studies and get my Masters in Middle English Literature. I'm sorry I didn't end up getting my PhD in the subject, and that I don't remember the language as well as I used to! But I truly had fun.

And finally, to my English teacher in high school, Mrs. Lang. Thank you for saying that I was a good writer. You set me off on a lifelong path with just those few words of encouragement.

About the Author

Hope Carolle is a professional book editor by day, and a historical romance/time travel writer late by night. She was inspired to write the series based on her own experiences getting a Masters in Middle English Literature before 1525 at King's College London as an American studying abroad. Now living in Charlotte, North Carolina, she is a proud mother of two young women, a giant rescue dog named Charlie, and looks forward to living abroad and walking more labyrinths soon.